ALLINGHAM: THE LONG JOURNEY HOME

This Large Print Book carries the
Seal of Approval of N.A.V.H.

ALLINGHAM: THE LONG JOURNEY HOME

JOHN C. HORST

THORNDIKE PRESS

A part of Gale, Cengage Learning

GALE
CENGAGE Learning®

Farmington Hills, Mich • San Francisco • New York • Waterville, Maine
Meriden, Conn • Mason, Ohio • Chicago

GALE
CENGAGE Learning·

Copyright © 2015 by John C. Horst.
Thorndike Press, a part of Gale, Cengage Learning.

Thorndike Press® Large Print Western.
The text of this Large Print edition is unabridged.
Other aspects of the book may vary from the original edition.
Set in 16 pt. Plantin.

LIBRARY OF CONGRESS CATALOGING-IN-PUBLICATION DATA

Horst, John C.
    Allingham : the long journey home / by John C. Horst. — Large print edition.
        pages cm. — (Thorndike Press large print western)
    ISBN 978-1-4104-8306-5 (hardcover) — ISBN 1-4104-8306-1 (hardcover)
    1. Frontier and pioneer life—Arizona—Fiction. 2. Arizona—History—To 1912—Fiction. 3. Large type books. I. Title.
    PS3608.O7724A83 2015b
    813'.6—dc23   2015019432

Published in 2015 by arrangement with John Horst

Printed in Mexico
1 2 3 4 5 6 7 19 18 17 16 15

Hell has three gates:
lust, anger, and greed

—Bhagavad Gita

CHAPTER 1
FLAGSTAFF,
ARIZONA TERRITORY, 1887

The newborn cried a good cry and everyone cheered. "It is a girl, Rebecca!" Rosario took the babe from the midwife and wiped her clean. She kissed the newest member of the Allingham clan on the forehead. "Hello, my little Frances." She smiled at Rebecca. "She is hungry." She handed the little one to her proud mother as Rebecca wiped the tears from her eyes.

"Oh, she's precious." She held the child to her breast to suckle and looked up at Allingham. "Look, darling, look at our little treasure."

Allingham smiled. "She doesn't look like me." He put a hand on Mr. Singh's shoulder. "Praise the Lord, she doesn't look like me."

Marta Ballard moved, without a moment's rest, all around them. The terse midwife's work appeared to be done. It wasn't an easy pregnancy, nor an easy birth, and the first successful one for the couple after three tries. She watched Rebecca's every move. She glanced at Rosario, now counting bloody rags. She nodded at the knowing look in the old Mexicana's eye, as Rosario had been on more than her fair share of births, both difficult and easy. None were ever so worrisome. The last rag did not appear so bad as the first.

Marta Ballard exhaled a little sigh of relief. She worked and watched and moved away to the parlor. It was best now to give the family a little time alone with the newest member of the Allingham family.

Allingham worried over them both. He'd birthed a baby or two in his time, as a copper back in New York's Hell's Kitchen, but, as it had been for Rosario, this was a worrisome time. He felt overwhelmed, as if he might cry, and as always, Rebecca could sense it, putting a hand to his cheek.

"No tears, darling, unless they're tears of joy. No worries, no more worries, we're both fine. Safe and sound as a pound." She smiled at her two fathers. "You see, she's beautiful."

Robert Halsted blushed. Embarrassed, he nodded, in a way of an apology, to Allingham. "Just like her mother."

"And grandmother." Hira Singh nodded.

"She is precious, Kaur. Congratulations on making such a beautiful jewel." The Sikh placed a little head covering on the infant that he'd been working on as they waited for the baby to arrive. "Now she has a proper crown. She is a princess, a Kaur, and she will always be such. Thank you daughter, thank you for such a grand gift."

They all, after a time, pulled themselves from the new parents' room. Mother and father and child needed some time alone now. Rosario stood in the corner, nearby in the event they'd need her. Now Allingham could cry in peace and he did and smiled and wetted Rebecca's cheek with his tears.

"I didn't think you could look more beautiful, but now" — he looked down at the infant suckling with enthusiasm — "you've outdone yourself this time, Rebecca. You've outdone it for certain, this time."

She smiled and closed her eyes. She was exhausted and her husband got up to leave, to let her sleep in peace when she grabbed him by the hand. "Stay. Please, darling, stay."

He did and they dozed together as little Frances emptied Rebecca's breast.

Allingham awoke to Rebecca laughing and pushing at the bedcovers. She smiled up at him with a queer, glazed look in her eyes. "They're *so* cute!" She grinned wider. "But they shouldn't be in bed with us, with the baby. Rosario and Miss Ballard'll have a fit if they find out."

Allingham looked at the bed. "What, Rebecca?"

"The puppies. They're so cute. They're adorable."

"Rebecca?" He pressed his hand to her forehead. "There are no puppies." He turned to brighten a lamp.

Rebecca shook her head and looked down again. She smiled, then shook herself again to wake up and clear the cobwebs from her mind. "I must be dreaming." She reeled and dropped down onto the pillow. "I, I don't feel very well, darling."

He pulled the lamp to and looked her over for any sign of distress, calling out for Rosario and the midwife.

"She's, she's delirious. She's . . . something's wrong!"

Marta Ballard pulled the sheets aside, regarding the blood pooling between Rebecca's thighs.

"She's bleeding. She's bleeding!" She sprang into action, massaging the fundus as Rosario took the babe into her arms. Allingham ran to the kitchen and was soon back.

"She's retained part of the afterbirth, she's bleeding out!"

The midwife nodded to Rosario. "Cold water, as much as you can manage, as cold as you can get it, please Miss Rosario, now!"

She turned her attention back to Rebecca. "My dear, you're bleeding. We're going to pack you with some cold rags, it's going to be unpleasant child, and it's going, not going to be comfortable."

Rebecca smiled, as one entranced. She was weak now, dizzy and only wanted to sleep. "It's okay, Miss Ballard. You go ahead, I'm just going to sleep for a while." She turned to lie on her side when the midwife called out.

"Don't let her turn! Keep her on her back!"

Allingham went into action. The color was fading as the life ran from Rebecca's body, she was dying before his very eyes. He grabbed her by the shoulders. In an instant he knew. Had known and seen enough in his time to know for certain that she'd soon die.

"Rebecca, please, please wake up. Hold on, Rebecca, hold on."

She turned and faced him. She smiled and reached up to pat his cheek and yawned. "I'm so thirsty, darling, please get me something to drink, some cold water, please."

"Yes, yes." He looked about frantic in the knowledge that something dreadful was about to happen to his love. "Get Hira, get Hira now!"

He held her, brushing the hair from her eyes. She was fading fast. It was only a matter of time.

"She's . . . not well, Hira, she's not well." His voice quivered as he called out. He searched the Sikh's face for something, anything that the Indian could do to make it right. "She's bleeding, my friend. She's bleeding. She's dying. She's dying." His eyes moved toward the bed. "She's going to die."

Singh reached down, stroking Rebecca's hair as he'd done when she was a little child. He held her, as only a father would his distraught child, moving closer and whispering into her ear. "Kaur, I want you to look into my eyes."

"Yes, bapu. I'm, I'm awake." She shook her head and smiled.

"Rebecca, Rebecca, you must, must, must think of God. Think of God, Kaur, think of God, my daughter. Just think of and be with God."

Rebecca Allingham fell back onto the pillow. She smiled a little and died.

■ ■ ■ ■

Mary Rogers was once a Christian and a schoolmarm. She was now Daya Kaur, wife of Hira Singh, a man old enough to be her father. She combed her husband's long black hair, now peppered with gray as he rested his head in her lap on the bed. She felt his tears wetting her thighs as she patted him with her free hand.

She'd give his hair three hundred thorough strokes with his kanga every night and they'd talk and love and be together and even the fact that the evil quack Webster had afflicted her with syphilis during her captivity, and made her barren, did nothing to diminish the happiness or love or desire they had for each other.

"I am sorry for your loss, my husband. She was a wonderful, wonderful daughter." She reached over and kissed him on the head.

He did not look up but rather spoke into her soft lap. "There is a story, an old story passed down from Baba Farid, that speaks of the midwife snipping the umbilical cord at birth; let me try to remember, yes, 'Better if she would also press a little the throat, one would not have to face the affairs of life

13

and bear its sorrows.' "

The babe whimpered, as if on cue, in the crib next to their bed and Daya looked on, thought of getting up when the newborn just as quickly settled down.

"Tomorrow, we'll see the wet nurse."

She thought of all she'd learned from her husband, all the teaching of Gurbani, the teaching of the Sikhs and how it had helped her through her terrible time, how it helped her understand what it was that made Hira Singh so wonderful, lovable, and she was now surprised at this seemingly contradictory statement. It was the opposite of what she'd learned.

"But, are we not just passing through, my love? And, wasn't Rebecca, wasn't she one with God at the end?" She began to tear up at the memory of her friend, passing on, just a few hours ago. The sister that she'd never had growing up. Rebecca Allingham was the kindest and gentlest person, aside from her husband, that Daya had ever known.

He sat up and dabbed his eyes. He hugged her and kissed her on the forehead. She smiled and admired him. Hira Singh was beautiful when crowned, but stunning when his locks were unencumbered by his dastar, the turban of the Sikh. She felt guilty desiring him at such a tragic time. She cast her eyes to the baby again.

"Rebecca was so certain this one would survive. After two miscarriages, and now, this. I worried so over the baby, I never imagined, even considered for a moment that Rebecca would die."

Singh looked on at the child. They both thought it, both hoped it, and would simply have to wait on Allingham. Their friend, their man Allingham, the new widower would have to decide and until then, they'd keep the little one for him. They'd love her and nurture her as if she were their own.

Singh looked on and considered his wife. She'd love little Frances as if she'd been the fruit of her own womb, he knew that. He wondered at how difficult it would be for her to give the little one up, if Allingham would so desire it. Once the bond was formed, it was all but impossible to break. He took a deep breath and pushed that thought out of his mind. There was too much sadness to bear right now; he did not need another thing to worry about.

"You are right, Kaur. Living is good, and suffering is a natural result, and an inevitable part of life, and it is what makes us closer to God. To suffer and endure it and to behave correctly in response to it

15

makes us closer to God. Without living there would be no possibility of knowing God." He reached over and kissed her cheek. He continued. "Human life is a serious affair; it is a valuable gift, a rare opportunity to identify and realize the moral and spiritual objectives. It assures us that we are the pinnacle of all creation; it reminds us that we are the embodiment of Divine Light itself."

"And you have had your share of suffering, my husband. You've lost your first wife and your child and now you've lost another. No parent should ever have to endure the tragedy of outliving his child."

And Rebecca was, without a doubt, his child. From the time she was born, he was in her life, back in India, when he and Halsted were two young lieutenants, one of the British Crown, and Singh an officer of the Sikh army. Together they helped to put the mutiny down, and for their heroics, were rewarded with the slaughter of each man's family. Singh losing his wife and children and servants, and Halsted about the same, except for little Rebecca. She'd survived the brutality of the mutineers, and was raised by the two bachelors ever since. Both men were good fathers, guiding her and nurturing her throughout her life.

Daya kissed him again and pulled him into

bed. She'd hold him and wait for him to fall asleep and then she herself would sleep and dream of baby Frances. She could not decide now whether to be happy or sad. She missed Rebecca Allingham terribly.

Chapter 2
Stosh Gorski

Pinkerton agent Stosh Gorski sat in the mahogany paneled office of Patrick O'Higgins Company. The office of the man who'd made millions since landing in Boston from Cork in 1847. Irishmen again. It seemed Gorski could not get away from the men of the Emerald Isle. He didn't mind. He liked the Irish. At least they were Catholic, well, at least the ones he'd encountered in his days on the meanest streets of New York.

The millionaire burst through the door and grabbed Gorski by the hand, shaking it as if they'd just now been reunited after a long absence. He grinned always, as he was a happy man. "Sorry to keep you waiting, Officer." He moved behind his great desk, sat down and just as quickly stood, as if he'd been ejected by the heavy springs under the leather cover of his upholstered chair. "Come over and have a seat, sir." He physically moved Stosh to the little parlor overlooking the street below. Bright sunlight streamed in and soon Stosh's head was swimming with the effects of good scotch and a fine Cuban cigar.

Another man soon joined them. "This here's my secretary." He pulled the man in by the arm and nodded for him to sit down beside Stosh. "Harold, this is our Pinkerton."

Harold Tomlinson was more austere, serious and guarded. His boss was too good for his own good, too trusting, and often too free with his cash.

The tycoon was uncharacteristic of the men of his ilk. He was not miserly. He did not covet or worship money. He considered himself blessed, lucky, and he would freely share his fortune with anyone and everyone, and because of this, Tomlinson took his job very seriously, not as the secretary, but rather as a kind of guardian, a guardian angel to keep good and kind O'Higgins from being fleeced too badly. He nodded to Gorski with a guarded countenance.

"So, Mr. Gorski, tell us what you know of your first assignment as a Pinkerton." O'Higgins spoke as he worked on lighting a fresh cigar.

Stosh shrugged. "Nothing, really sir. I am

a brand-new Pinkerton and saw the assignment in northern Arizona. I know a fellow there, and well, I signed up for it, and here I am."

Tomlinson became more serious. "First assignment? What are your credentials, sir?"

"New York City police for fifteen years, first a constable, then a sergeant."

"Where?

"The Five Points."

Tomlinson nodded his approval at O'Higgins. They both knew well enough about Hell's Kitchen. It was the stuff of legend. Any copper to survive it for so long was tough enough, competent enough to handle the job at hand.

"Then you are our man, my fine fellow, you are our man." O'Higgins smiled broadly.

Gorski liked them both right off. He'd heard of the famous prospector. O'Higgins found a silver strike in Colorado. He became a millionaire overnight. He was generous to a fault, a bachelor without family and no real interest in money or wealth. In this he was a very unlikely tycoon, but tycoon he most certainly was. For his ambivalence toward money, he was rewarded by providence, or the gods, or fate, with a kind of Midas touch. Everything he invested in paid off handsomely. Everyone he backed, well, almost everyone, returned his money to him many times over. He fairly tripped over dollars and did not care much about any of it.

He was a man dedicated to his fellow man, and would never turn down an opportunity to help another. It was why he'd gotten involved in the cattle business in Arizona, and why he now had Stosh Gorski sitting in the lounge of his office overlooking the busy Chicago street below.

"Harold, tell Officer Gorski, tell him why his services are so desperately required."

"Mr. Gorski, what do you know of the Arizona Territory?"

"Oh, a little. Read about the land, its riches, its prospects, how it has become a bit wilder than it should be because of these things, because of the lack of law, the wild Indians still moving about, the place can be a paradise or a Sodom and Gomorrah, depending on the men who populate it."

"I read in your dossier that you helped Marshal Allingham with that terrible business a couple of years ago, with that murderous bastard and destroyer of redheaded women." O'Higgins became a little serious, a little sad.

"Yes, that butcher and quack Webster. He

wasn't even a doctor, you know, a mortuary surgeon and a lunatic. Allingham got him, he always got his man."

"He's retired, I understand."

Stosh Gorski looked out the window, deep in thought. He poured a glass of water and drank it. Allingham. He thought hard about what to say about Allingham.

Stosh looked back at the men with the same sadness in his eyes that had just now seemed to hang over all of them, hang over the room like a wet shroud. "His wife passed away. Seems it was just too much for him to bear."

"Are you married, Officer Gorski?"

He felt his face flush. He nodded. "No longer. I lost my wife to female troubles, two years ago this June."

"I'm sorry."

Gorski watched the man look forlorn, even as if he might cry and this touched the veteran lawman. Patrick O'Higgins was significantly affected by such things, any suffering of the human spirit or mind. Stosh continued.

"No matter. Please, Mr. O'Higgins, tell me, what may I do to help you?"

"It's Paddy. Paddy is my name, and it's what you call me, and you are Stanislaus?"

"Stosh."

"Well, Stosh, here is our dilemma. A few years ago, we started a ranch right down in a place known as Pleasant Valley . . ."

"In the Tonto Basin," Tomlinson added.

"Yes, yes. Harold found out about it, told me about it, told me that it was good land, land that could be populated and helped by my fortune. Lots of folks just scratching out a living there, just getting by, and I thought, well, a place called Pleasant Valley, that must be a fine sort of place, and my money might help bring it about, bring something to it, make it good for the folks living there, so, by gum, we went ahead and invested, got a nice herd of a few hundred . . ."

"A thousand," Tomlinson chimed in.

"Yes, a thousand cattle." He smiled. "It was going well, Stosh, me boy, but then, well, now the fellows with the sheep have invoked the ire of the others, and they're all squabbling over it like a bunch of schoolboys."

Tomlinson interjected. "There's plenty of land for them to move about peacefully, but water is dear. The water should sustain them all well enough, but the old greed has taken many of them over, and now there's a regular range war brewing."

"More than brewing." O'Higgins went to his desk, found a file and handed it to Gorski. "Look at this, look at this, Stoshy, me boy."

There were newspaper clippings, photos of men lynched, hanging like dreadful fruit from the vine, along the rail lines, swaying from telegraph poles. There were images of ranch houses burned, and one particularly disturbing photo of little children slain in the front yard of a destroyed home. Gorski closed the file and looked into O'Higgins's watery eyes.

"It's got to stop, my friend. It's got to stop."

Stosh stroked his chin. "What of the law?"

Tomlinson laughed in a way that revealed his cynicism. "There is no law. The county sheriffs are good at collecting taxes and getting reelected. The land's too vast to keep the bad men in check, the courts too limited, and some corrupt, so that no one is ever punished or brought to justice. Your man Allingham, retired, wasting his talent and his mind. We cannot expect anything from him." He shrugged. "Mr. Gorski, it is up to us, up to you."

"And, the men on your ranch, what of them?"

Tomlinson laughed cynically again. "Gilliland! Complete imbecile!"

"Now, Harold." O'Higgins put up a

cautionary hand. He did not like to talk ill of his people. "Gilliland is a cowhand, a range boss. Granted, he's not the smartest fellow, but he's loyal and of a good character." He looked at Stosh and continued. "I hired him out of Texas. He was my manager there at one of our operations, and I moved him on to Arizona. The men have been safe, operating without difficulty, but they are no vigilante force."

"Ha! Vigilante force is an understatement. It's what we don't want spreading, Mr. Gorski." Harold waved his hand in the air. "That's what's been responsible for so many of the lynchings. Too damned many men riding about, taking the law into their own hands. Damned lynch law, more a scourge than a form of justice."

Stosh cringed a little at the thought. He'd investigated more than a few lynchings in his time, the poor Negro dockworkers, every time there was a labor dispute, there was at least one lynching.

"They are no law at all, my friend, no law at all."

"No, Stosh, my boy, you'll get no help from the men on my ranch, no help from Gilliland or any of the hands, and that's probably a good thing. Truth is, we've not got much to offer you but danger and hard toil and despair."

Gorski stood up and both men fully expected him to tell them to go to hell. Instead, he put his cigar down with great care, in the fine crystal ashtray.

"When do we begin?"

CHAPTER 3
BASQUES

Lucía Etxebarría de Asteinza picked up the basket of peaches, along with the clean pie tin from the back stoop of her cabin door. He'd always have them for her in season. Out of season, he'd leave preserves or canned peaches or ones that had been dried. She'd not spoken a word to him but knew well enough from the folks about that he was a good and kind man. A hermit really, as he lived alone and spoke to no one. He kept to himself and his orchard and she never tried to engage him, even though she'd seen him a time or two, in the wee hours, quietly lurking about, making his gift deposits when he hoped no one could discover his little conspiratorial acts of goodwill and kindness.

Xavier Zubiri, Lucía's husband, was the one to suggest baking pies for the mysterious visitor. The Basque was a kind man and thought that some kindness was due the peach-growing hermit. He'd heard rumors about him, heard that he'd lost his wife, was once a famous lawman but now alone and isolated, and perhaps a little addled of mind. At least the couple could offer gifts in kind, and the pie tins were dutifully returned within a couple of days, always spotless, like clockwork.

Lucía smiled and held one up for her husband to see. "I have never seen a man clean a dish so well." She put it away and felt the peaches and they were ripe. She put one before her husband as he sat down to breakfast.

They were happy here. Finally, after three years in the States, they'd found a good boss in the form of Pierce Hall and his partner Old Pop. They were good cattlemen and, by the urging of the older one's wife, decided to add sheep to their operation. Rosario remembered that Mexican ranches always had sheep and cattle, and knew well enough that it would work up in el Norte just as well as down south in her homeland, in old Mexico.

The ranchers hired the Basques as soon as they learned that the couple were in the territory, and now the two were well on their way to making their own way in the world, well on their way to creating their own flock.

Perhaps there'd be babies in a year or two. They were hopeful in this Arizona land, this land that bore the Basque name.

"He has brought us many peaches. I'll make a pie for Señora Rosario with this batch. She will like that, I think."

Xavier nodded. The Mexicana matron of the Hall ranch was a Godsend, as she was so much like, in both temperament and wisdom, Lucía's mother back home in Spain, that it made the transition to the new world easier for both of them. They loved Señora Rosario and knew they were lucky to have such a good boss and friend.

He reached for her as she sidled past him and pulled her onto his lap. He'd already worked three hours and the sun was just coming up. A little time with his wife would not be such a terrible waste, or a significant distraction from his day's toil.

She plopped down, in mock exasperation, then kissed him on the head. "You will never get your work finished this way." She did not resist much. "You are worse now than when we were first married."

"Because I am happy and because I need help. We need to get busy, my wife, we need strong children because we will have the best baserria on this side of the ocean. We will have a house, three stories high, all of

29

stone, and a proper roof made with tiles."
He looked up, a little disgusted at the
ramshackle roof over his head. Every time a
wind blew, little bits of dust fell on them.
"It will be just like back home. And we will
have sheep, many sheep, and you will see,
my wife, we will have the finest home in the
land."

He ran his hand up her thigh and she
pretended to push him away.

"But we need to get busy. A child is nothing but a burden the first four years of its
life, and I plan big things, many big things,
so we must get busy, my love."

She stood up and took him by the hand,
leading him to the bed. "You are like a
young ram."

"It is not my fault," he spoke as he pulled
the suspenders from his muscled shoulders.
"You should not have been born so beautiful, and then I would not be thinking of you
all the time."

The mule brayed as Xavier pushed an errant ewe along toward home. The sound
startled him as he was deep in thought, and
not much paying attention to his surround-
ings. The hermit smiled and pointed with
his head, in the direction of the animal, as
he pulled another trout from the stream

running through the shepherd's valley.

The Basque recovered and nodded. "Good evening."

"Evening." The angler nodded and smiled and again regarded his animal. "You'll never sneak up on a man with a mule."

"No doubt." Xavier regarded the animal and patted it on the neck.

"Got him from a breeder down south, outside of Tombstone."

"Thank you for the peaches. My wife is very grateful, and so am I."

"Thank her for the pies. I am very grateful."

The Basque extended his hand. "Xavier Zubiri."

"I know." He wiped the fish slime from his palm on his old tattered work shirt. "Clarence."

"Pleased to meet you, Mr. Clarence."

"Just Clarence, please."

"Xavier."

"Care for some trout?" He held up a willow branch with a dozen fish strung up through the gills. "They're small, but good eating."

"Only if you will join us. If you eat them with us."

The hermit looked off into the water, as if he were, all at once, in another world.

"Perhaps some other time . . ."

"Why? Why, mister, won't you . . . ?"

"Clarence, please, it's Clarence."

"Why, Clarence, will you not share a meal with us? We are good neighbors, we are Basques, and Basques make good, the best of neighbors."

The hermit shrugged. "I'm certain of it, but . . ." He just as quickly changed his mind. "I'd be honored, Xavier."

He smiled and Xavier could tell he was back with him, back in the present, no longer distracted by his musings. The hermit had a friendly smile.

They walked in silence to the cabin, Clarence leading his mule as Xavier pushed his sheep along, the shepherd snatching glances at the strange man every now and again. He was a giant compared to the Basque, with hair worn long around his shoulders and a beard reaching halfway down his chest. He was clean but dressed plainly, almost poorly, with old dungarees and a work shirt of homespun, bleached beige by the sun. He wore no belt or suspenders, but rather held his trousers tight to his bony hips with a length of old hemp rope, as his clothes hung off him as if he'd recently lost a great deal of weight. He looked a bit like an odd scarecrow that had been dressed in an outfit many times too large. He wore a Mexican hat of straw and this was tattered and frayed. It made him look small for such a tall man.

He walked with purpose, however, Xavier even noting a bit of a spring in his stride.

When they were finally home, Xavier took him by the elbow, ushering him into his humble home. "Lucía, a visitor."

The Basque's wife smiled warmly. "Finally, we get to thank you." She held out a hand and the hermit bowed nearly doubled over as he removed his big sombrero, tucking it under an arm. He grabbed the woman's hand in both of his great fists. Like a cavalier of old, he kissed her on the knuckle and smiled bashfully. "I have fish."

"Oh, and such grand fish. Trout like at home, Lucía."

She took them from Clarence and began preparing them for supper. She smiled. "And they are so nice and clean."

Xavier sat back and enjoyed watching his wife move about the little kitchen. He set the table, then poured for the three of them. "This is txakolina; the drink from our home, Lucía makes it for us." He placed a glass next to his wife and then handed one to the hermit. "Your health."

"And yours."

Xavier ate with the appetite of a farmer, scarfing down one fish after another. "Trout in my back pasture, and I never have bothered to catch them."

Lucía shrugged. "As if you have time for such things." She looked at the hermit and then nodded toward her husband. "He works night and day, mister. He never stops." She smiled at her man. "Perhaps you should take some time for a little fishing, my husband. My father always said that fishing is good for the soul."

The hermit ate little and said less. He watched the woman with a certain reverence and Lucía could not help but note a significant sadness about him, a sadness in his gaze. It made her pity him and she would, every now and again, smile and check to see if there was anything else she could do for her special guest.

After a while, Clarence stood up and began clearing the table. Lucía held up a hand. "It is my work, mister, you please, sit back down." She smiled at her husband. "Xavier, a little music, please."

He waved her off with his hand. "No, no, our friend does not want to hear our peasant music. It would seem crass and silly to him, I think."

"I'd like very much to hear it." The hermit nodded encouragement.

Xavier pulled out his dultzaina, a bagpipe-like instrument, and began playing a happy tune. The hermit sat back, pleased. He worked on his wine. Without any warning, his eyes welled up, and, to Lucía's dismay, he began to cry.

"Oh, mister, tell us, tell us what is wrong." Lucía reached over and touched him, with great compassion, on the arm.

"Oh, nothing, nothing." He shrugged and smiled as he dried his eyes. "Just remembering some happier times. I'm sorry, please do forgive me."

He stood up and nodded his head. "I thank you both for letting me share your happy home." He headed for the door and his mule. "This was truly grand, truly grand."

Before they could say another word, he was gone.

CHAPTER 4
THE FLORIDIAN

Joshua Housman sat in the parlor and waited for his boss, Señora Rosario, to bring him tea. With great care, so as not to scratch the furnishings, he removed his spurs, then rubbed the dust from the tops of his dirty boots with the backs of his trouser legs, first left, then right. He was also sure to keep his ass planted squarely on his scarf, which he'd laid flat over the seat's fabric, as he did not want to soil the lady's settee.

He held his hat in his hand and tried his best to calm his hair, using his fingers as a comb. He became distracted by the pencil drawing hanging on the wall between the two windows. He was tickled, as the lady had taken it to be framed down in Phoenix, and it was the best treatment any of his doodles had ever been given. Most of them, he expected were to just be thrown away. But Rosario had framed this one.

"Do you like it, my boy?"

He jumped to attention and watched the round Mexicana put the tea service on the table in front of his dirty scarf. She smiled and this always made him blush, as Señora Rosario was better than the best surrogate mother a young man could ever hope to have.

"Oh, fine, ma'am. Just sorry I used some old brown butcher paper to draw on. I never imagined it would decorate your wall."

"It is beautiful." She regarded her likeness again, as if she were looking it over for the first time. "You are a great artist, my boy." She turned and looked at it again. "My boy, you made a great likeness, your technical skill is muy bien, but that is not why I love this picture so much. I love it because you have captured my soul, and this is what makes it great."

"It's easy when you have such a nice subject." He blushed and she didn't mind that he'd flirted with her a little. There was no harm, no offense intended and none taken.

They drank their tea and dined on Rosario's cake in silence for a while, as Joshua was not a talkative man.

He looked at the pencil sketch of Rosario, hanging behind her, just above her head and compared it to the real thing. He was pleased with himself. "Back home, you know, my brother has a cigar outfit. I used to do the art for him, on the boxes."

"You did?" Rosario smiled. "I have seen many of these boxes, muy bonita, my lad. Did you have many such beautiful women to model for you?"

"No, ma'am. You're the first one." He grinned bashfully. "Mostly we just made it up in our heads, or took inspiration from other work, or posters, or out of books. Sometimes we used cigar-box art from other outfits, but my brother didn't like that much. He thought that was cheating, and he worried over infringing on some other man's art." He shrugged.

Rosario liked Joshua best of all her cowmen, and she loved every one of them. They were good men, but Joshua was special, as he was very smart and kind and had the work ethic that Rosario had lived by all her life. He was also handsome, with blond hair that had been bleached in the Florida sun, and eyes the color of the sea surrounding his childhood home in the Keys.

He'd come out to Arizona when the Hall ranch was run by the old Scotsman, and everyone, especially Pierce Hall, was surprised that he'd stayed on, as, like Pierce, Joshua Housman was the source of much ridicule and teasing by the bad Hall men, Donny, and Thad and the old man alike.

It seemed Joshua had benefited from the death of these men just as certainly as had Pierce and Old Pop, and now, of course, Rosario. The young Floridian was happy with his new bosses and glad he'd endured the others through to the end. He had good patrons now and was happy in his work as top hand.

After tea he opened his brand book and some other notes, sketches and documents. He fidgeted a little nervously with the counterfeit stamp iron and a saddle cinch ring that had no doubt been intended to be put to use as a running iron. These he carefully placed on a thick pad of burlap to protect the table between him and his boss.

He stood up when Pierce Hall and Old Pop made it into the room, the older boss grabbing the young man energetically by the hand. "How are you this fine day, my boy?"

"Fine, sir. Brought everything as you asked." He looked doubtfully at the objects as Pierce surveyed them with suspicion.

"You found these on our spread?"

"Yes, sir. Looks like they've been put there as a plant, to set us up. Out at the old place. And" — he opened his sketchbook —

"looks like some of our stock's missing. And, well, sir . . ." Joshua Housman became, all of a sudden, a little self-conscious. He looked down at his hands.

"What is it, lad?" Old Pop pressed him.

"Some of our calves have been stolen, and well, replaced by ones from another herd. These, I swear, have been over-branded to make it look like our brand. To make it look like we stole calves and changed the brand to ours."

"How do you know this?" Rosario smiled a little, always impressed with Joshua's intelligence and keen eye.

"My brother, ma'am, used to say I have a gift. He said I had a camera in my head, could take pictures with my brain and remember every detail of a thing. Kind of a gift for remembering a face, even a face of an animal, a unique thing about a particular animal, and well, ma'am, I can just remember. I even remembered a shark that bit my brother one time, a long time ago, bit off part of his foot when we were salvaging. All our friends went out hunting for that shark, brought a whole slew of them in, and I was able to pick out the one who'd done the deed, even after they'd brought in over a hundred of them. They cut that shark open, and found my brother's toes." He continued.

"Well, I remember all our calves just the same way, ma'am. Every last one of them. I don't even need to see the brand, know our calves as well as I know my own family." He shrugged. "And besides, none of the ones we have now are going for their mothers. They just kind of mill around. You know a calf'll hang with its mother, never far from the teat, but not these."

"Then, they can't be ours." Pierce Hall looked a little more nervous than usual. He did not like the sound of this at all. He looked at Old Pop and then at Rosario.

"It's that bastard from Texas, Gilliland. I knew it, knew it right off he had a brand too much like ours. Knew he was no good, knew it was a setup all along. Jesus, Old Pop, he's fixin' to frame us up and make us out as rustlers, I swear it."

Pierce was likely right. Things were getting uglier in the valley by the day, and even though they'd been there the longest, and were the fairest to trade with, and had nothing to do with the killings or lynchings, they had many enemies.

Damned blacks, they were called, due to Pierce's Indian blood and Rosario's Mexican blood. Then there was the whole issue with that Mexican Ramon la Garza

41

and the Halls bringing up the damned Mexican horses from down south. The Halls were neck deep in that, upsetting even the horse trade business in the area. The jealous asses could not let it alone, and then, to top it all off, Old Pop marrying a dark Mexican, a former washerwoman and housekeeper and maid, making her the matron of the ranch, it was downright scandalous.

But it was really just good old-fashioned greed that made the war. Greed and the worry that someone might be getting something more than they were due, and the thought that someone might be getting more water than they were due, or that the foreigners were coming in, with their odd ways, and horror of horrors, sheep, which was completely the fault of the Hall ranch, and that was just plain going too far.

Now they had the odd people from Spain or God knows where, moving in, the Basques. And everyone knew, once they had a foothold, well, then the sluicegates would be opened, and the land would soon be chock full of the foreigners with their odd ways and odd lingo and it would just ruin everything.

Old Pop looked at Rosario and shrugged. He was not certain what to do.

She looked everything over. "My love, I

am sorry to say, but I believe we have a Judas among us."

Joshua Housman nodded. He didn't want to admit it, couldn't even think of a good suspect among his men, but his matron was right. "Yes, Miss Rosario, you're right about that. Someone's planting these things, or they're helping the blackheart responsible, I'm sure of that."

Joshua Housman sketched as he propped himself against his pillow in bed, and finished a doodle. He pitched it, like a playing card, at the hand who'd been his subject for more than an hour. The model took it up and held it out against the lamplight. He grunted his satisfaction and carefully put it away. "Thanks, Josh, my ma'll like it well enough."

Another man, a stutterer named Harry handed his boss a cup of coffee. "Whe—when you headin' out, Josh?"

"Early, early. Heading to Flagstaff, going to see Miss Rosario's old boss, Robert Halsted. He's still got some pull with the Safety Committee there. Hope we might get some help."

"T—too b—bad Allingham isn't around no more."

"Oh, he's around all right." Long Jack

spoke through a cloud of smoke and blew his answers with smoky breath. He eyed them all cynically, as Long Jack liked to find fault with everyone and everything. He was, for all intents and purposes, a killjoy, but ultimately a good man and a loyal friend. He worked hard and was competent. He'd never let a man down, and his constant complaining, for the most part, was his only vice. He looked at the stuttering man as he folded his arms across his chest. "He's around, just don't do law work anymore. Lives with a mule, I hear, in filth, on some peach orchard down in Walnut Canyon."

"Oa—oak Creek Ca—canyon."

"Yea, yea, well, might as well be the Grand Canyon, he ain't a law dog anymore."

Everyone ignored Long Jack as Joshua pulled his trousers, then shirt off and settled into bed. The stuttering man worried a bit.

"D—damned b—bad business."

"Sure it is, but what do ya expect?" Long Jack was in an especially dour mood this night. "Damned sheep. That's what done it. I told 'em, told 'em to leave off the sheep. Sheep are nothing but a nuisance. Sheep are the worst thing possible for grazing land."

"No they—they're not."

"Yes they are, eat the grass down to a nubbin' and kill it, kill it every time. Damned nuisance. That's why they got to run them up in the mountains, you know. Damned nuisance. I told the bosses, told both of 'em, told 'em, but will they listen to me, no, never."

"Long Jack, you sound like an old woman bitchin' all the time," Josh spoke at a knothole in the ceiling above his bed. "No one *ever* listens to you, let alone the bosses."

They all laughed. Even Long Jack could not disagree. Sometimes his complaining even got under his own skin.

Joshua rubbed his temples and continued. "It's a load of bullshit anyway. Sheep like certain things, they're browsers, they eat forbs and brush and the like. Don't even eat the grass cattle like. Fact is, the land's better for it. Keeps the vegetation from being overgrazed and gives all the plants a chance to grow evenly."

Harry looked on his boss with reverence. Josh was the smartest man the old hand had known. He was smarter than the big bosses, really, and Harry liked to hear him talk. He looked dismissively at Long Jack. "A—and be—besides, ain't' your place to question the bosses, L—Long Jack. Ain't your place by a mile."

Ang Lee, the cook chimed in. "You are

right, Harry." He did not look up from the potato he was peeling. He bobbed his head in the direction of the complainer. "Not your business to question bosses, Long Jack. Bosses good men, and lady, Miss Rosario. If they want sheep, they have sheep. That an end to it. You keep mouth shut tight."

Joshua settled back in his bed and watched the men mill about. He was happy here. They had a good clean bunkhouse, the best grub they could ever want, and good men to work and live with. The Hall ranch was the best in the territory, maybe the best in all the West and he was going to do what he could to put an end to this nonsense.

He closed his eyes and began immediately to dream a little about his home in Key West. He thought of his brother and cigars and pretty women adorning the artwork on the cigar boxes. He dreamed a little of Miss Rosario. She must have been a stunner in her day, as she was still pretty and he liked her very much. He liked them all on the Hall ranch. He'd help to make things right.

CHAPTER 5
W. DRUITT AND COMPANY

Walter Druitt abruptly sat up, then threw his legs to the side of the bed. He belched and pounded with his fist the spot that burned in his chest, seemingly through to his spine, as if he'd swallowed an ember. He gulped water, then made it to the kitchen and gulped buttermilk. Nothing helped, nothing worked. He ate half a loaf of bread and smoked a cigar and paced the length and width of his library. He saw the ledger on his desk, and then the letter from the bank and that made his stomach churn. At least the upset in his stomach distracted him from the heartburn.

He gulped three scotches. Now he was a little drunk and sweaty and fully awake. It was not yet two in the morning. He cried when everyone was asleep.

Eventually he tired of crying and wiped his eyes with his smoking-jacket sleeves and sat back in the big leather chair near the fireplace and wondered how he'd gotten himself into such a mess. He looked around the vast study, at the opulent furnishings, the leather-bound books, the massive foyer beyond the great mahogany door separating his room from the rest of the house. All mortgaged to the hilt. Even the land it was built on belonged to someone else.

He'd be thirty-nine next month and wondered when it would all catch up to him. Now it had, it seemed, and the letter was proof of that. The bank was demanding full payment, calling in all the loans unless he played ball with them. It was all so unfair, but unfair was the hallmark of the Druitt family, ever since that damned war.

They were plantation owners and slaveholders and some of the grandest landholders in Mississippi and as a young boy he was accustomed to all the grandeur that such wealth could provide. None of his people fought in the war. He was too young, by his mother's estimation, and his father and older brothers too important to the funding of the CSA to be wasted in battle.

They'd done well, financially all the way up till the end. They even survived the King Cotton debacle. His father helped procure weapons from England, and made a tidy sum from brokering that. At the very end, his old man even worked with the Yankees to supply cotton to the north, so he was working for both sides, clothing Yankees in his southern cotton so that they could be marched down and shot by Rebels armed with his British guns.

But it all unraveled. The patriarch, despite all his cleverness and wealth, could not overcome the great leveler. Time and the hardening of arteries were an equal-opportunity killer, and they did not care how important or wealthy the patriarch of the Druitt clan was.

He died of a stroke in sixty-six, leaving the family with significantly more debt than cash, and without a man bright enough to keep the ball in the air. And that is why Walter Druitt was in Arizona, sitting on a mortgaged ranch with a hole burned through his esophagus.

His attention turned from self-pity to his wife up the stairs, in the bedroom she kept as her own for more years than he'd like to remember. Her nightmares used to worry and scare him. He'd rush to her side, pat her gently on the hand and comfort her, but that was a long time ago. Now he found them a little amusing.

He lit another cigar and listened to her stifled screams. Babbling would come next and then she'd be awake and up and he'd hear her pace about the room. He envisioned her bare feet on the heavy Oriental rug and thought about how pretty she once was, still was, really, but he'd not enjoyed her carnal offerings for quite a long time. He sometimes forgot what she looked like under her clothes.

He'd blame her for his money problems had he been a little dimmer, a little more delusional. She did her best to lead him to ruin, but, if it hadn't been her, it would have been someone else. He'd have found another carbon copy of himself and they'd hurdle down the path to financial ruin together. It was in his nature, and in the nature of everyone he'd ever known.

The real problem was that he was too honest for his own good. And too ambitious and too deluded into thinking he had the potential for greatness. Lots of men just like him lived the high life, fleeced the banks, set up bogus companies, lived lavishly on credit, and moved about constantly, one step ahead of the debt collectors. At least there were no longer debtor prisons to worry about.

He could have done it as well, except for the nagging desire to make his own way in the world. He wanted, always wanted, to be an empire builder. He wanted to generate wealth and have real means and have real tangible things to own, possess. He wanted land and now livestock and properties, and perhaps even to one day own his own bank. That was what Walter Druitt wanted, but the dream constantly evaded him. He was always a day late and a dollar short, which was the story of his life.

She wanted to spend a year in England. He had not the guts to tell her that he had no way of paying for it. Didn't have even enough for the ship's passage for a one of them, let alone all the things that the boy and the girl and himself and his wife would require once there. And *what* she'd require once there! Many, many opulent and expensive things, certainly. That was a given.

Walter Druitt had many a pot to piss in. Problem was, they most definitely, along with the window to throw it out of, belonged to another man, down to the last item and detail.

He worked hard on the cigar and smoked it down to a point where he could let it die without feeling regret. If she got up and smelled it, he'd risk having her come down and speak to him. It was far too early for that.

He fantasized a little about the trip to

Britain. He could send them and stay behind, and then, while they were all gone, burn the place to the ground. The great, wonderful thing about mortgages was that the banks almost always required insurance. A little careless flame would do a body good. At least he'd be shed of it all.

He thought about the cousin in Lancashire. He ran a huge cotton mill, and Walter's family used to supply cotton to it. But that was a long time ago. They'd stay with him and he'd rub their faces in it. That sounded like a lot of fun. He sighed and wished he hadn't let the cigar die. She didn't come down. He had another scotch.

He looked at his watch and it was already past three. She quieted down, back to sleep. He thought about the meeting later in the day. What was he doing? He had nothing against the Hall men. He liked them, really. What would he say to this Pinkerton? He drained the bottle and shuffled, like an old drunk, or a man headed to the gallows, off to bed.

Stosh Gorski was up early and surveyed the town of Holbrook. It wasn't a large place, kind of quiet, and at this early hour, even quieter yet. The farmers and ranchers were doing what they did on their own spreads, the party-goers and gamblers and whores were in bed, and the shop owners were not yet required to start their day.

Stosh rubbed the joints of his sore knees as he waited for the pain to subside. He hated riding a horse, and it was the one thing he dreaded about his new job in this wild land. Horses were for pulling and plowing in his home country, and he never had a need or use for them in New York. The sharp pains running through his joints were a good reminder of why he disliked riding them so much.

Down the street stood a grizzled man preparing a horse, a mule and a burro for some rough travel. He eyed Stosh and tipped his dusty hat, nodding a good morning as he worked.

He was just the kind of man Stosh intended to meet as soon as was practicable, and as there were several hours to kill before meeting the cattlemen, he thought he'd try for an audience with the old fellow now.

"Have you had your breakfast, sir?"

Hugh Auld looked left and then right over his crooked shoulders. The dude was certainly addressing him. He nodded a little defiantly, as Hugh was not certain of the foreigner's intentions. The man looked a bit like a law dog, and though Hugh was no desperado, not by any means, he generally did not mix with such men. He spoke at his saddle as he worked. "I have."

Stosh Gorski knew how to get men to talk. It was his gift. It was why he was a good lawman and why he rarely had to hurt or risk being hurt by bad men. It was why he had yet to kill a man.

"I'm new to this land, mister." He grinned a little and regarded his own outfit and how different it was from the one worn by the prospector. "Certain you can see that."

Hugh Auld ignored him and kept working. He listened, nonetheless.

"I'd like some advice."

"Go back to New York or Chicago, or Cincinnati, or wherever you came from."

"Not that kind of advice."

The prospector turned and looked the man over. "You some kind of law, mister?"

"I'm with the Pinkertons."

"Hah! I met him. Pinkerton." He spit on the ground between his horse's feet. "Big horse's ass."

Stosh smiled. He liked the surly man. "I'd like to pay you for some advice."

"What sort of advice?" He stopped and looked Stosh Gorski up and down. "And more important, how much?"

"How to move about the land. How to

keep alive." Stosh pointed at the man's outfit. "I can see you've been around a bit, around this terrain for a while. See you know the way and lay of the land. Buy you a drink and a meal and pay you for your time, you name the fee, if you'll have it."

"Don't drink." Hugh Auld smiled. "But I'm mighty fond of cake."

They wound up at a lunch counter run by a Chinese named Chin who knew Auld well, as he had the best cake in the territory and Hugh Auld had the grandest sweet tooth in the land. He finished the third piece as Stosh Gorski watched and waited for an invitation to begin his inquiry.

Auld wiped his mouth with a napkin and this impressed Gorski as the man was neither uncouth nor unintelligent. He was, in fact, the opposite and it was encouraging to see such a bright and dignified man doing such rough work. Gorski did not know very much about prospectors.

"What would you like to know, mister . . . ?"

"Gorski." Stosh extended his hand and the prospector shook it.

"Auld. Hugh Auld. Call me Hugh. Everyone else does."

"Stosh."

"What are you, some kind of foreigner?"

"I am from Poland, Hugh."

"I had a grandmother from Poland. Grand cook. Grand old gal. Couldn't understand a word she said, but she was a fine gal."

He held up his cup for the cook to refill and looked at Gorski. "All right, my fine man from Poland, what would you like to know?"

"I'm traveling rough and don't know this land. Don't really know how to travel rough. Lived in cities all my life. Tell me how to keep alive."

"I see." Hugh smiled and rubbed his stubbly chin. He began.

"Always have enough water. Even when it isn't hot. Get canteens big enough. Lots of them, and I mean big enough. If you can fill a canteen with a good piss, then it isn't big enough. Don't drink spirits when it's hot. Don't stop or camp or lie down in a dry riverbed, ever. Don't stick your hand anywhere that you can't see. Don't camp where there's Apaches. Don't have any dealings with Apaches. In fact, just plain avoid Apaches at all costs. Always buy things from Navajos. They're the Jews of the Indian world. They're always selling something, blankets, jewelry, horses, something. Always selling something. Buy something from them. They'll be your best friend once you've done that. Pimas are darlings. So are Hopis. Hopi women are the prettiest, but they don't cavort, so don't waste your time trying. You'll have to take one for a wife *if* she'll have you, which is unlikely, no offense, but that's the only way you'll ever bed one. Put a rope around you when you sleep rough. Rattlers won't cross it."

"That a load a shit." The Chinese cook spoke without looking at either man. The prospector ignored him and continued.

"Shake your boots out before putting them on, always, even in a hotel room."

Hugh looked at the Chinese man a little cynically. "Tell me that isn't right."

"No, that right."

"Scorpions are fond of boots. If you get bit by a brown spider, you got to cut a good chunk of your flesh away, all around the bite or your whole body'll rot away, starting where it got you. Always have at least two beasts of burden. Get yourself a mule. A good breeder down around just north of Tombstone, Walsh, Arvel Walsh, has the best mules in the land. Trust your mule. If your mule won't go someplace, take his advice. Don't go yourself. A mule's smarter than most men. If you can't get a mule, get a burro. Get yourself a Winchester. Get it the same caliber as your six-shooter. Then you won't get the cartridges mixed up or run out of one or the other. Both the same." He stopped for a moment and looked Gorski over carefully. "Get a better hat than that. Get a scarf for dust, silk's the best, catches the dust and dries out quick when you get it wet. You get into a dust storm you'll know it. You get a lung full of bad dust, you can die."

Hugh paused again and looked at the cook. "Mr. Chin, what did I miss?"

The cook looked serious and wagged his index finger back and forth, in front of Stosh's eyes. "Never trust an Irish or China-man."

Auld smiled. "Mr. Chin used to work for the railroad. He's been around."

He continued. "Have enough food, matches, a map, a compass, know where you are at all times. Watch out for bandits. There're lots of bandits. Usually can tell a bandit pretty well, they have no purpose in life, but, you being a law dog, you know that well enough. Decent folks are always doing something, bandits are not. They're just bumming. Bumming and looking for an op-portunity to do no good. There's a lot of that out here, Stosh. You meet a prospector, share a meal with him, and keep a fairly recent newspaper to share. Some of these boys stay out for a long stretch at a time. They often like the company of a white man. They'll help you. All the decent folks'll help you around here. There are no bad neighbors in Arizona, mister. But there are many bad men."

Hugh twisted a cigarette and Stosh did the same. Mr. Chin worked on his pipe as it was too early for much commerce just now. The prospector looked Stosh in the eye. "So, what's your business, then, Stosh?"

"I was hired by a cattleman, O'Higgins." He smiled at Chin and the memory of his warning not to trust the Irish. "To deal with this range war."

"Hmm." Hugh shrugged. "That's a bad business. Shame Allingham isn't on it."

Stosh brightened. "You know Allingham?"

Mr. Chin nodded resolutely in the affirmative. He watched Hugh respond.

"Oh, sure. Everyone knows or at least knows *of* Allingham. He cleared my friend Eli Crump, back in Canyon Diablo. Caught that damned murderer of redheaded prostitutes as well." His eyes brightened and he smiled at Chin. "Remember old Eli, Mr. Chin?"

Chin wagged his head in the affirmative. "Stinky bastard."

"That he was. But a good man. Loved the

whores." Auld looked a little seriously at Gorski and turned his head slowly from side. "Don't know why a man lies down with whores. If that little quim doesn't squeeze back, well, hell, no better than your hand." His face reddened and he cleared his throat, a little embarrassed by his own pontificating. "Sorry, that was a bit crass."

Gorski ignored his diatribe on whores. He was intrigued over the fame of Allingham. "Tell me about Allingham."

"Oh, well, with Eli . . ." He looked at Chin again. "He *was* a stinky bastard. Don't know why, he wasn't really all that dirty."

Chin spoke up. "He had a rotten mouth."

"Yes, that he did, but it was more than that. He just plain stunk. Stunk like rotten fish, *all the time.* Anyway, that's neither here nor there. Allingham figured out he didn't murder some whore in Canyon Diablo."

"The princess." Chin remembered her well, as she was rather famous in her own right.

"Yes, yes, the princess, that was what they called her. Everyone else would have pinned it on old Eli, sure as hell, but Allingham figured it out. Poor old Eli, he rode a dead whore, and that was too much for his simple mind. He shot himself through the head over it."

"Rode a dead whore?" Stosh was intrigued and simultaneously not a little confused.

"Yea, well." Hugh scratched his forehead. "It's kind of complicated, but the way I hear it, old Eli was ready to do the deed, made a bargain with the princess, got cleaned up the best he could and then, right when he was ready to consummate the deal, nature called. He went down to the jakes to conduct his business, then when he came back, the princess was dead."

Chin spoke up and ran his finger under his chin, from left to right. "Throat cut."

Auld nodded and continued. "Someone had stepped into her room and cut the whore's throat. Old Eli came back in and went to town, as it was dark in there, dark probably so the whore could get through it. Eli not only stunk, but he wasn't much to look at, either. It was only after he was finished that he figured out she was stone dead the whole time. Eli, all covered in blood, he ran off and then shot himself through the gourd."

Chin interjected, shaking his head from side to side. "Fornicating with a corpse, bad, bad."

"But his honor was intact. Allingham assured that. His honor was intact, cleared of killing the whore." Hugh shrugged. "Old Eli was a pretty good prospector."

John Gilliland was indeed not smart, just as Stosh had been warned by his bosses, the bosses of both men. Gorski could not understand O'Higgins in this regard. Something about the Texan appealed to the tycoon, though, and for that reason, Gilliland was in a position of power and responsibility far beyond his capacity.

Gilliland nodded toward the seated men, as a way of introduction. "Tom Graham, Walter Druitt."

Gorski sat down and worked on twisting a cigarette. "Gentlemen." Stosh was still not certain of Gilliland's reason for having this little conference. He decided to do more listening than talking, and Graham, obviously the most energetic and aggressive of the group, did not disappoint him.

"I'm sure glad they brought you in here, Mr. Gorsham."

"Gorski." Walter Druitt corrected his fellow cattle baron. He took a long drink and looked for a waiter to refill it. He always drank with great enthusiasm when the bill was covered by another man, and Gilliland, courtesy of O'Higgins, was picking up this tab.

"Gorski." Graham shrugged as if he didn't

care one way or the other about getting the Pinkerton's name right. He looked a little accusingly at Stosh. "What are you, some kind of foreigner?"

"I'm an American, just as much as you!" It was the first time Stosh had gotten his back up a little, but this Graham fellow was already beginning to wear on his nerves, and he'd known the man not much longer than a minute. He did not like Graham and Graham could sense it. They all could sense it and Gilliland did his best to settle them all down.

"Mr. Gorski's a good lawman." Gilliland looked over his shoulder and back to the corner of the hotel dining room. He was there and none of them liked it much. "Better than that long-haired Wild Bill Hickok impersonator."

"Oh, Jesus." Graham craned his neck and turned to look behind him. "Commodore Ass Owens. What the hell's he doin' here?"

"Oh, he knew we were meeting." Druitt spoke into his glass and downed another. "He knows everything that goes on around here."

"Goddamn it, here he comes," Graham sneered.

"Gentlemen." Sheriff Commodore Perry Owens strode up to the table of cattlemen.

He nodded and did not wait for an invitation, but rather pulled up a spare chair and sat down, next to Stosh Gorski.

"This is a private party, *Commander.*" Graham smirked a little at his own joke.

"That's Commodore, but you can just call me Sheriff Owens." He extended his hand toward Gorski, looking Stosh in the eye. "I don't know this man."

Stosh took the sheriff's hand. "Stosh Gorski, with the Pinkertons, Sheriff, here to investigate this range war at the behest of Mr. O'Higgins, up in Chicago."

"Oh, sure. I know him, or should I say, know of him. He's your boss, ain't he, John?"

Gilliland nodded just discernibly.

"Don't you have Indian children to shoot, or something, Sheriff?" Graham grinned at the now drunk Druitt. He glared back at Owens.

The sheriff remained unflappable. He ignored the gibe. "Oh, I've got plenty to do right here, with three of the most interesting players in the cattle trade all in one place." He eyed Graham with just the hint of contempt, but held his temper well.

Gorski was impressed by him. He was a fellow lawman, even if he looked like a throwback from the seventies, a kind of cross between Wild Bill and General Custer, with his long auburn hair hanging down off his shoulders. He dressed like a dime-novel hero, and Gorski was intrigued by his outfit, consisting of low-slung six-shooters on each hip, butts forward. He even sensed a slight hint of lilac in the fellow's hair. A man who looked and smelled as such was either a fool or a regular tough customer, and Stosh Gorski was convinced that it was probable that he was in the presence of the latter.

Graham spat his response at the table. "Ain't us you need to be worried about. It's them damned blacks. Damned Halls are the ones. You want to stop this range war, stop these killings, go knock on their door. Sheep-herding nigger bastards."

Owens stood up. He was finished with them for now. He nodded to Gorski. "Welcome to Arizona, Mr. Gorski. Good luck with your investigation." He grinned at Graham. "You're going to need it."

Chapter 6
It Begins

"Sometimes I think your partner would leave his head behind if it was not attached." Rosario looked at Old Pop's wallet as she shook her head in mock disgust. Her husband was always forgetting something.

Pierce finished his breakfast, looked at his watch and nodded. "He and Josh ain't more than an hour down the road, and they got them calves to slow 'em down. I'll run it to him, ma'am."

"You be careful, my boy." They were all, every one of them despite their age or station in life, Rosario's boys.

"Yes, ma'am." He got up and wiped his mouth and kissed her on the cheek. He might have been the principal owner of the ranch, but everyone knew that Rosario was the brains of this operation.

He was soon in the saddle and she watched him from the ranch house porch. He nodded. "Back by lunch, ma'am."

Pierce Hall was more and more prone to sullenness and worry these days. Something always, a dark cloud or a feeling in his gut would nag him. Rosario thought he needed a wife, and that was probably true. One time she even came right out and said it. Regular relations with a woman were the only thing that kept a man sane. He remembered well how that made him blush. The image of Old Pop and Rosario, naked in bed flashed in his mind, and he did not like that very much.

But things had been going so well for so long and now this. This business with the other cattlemen now seemed to prove that his inclinations and premonitions were all founded, a shit storm was brewing, and he knew it was going to be a big one.

He wondered as he loped along, why men could not just live in peace and behave like decent human beings. He'd treated everyone square since taking over the ranch from his dead father and brothers. He had good hands working for him, a good manager in the form of Rosario, a grand partnership with Ramon la Garza down in Mexico. Everyone respected his stock, his beeves, and his horses, at least, his horses in the sense that he brokered the deals between the Anglos and the Mexican Jefe. Now he was doing well with sheep, and they weren't in the least a problem. Ask any man of science and they'd tell you, sheep don't hurt grazing land any more than cattle do. It was all preposterous to suggest sheep ever hurt the cattle industry. La Garza convinced him of that last time he'd come to visit. Rosario was right; many of the big ranches had run cattle and sheep on the same spread. La Garza's family had done so for years. It was a myth made up by the greedy asses and hateful bastards who wanted to cause trouble. And it worked.

The Hall ranchmen were fair to all the newcomers, too. They never begrudged a man the use of their lands, their water. No fences would ever go up as long as the Halls had control. There was enough to go around, and he and Old Pop and Rosario were not greedy people. There absolutely was enough to go around.

He considered this latest mess. This frame-up job. Who'd do such a thing? They had no need to steal cattle. Hell, they were rolling in money, thanks to Rosario and Hira Singh and Robert Halsted. He smiled at the thought of him and Old Pop working out the business end of things. It would have been a disaster. They were good with the stock and running cattle and all, good with the men and knew how to make a herd thrive, but handling money was a different matter. Rosario was the one to make it all right. She was the smartest woman, smartest person, for that matter, he'd ever known. She was a good wife to his adopted father and a good matron and a good friend. She was the mother that Pierce had never known.

He kicked his mount again and moved a little faster. Today his guts were giving him a fit. It was a gift, or curse, depending on how you looked at it and Pierce had it since childhood. Every time something bad was about to happen, the little roll of his gut, the little, almost ticklish pain would grab him, as surely as rheumatism foretold rain in an old man's joints, and he'd know, sure as hell, something bad was about to happen.

He thought about the Floridian, Joshua Housman. He was a good man, a smart and honest and decent fellow and he was glad Old Pop had him with him on the ride to see the Halsted people in Flagstaff. They needed to turn those stolen calves over as soon as possible, and Josh was a tough customer. Pierce knew he'd be more useful than he himself could ever be to Old Pop if things were to get ugly. He wondered at that. Why did he freeze up in a gun battle? He wasn't afraid. He was no coward, but every damned time, he'd freeze. Didn't want to kill another man, that's what Rosario told him. Rosario, a lady, and a fine lady, who'd have a whole damned stock full of notches on her ten-gauge, had she gone in for such things. How could a lady best him when it came to killing bad men?

He was proud to know her. Rosario was no ordinary lady, no ordinary human being by a long ways, and he took solace in that. Rosario was a force of her own, and he would have to be satisfied, comfortable in the knowledge that few men could ever live up to her measure. Few men could come close.

He looked at the sun and thought he'd certainly be catching them up by now. Over the next rise, it all opened up to a nice plateau and then cottonwoods, and then there'd be the train tracks to cross, then follow, follow the rail and the miles of telegraph wire and then they'd all be in Flagstaff. Well, at least Old Pop and Josh. He'd have to go back so as not to worry Rosario.

At first, he could not believe his eyes as he beheld the dancing form, jigging, flailing, gesticulating, up high in the air, suspended, as if by magic under the pole holding up the telegraph wires. Men stood or sat ahorse below, laughing, depraved, primitive in their puerile glee.

Screaming could be heard, tearing at his eardrums, a primal, inarticulate voice, high pitched, as if in a nightmare, as if the scream was screamed by vocal cords not in control, paralyzed by slumber. Then a shot, past his ear, and Pierce now understood, comprehended that he was racing, the screaming his own, his six-shooter, as if by magic, in his hand, firing at the clump of men, at the whole rotten affair, firing wildly, as a man fires, unthinking, consumed by emotion, at a pack of coyotes feasting on a not-yet-dead steer.

His mount crumpled beneath him, a bullet to its brain, he spilled onto the desert floor, then silence, then confusion. The men were, as if by magic, all gone, the jigging man beginning to relax in death; legs, boots, trousers, chaps, drenched in his own fluids, face purple, eyes bulging. Pierce Hall worked to cut Old Pop down.

The old fellow dropped a good ten feet, feet first and crumpled lifeless to the dusty ground. The thin horsehair rope imbedded in blood-soaked flesh. Pierce worked it out of, off the damaged tissues. The young man could barely see for crying.

He sat back, numb, unthinking, trying to take the whole thing in. Joshua over to the side, half his face gone, his blond hair no longer blond, now red with dark, thick, coagulated blood. One beautiful blue eye gone, the other moving about as if to make sense of it all. Blood poured from a wound just above his gun-belt buckle.

Pierce was on him. He spoke in a soothing voice. "Hey, Josh."

The top hand worked his jaws, as if he'd gotten a cramp or awakened from long sleep. He reached up and felt the terrible wound and his empty eye socket. He winced in pain at the gut wound. He held out a cautionary hand to Pierce. "Don't, don't touch me!"

"No, no. I won't, friend, I won't." Pierce shook the cobwebs from his own shaken mind. "I'll just find your hat, get you a little shade, Josh. Don't worry, I'll take good care of you, friend. I'll take good care of you, you're goin' to be all right."

Josh sat up a little. He was comprehending now. He nodded to his boss. "Do for Old Pop. Don't worry about me. He can't be dead. He just can't be dead."

Josh gathered his legs beneath him and pulled himself to his feet. Holding his gut closed, he dragged himself to the old man's side.

"Look, Pierce, look, his chest's moving. Look." He pointed with a bloody finger. "His color's coming back, Jesus, man, he's alive."

And, as if the young man's words somehow were capable of conjuring the dead, Old Pop gasped and made a sound like a newborn calf, a rushing sound of wind filling up lungs. Old Pop had survived a lynching. Joshua Housman, played out, crumpled to the ground.

CHAPTER 7
LAMBS

"Hello, darling." Rebecca Allingham whispered into his ear. He awoke and stretched and smiled. He looked at his clock. One on the dot, she never failed to visit him at the appointed hour.

"Hello, Rebecca." She sat in the comfy chair, her chair, the one he'd brought from Flagstaff and dutifully placed next to his bed, replete with the little pillow she used to place in the small of her back, everything was just as she liked it.

As always, she held up a cautionary hand when he tried to get out of bed. "You'll get cold."

"Aren't you?"

She smiled her wonderful smile. "I'm fine, darling, just fine."

"I miss you."

"Now, darling, no sad talk. Our rule, remember, no sadness, only happy thoughts."

He nodded and smiled and looked his beautiful wife over from head to toe. He thought hard to change the subject, to think of something pleasant to say. He remembered something good and nice.

"I'm to help the Basques tomorrow. They're separating the lambs."

"I love lambs, they are *so* adorable. Give them a kiss on the head for me, will you?"

He blinked hard to stay awake, focus on her. Her visits were always too brief. He began to say something and she interrupted his thoughts.

"Eating okay, darling?" She turned her head slowly from side to side. "You are so gaunt these days. And pale."

"I'm fine, Rebecca. I'm happy, as long as you come to see me, as long as I have the men in the orchard, and as long as I have my memories and thoughts of you." He nodded. "I'm happy." He remembered something. "The baby, Rebecca, Rosario's bringing Frances for a visit." He smiled. "Is there anything you'd like me to say for you?"

"No, darling, just kiss and hug her for me."

She got up and tucked him in. "Now, close your eyes, get some sleep. Dream, darling, dream good dreams. I love you. Good night."

Xavier Zubiri turned his Lucía, blindfolded and laughing, round and round. "Stop!" She giggled. "You are making me dizzy."

He nodded to Clarence who dutifully held up two lambs, one tucked under each arm. They bleated in turns.

"We will make it fair to us and fair to the Hall ranch. Lucía must pick them at random."

"You could have let me. I don't know a good lamb from a bad donkey." Clarence grinned.

"But it is more fun this way." He reached over and kissed his wife on the cheek. She seemed more beautiful to him wearing the blindfold. He could not understand why.

She reached out and felt them. She chose the one that licked her hand.

Xavier nodded in victory. "It is ours."

They worked through the morning until all were sorted and then dined in the yard, amongst the flock. Half of the offspring would belong to them, the other to the Hall ranch.

"In five years, we will have our own great flock."

Clarence nodded as he drank freely from

his own bota, a recent gift from his new friends. The latest batch of wine was especially good. He held up the wineskin and nodded to Lucía, shooting it into his mouth as he'd been taught. "You've done well, my dear."

He remembered something, and walked into the pen among the little ones that would bear the Zubiri name. "Rebecca told me to kiss them for her."

Lucía became quiet. She did not like to hear about Clarence's delusional conversations with his dead wife. She rubbed the goose bumps raised up on her arms.

"Oh, Clarence!"

She suppressed an urge to cry as Xavier held up a cautionary hand. His hermit friend was fragile, and sometimes his wife could be a little too forceful in such matters. He did not want Lucía admonishing Clarence for such fanciful talk. He turned his head from side to side, putting a finger to his lips, warning her to keep her tongue as Clarence continued his ministrations to the little ones.

He was back with them in short order and sat beside them again. "Rebecca loves lambs." He remembered something. "Rosario's bringing Frances for a visit. Will you come see her?"

"Of course, we will, my friend. Of course we will."

They sat for a while and said nothing as Clarence worked on a cigarette. He drank again from his bota and, with no warning, began to talk, looking off in the distance, he spoke toward one of the mountains.

"I know she's dead." Tears ran down his cheeks and he didn't try to hide them. He didn't bother to wipe them away. He watched the lambs nap and thought of Rebecca again.

"When did you see your child last?" Lucía leaned forward and rubbed his back, almost the way Rebecca used to do when he was tired or weary or worried over something.

"Oh, I don't know. A while ago." He smiled. "Truth is, she looks too much like Rebecca for me to stand." He looked into Lucía's pretty eyes and watched her heart break for him. "She's well cared for, you know. To tell the truth, I intend to just turn Frances over to Hira and his wife. They are Sikhs, you know. She used to be Mary Rogers, Hira's wife, and now she's . . ." He stopped for a moment, a look of puzzlement on his face. "You know, I can't remember her new Sikh name. But she's a good woman and she's a good mother but can't have babies of her own now because of what

Webster did to her." He sighed. "I don't know, don't know how much longer . . . just don't know."

"Clarence, I am a young woman and have not been on this earth very long, but I know a little of such things, and I can say, the baby has a good father and would do well with you in her life." She was crying now and they cried together and Xavier was starting to get worked up himself. It was turning into a regular miserable afternoon for them all.

Clarence stopped them. He jumped up and patted Lucía on her knee. "I'm just being silly and I'm sorry to bring all this up. I might just be plain insane, you two, and that is why I see her, my Rebecca, all the time."

"Grief manifests itself in mysterious ways, my friend." Xavier nodded, reassuringly. "I do not think you are mad at all. I believe you are a very sad man who loved his wife very much." He grabbed Lucía's hand and gave it a loving squeeze. "We are blessed with such love, and Lucía and I understand the love you had for your wife, because we share such love."

He became embarrassed at his own sentimental talk, but felt some relief in making such a speech to his friend.

Clarence sat in silence again and worked

on his bota. He at least was not crying any longer. He turned and looked them both over thoughtfully, then grinned a sheepish grin. "I might still be insane." He felt good talking about it. He'd talked so little for so long, and kept so many ideas and thoughts and emotions locked away. The conversations with his new friends now served as a kind of catharsis, an outpouring of emotions and thoughts, a sharing of all he'd bottled up for so long.

"You know, back in the war, I was a soldier. I got wounded in a peach orchard, at a big battle outside of a little town called Gettysburg, in Pennsylvania. I was a young man and I was hit and lying in a great field of dead and dying men, from both sides. Boys and men were dying in that hot sun and some were so thirsty that they ate some of those unripe peaches. Peaches everywhere, all over the ground, knocked down by shot and musket fire, great big branches of peaches, lying all around. I never understood how those trees could survive, being all shot up like that. But I heard they did. Heard that orchard is still there. But those men and boys, the ones who ate those unripe peaches, they were worse off than if they'd had nothing. A belly full of unripe peaches is no good, and you know, sometimes, when I lie down in my orchard and look up through the branches of my trees, I'm transported back there, some twenty odd years ago and some of those dead men come up and talk to me and I give them some of my peaches and they're ripe and the dead men thank me for them. I keep buckets of water around the orchard with a ladle so they can slake their thirst. God it was hot that day. So hot, and the fire and all that smoke. The air thick with smoke, the salt from the powder, it gets on your face, on your hands, in the wounds, mixes with the sweat or the blood and burns. Burns just as if you'd had acid thrown on you. My eyes burned so, my God it was hot."

He stubbed his cigarette out and looked at it and held it up for Lucía to see. "Look at that, just the way Webster, that murderous devil, used to put his out." He turned back and looked off at the mountain again. "Sometimes, those dead soldiers talk to me. They tell me how lucky I am. The rebels are some of the funniest about it. Men from the south, they have a funny sense of humor, kind of like the Irish. Guess a lot of them are Irish, don't know. They say they're sorry to be dead and especially sorry to be buried so far north, up in the Yankee land. They say I'm lucky because I got to live and get married and have a life and find a good wife and have a child." He stopped and took another drink from his bota. "But sometimes, my friends, I wonder. I wonder if, if it would have not been better had I not made it out of that orchard in Gettysburg. At least I would have never known this loss. Maybe it would have been better never to have known Rebecca at all."

Lucía became a little terse with him. "You must *never* say that again!" She cried and Clarence felt sorry for making her cry. "You are my friend, *our* good friend, and we love you and you should not wish to be dead. Promise me, Clarence, promise me right now that you will never say that again. Promise me that you will never think that again. Promise me. Promise me right now!"

He blushed and looked at the ground. He felt that flutter in his heart, the outpouring of love that he'd not known since Rebecca. He smiled and held out his hand. "I promise, my dear, dear Lucía. I promise. You have my word. I'll never say it again."

CHAPTER 8
A COZY ARRANGEMENT

Walter Druitt watched Betty wash up at the chamber pot at the foot of her bed. It was with Betty when he felt least miserable. He could never feel happy, because happy never entered into it for Walter Druitt. There were only levels of misery, from completely miserable to not very miserable/almost happy. But there was never a happy and the concept of joy was completely out of the question.

But dalliances were a family legacy, and Druitt learned of them from a very tender age, as he was many things, but he was most definitely not stupid, and by the time he was sixteen, his suspicions were proven to be fact, as his father figured that at that point in his son's young life, talking about it openly to him and his brothers was the right and manly thing to do. The sooner they learned, the better, as it was expected in their strata and as inevitable as the turning of the earth.

It was, according to the patriarch, not only expected, but a necessity. The old man said that outright. Man was not a monogamous creature, despite what the bible and the ministers said. It was unnatural, just as a rutting buck or bull would not be expected to live in such a way. Man was drawn to act in his most natural state. And a man of means, well, he needed distractions. Just as obtaining fine racehorses, or fast carriages, or excellent hunting dogs, a man had to collect pretty women as well, and preferably the kind who did not mind being placed in the category of the baser level of the species, as women, most certainly, to the senior Druitt's mind, were definitely of the baser sort.

Walter Druitt remembered wanting to fight his father over that. He wanted to duel him and shoot him between his beady eyes when the old man spoke in such a casual, offhanded way about his marriage and abuse of his wife. *His* mother. The old man was merely married to this woman, but she was Walter Druitt's mother. *His* mother and he loved her very much. The thought of his father doing that to someone other than his mother made him angry and repulsed and sad. His mother deserved better treatment than that.

But once he was married for three years, and once his own wife had decided that one boy and one girl were enough, Walter Druitt finally understood. It was better all around, for husband and wife, and children alike, to go with the conventional, and that was when Walter Druitt took on his first Betty. There'd been twenty-three of them since the present Betty, and frankly, he could remember his hunting dogs better than he could any of them.

But a marriage without love and mutual respect and consideration needed such an arrangement. It did not matter that the dalliances were a monumental distraction. It did not enter into it that, if perhaps, by some preposterous notion, he'd chosen a different path, been present, engaged, shown some gentle kindness, shown the woman he allegedly loved, at least initially, that he still desired her, that she was still desirable to him after the ravages of time, gravity, the addition of a bit extra weight around the middle and thighs, after the excitement had worn off, that he still wanted her for his mate, that he still wanted her in his bed, that he worshiped and cared for her as the marriage vows promised, declared he would all those many sad years ago, things might have been different.

But none of that would happen, and that is why Walter Druitt sat back and considered Betty in her little apartment in the middle of the night.

Betty would never remotely think of herself as a full-fledged prostitute. But no one could call her a concubine, either. She was somewhere in between. Perhaps a mistress, but most definitely not a courtesan. She was not bright or clever enough for that. She could never be counted among the great seductresses, and that is why she only rated a Walter Druitt. They were, it seemed, made for each other.

Still, he was not a hideous man, kept himself clean, spoke in a respectful manner to her, did not beat her, and gave her a hundred and fifty a month for pin money, which of course was not ever intended to be used on either needle or thread. He also paid for her room and board in a nice place just next door to his office. It was a cozy arrangement indeed, and one that allayed Mrs. Druitt's suspicions, had she been interested in finding out where her husband spent so much of his time, which she was not. *At the office* would suffice.

For such kind consideration, Betty engaged in activities that Druitt's wife stopped engaging in a long time ago, and it helped that Betty was beautiful in a way that twenty-five-year-old women were beautiful, beautiful in a way that Walter Druitt's wife was, two children, twenty-five pounds, and fifteen years ago.

Betty also engaged in such scandalous behavior as talking openly and casually about sex, washing her pudenda in his presence, not wearing undergarments most of the time, and being the possessor of a certain repertoire of gymnastics between the sheets that men only read about or heard were possible to experience in the more exotic places of Paris or in the subcontinent of southern Asia, in the bibikhana or ladyhouse of East India Company fame.

She finished and crawled back under the covers, running her fingers down his body as if she really wanted him. Betty was also an accomplished actress.

"What's wrong, lover?"

"What do you mean?" Betty was not nearly so stupid as she looked or acted most of the time.

"You've been in a terrible funk all evening. And . . ." She reached over and lit two cigars, placing one in his mouth; she blew clouds of smoke at the ceiling with the other. "You usually send me to the moon." She lied. "But tonight, you just didn't seem very interested."

He rubbed his temples. "Just have a lot on my mind, Betty."

"Talk about it." She supported her head on her hand, an ample breast resting on his hairy chest.

"It's nothing that would interest you."

"So, the bank, have they backed off?" She gave him a knowing grin.

He was always impressed with the depth of information she possessed. He knew he ran his mouth too freely around Betty.

"As long as I play ball."

"As it relates to the Hall ranch?"

He shot up into a sitting position. "That's going a little far, Betty."

She turned onto her back and blew cigar smoke at the ceiling again. "I might be a good roll in the hay, and a great pair of these" — she pointed at her breasts — "Walter, but I've also got ears . . . and a brain. Not stupid."

"I know you're not." He had to think fast. He'd always been a terrible card player. This was why. All the stress of the past weeks had made him vulnerable, had loosened his tongue, and he'd run his mouth way too much. He always, always showed too much of his hand. He sat up and looked her in the eye.

All of a sudden, he wanted to be held, not necessarily by Betty, but by someone, someone with some compassion, someone who'd make the panic go away. But that did not happen and instead, his mind raced to come up with something to say. It seemed he could trust no one these days.

"I'm going to try to buy them out, Betty. That's all. No violence. This war has got to end. This is just, all just too much and I'm no killer. I hate killing. Hate to hear about women and children dying, hate to hear about lynchings. It isn't right." He felt funny speaking about things in moral terms. "And I'm hoping I can put an end to it all."

She gave him a broad smile and looked him in the eye with a gaze that was all about reverence and adoration. Betty was indeed a great actress. She pulled his hand to her breast and kissed him on the mouth. "If there's a man for it," she lied again, "you are him."

He smiled cynically and pretended to believe her. He looked at his watch and grimaced. Four more hours until he'd hear from his men. He did not know if that was good or bad. He was not sleepy, nor was he happy to have Betty so wide awake.

But after the cigars were finished along with a half bottle of port left over from dinner, Betty did some things that were both novel and distracting for the better part of an hour and afterward he slept well for another three and a half.

He awoke alone to bright sunlight streaming around the curtains and a sliver of sun burrowing through his right eyelid until he was fully awake. His tongue felt much like the ashtray holding the cigar butts. He looked at his watch and then out the window and saw the men milling about the boardwalk in front of his office. He jumped out of bed and dressed quickly as Betty walked in, stretching her back in her sheer nightgown and sipping tea. She kissed him and asked him when he'd return. He did not hear her question and she did not much care. She had some shopping to do.

CHAPTER 9
A GOOD SOLDIER

Pierce Hall could not sit still, nor could he stop the shaking inside. He gulped cup after cup of hot coffee and Rosario would pat him on the shoulder whenever she'd pass him by, which was often, as Rosario had much to do with two invalids, one her husband, and the other her dying top hand to comfort and worry over. Both men were in the best of hands.

Mr. Singh made the young man tea and took his coffee from him. "Tea is much better than horrid coffee at a time like this." He smiled with his typical kindness at the young man.

The Sikh understood what he was going through now, as Mr. Singh had known such times in his life, fresh from battle. The mind goes over and over everything that transpired, looking for answers, looking for reasons to feel that one had not done his part, done enough. He decided to sit with

Pierce with little Frances in his arms. The presence of a child would be a comfort to Pierce Hall now and, the fact was, Mr. Singh needed it as well. The comfort of human contact was essential to the Sikh now. He ran his fingers through the child's hair as she sat and played on his lap, spinning the steel bracelet on his wrist. He waited for Pierce to speak.

"I, I, God, Mr. Singh, I didn't, I didn't . . ."

"You've done nothing wrong, Pierce. You acted with bravery and you were just not there in time. But if you had been, the bad men would no doubt have done worse to you, and you would not have been able to save Old Pop."

Pierce ran a trembling hand through his hair and felt the tea soothe his churned-up guts. "He's goin' to die, you know, I mean, Josh. The doc says no cure for bein' gut shot. Nothin' they can do for that, but wait for him to die."

"But your father, Old Pop, will survive, thanks to you."

"Yeah, and crippled up, because of me. Cuttin' a man down like that. Jesus, what the hell was I thinkin'? What the hell was I thinkin', Mr. Singh?"

The Sikh smiled. He'd have to choose his

words with great care. The young man was riddled with guilt and none of it founded. Pierce was a hero, and Singh would have to make him understand that without patronizing him.

"Pierce," he spoke at the top of his little girl's head. He kissed her auburn locks and she looked up and patted his beard. "Pierce, the men were the bad ones. They did a horrific thing, and it could have been much worse. Young Joshua would have lain in the sun and died a horrible death, but now he is in a comfortable bed, with pain medicine to lessen his suffering. Old Pop will live, and we don't know if his paralysis is permanent. Time will tell. Sometimes the spinal cord is only bruised, or the injury is only temporary. But he is alive and he has his senses and soon he will be able to even talk. And you are the reason for this. You were very brave, Pierce. You were a good soldier, and I for one, am very proud of you."

Pierce blinked away his tears. It was a great honor to be thought of in such high regard by the Sikh, and Pierce knew that Mr. Singh did not say such things without meaning them. Hira Singh did not speak ill of anyone, and when he had nothing good to say of a man, he said nothing at all.

The young man took a deep breath. Without thinking, he reached over and stroked little Frances's head. The noble man's words were getting through to him. He began to relax a little. "I thank you for your kindness, Mr. Singh."

Rosario watched the two men through the doorway from her vantage point in the chair at the bed next to Old Pop. It was the same chair she'd used when keeping vigil over Hobbsie, the husband she had lost a few years before. It was heartening to see the great lion take care of young Pierce. He'd need that now and need Hira's guidance and counsel for all that he'd face in the coming days. Rosario knew, this trial was far from over. It was just beginning for Pierce and the rest of the clan.

She turned her attention to her current husband and watched him sleep until he awoke and gave her a little smile. He mouthed a hello to her and winced from the pain. It was the worse sore throat he'd ever had.

He motioned for a mirror and she gave him one so that he could look himself over. His face was mostly still purple, going toward a yellowish green from so many broken blood vessels. Rosario had stitched closed the big gashes just above the Adam's apple, applied a poultice to his neck wound, and had a cotton dressing wrapped around the whole affair to keep it clean and dry. He began pulling at it to see what damage it hid and Rosario stopped him.

"Now, now, my love. You will see it soon enough. We must keep it clean to ward off an infection."

He nodded and then whispered. "I look like George Washington."

She kissed him on the forehead. "No more talking for now." Of all of the husbands she'd had in her time, Old Pop was, if she were honest with herself, her favorite. She loved all the others very keenly; loved Hobbsie of course. But Old Pop was extra special as he was the kindest and gentlest man she'd ever known. She watched him wince in pain as he tried to move his legs.

"My darling, you have a broken back, too. Your legs are not yet working."

He nodded. He also knew that Rosario was making this terrible news as good as it could sound. He wondered what it would be like to spend the rest of his days in bed, or in a rocker, or being pushed about in a wheelchair. He wondered if he'd ever ride a horse again, and a wave of fear washed over him. He swallowed hard and put his fingers to his throat as if the noose was still cinched about his neck; still strangling him and he needed to get it off. But of course, there was nothing there but Rosario's clean white stock of a dressing, loosely fitted to make him as comfortable as possible.

He tried to speak to her again and Rosario stopped him. She held up a slate and chalk. Old Pop was half embarrassed to use it, as writing was never his strong suit. He complied and began scribbling. He held up the board. "Love you."

"I love you, too, my darling."

He looked around and wrote: "I remember this room."

"Sí, you are at the Halsted home. Pierce brought you and Joshua here yesterday."

"Pierce okay?"

"Sí, he is good. He got a bump on the head, and his horse is dead, but he is good. He is a great hero, and you must tell him that when you see him, my love. He is with Hira now, and I will get him for you."

He wrote again: "I was so scared. Saw God, I think." He smiled, a little embarrassed. He wiped the slate clean and wrote again. "Josh dead, shot in head."

"He is still alive, my love." Rosario would not lie to her husband. "He is in the next room, but he does not have long. He is dying, my love. He was shot down low, too, and there is a bad infection, and the doctor says it is just a matter of time. I've sent for his brother in Florida."

Old Pop scribbled: "Suffering?"

"No, my love, not much. He has much laudanum. He is comfortable and he has much paper and pencils and he's drawing as he can. It is a comfort to him."

She called out to Pierce. "Old Pop is awake, my boy. Come and see him."

He did and sat down in Rosario's chair and Old Pop smiled at him. He reached out and patted the back of the young man's hand. He nodded and mouthed a thank-you.

"Jesus, Pa, I'm sorry. I'm mighty sorry." He began to cry and could not get control as his old friend and adopted father looked like hell.

The old man grabbed him and held him in his arms. He patted him on the shoulder and whispered in his ear. "Thank you, my son. Thank you."

He wiped his cheeks. "Jesus, Old Pop, I thought I lost you. I thought you were gone, and I broke your back. I'm mighty sorry for that. I'm such a boob."

"No, you're not." He winced again and took a drink of water. He mouthed the words. "Better'n a one-way trip to kingdom come." He grinned and pointed skyward. Pierce finally smiled.

"Who did this to you, Old Pop? Who did it?"

The old man shook his head slowly from side to side, then shrugged. He picked up the slate and wrote: "Had scarves over noses." He shrugged. He was exhausted and lay back.

"You rest, Pa. Go ahead and rest."

Rosario repacked the crater that had once held the beautiful, sea-colored eye. Joshua Housman did not flinch or cry out. Instead he worked on a sketch. He waited for Rosario to finish.

"A man with one eye can't draw worth a damn, ma'am." He held up a sketch for Rosario to see. She could not tell if his art was suffering due to the pain, the fever, the partial blindness, or the narcotic haze, but it had most certainly suffered. The young man was dying and his art was dying with him. He continued. "No depth perception. That's the problem."

"Keep drawing, my boy. Your brother will be here soon. He wired me. He is on the train."

The young man shifted in bed and the gut pain tore through his very being. He took a deep breath and cried out. He smiled as the pain let up a little. "Sorry ma'am. Regular little baby, aren't I?"

"Not a bit, my boy. Not a bit." There wasn't much time and Rosario knew it. She didn't want to appear indelicate, but something had to be done.

"My boy, what can you tell me of these assassins?"

"Oh," he grimaced again as he pulled himself up higher in the bed. "Not much. They were all wearing scarves tied over their faces. They knew we were coming. It was all set up. They found the irons and they took the calves. Said that we were rustlers. Old Pop tried to reason with them, and they threw a rope around his neck. I pulled my six-shooter, and one shot me in the eye. When I was down, they shot me in the gut. They thought I was dead and left me alone, and I might as well have been. I couldn't move. Couldn't move a bit, ma'am, couldn't help Old Pop and I'm sorry about that."

"How many, my boy?"

"Seven." He was pale now and Rosario could tell he'd had enough. She left him alone to sleep.

He slept through until evening and awoke to find some broth on the table by his bed. He was not hungry but did imbibe of the laudanum. It didn't much matter anyway. He knew it. He was dying. He could smell it. His gut wound was gangrenous and he knew the odor of gangrene and it permeated the very room. He hoped he'd live long enough to see his brother.

He remembered his dream and most of it was good, some was bad. He dreamed that Rosario crawled into his bed and, all of a sudden, was a stunning cigar-box model and a good eighty pounds lighter and thirty years younger and she made passionate love to him and it was good. He liked that dream very much and thought that he'd have to try his best not to blush or admire her ample bosom when she next changed his dressings. He had all respect for her and even thought that perhaps he loved her, not in a carnal way, of course, but he was still glad he had the dream and hoped that this evening she'd visit his bed in his dreams again and they'd make love again.

He dreamed of the sharks and his brother losing his toes. That was the bad part of the dream, and then he dreamed of the lynching, but instead of Old Pop, the bad men had strung up a great shark, like how they used to do at the big fishing pier down on Front Street in Key West. Someone very strange, perhaps Mr. Singh, walked up and cut the shark's belly open with a great fancy sword like what he'd seen in pictures in a book about the Arabian Nights, and a calf fell out onto the ground. It bleated because the shark had birthed it and it ran off and one of the bad men branded it with the Hall ranch brand.

In a moment of clarity, he remembered some details, details of each man, and he began furiously sketching each one. His mind was wandering now, and the fever was beginning to ravage his body and soon he felt very confused, but he still kept drawing and when he was finished, he looked around a little wildly and found more paper and some envelopes put there for him by Rosario, in the event he'd like to write to someone.

He did and put the sketches and letter in the envelope and sealed it. He wrote his brother's name on it and fell back onto his sweat-soaked pillow. He was exhausted and drifted off.

He heard a voice talking and then realized it was he who was talking to no one. He didn't much care. "It's done, it's done." He arched his back and tried to move away from the gut-wrenching pain, but couldn't. He vomited from the pain and that made it hurt worse and now his throat was, in all likelihood, as sore as Old Pop's. He took a big drink of the laudanum. He needed more and more already as the pain was too much to control and his body already acclimated to the drug. He drained the bottle and thought of calling for Rosario or Singh or Pierce, but the drug finally, mercifully, hit his brain and was now taking hold and he quickly felt very sleepy again.

He dreamed of Rosario again and she was as young and beautiful as before, standing naked by his bed. She reached out for him and he took her hand and followed her out through the bedroom door and then outside and they were on the beautiful beach in the bright sunlight out in back of his home back in Florida. It had not changed a bit in all the years he'd been away from it. His brother handed him a cigar and nodded to them both and they turned toward the ocean and watched a pod of porpoises beach a big shark, pushing it far out of the surf and onto the sand at their feet. The shark became Old Pop and he was fine now and stood up and brushed the sand from his legs and then walked up to them and took Rosario by the hand and away from him. They both waved to him as they stood arm in arm, and then young Joshua Housman was dead.

CHAPTER 10
HE IS BROKEN

Stosh Gorski admired the Mexicana as she handled the horses pulling the buggy so well. She had the conveyance fixed with a scabbard to hold her ten-gauge close by, secure, always ready to do good service when needed. He observed the grip of a six-shooter poking out of the right pocket of her elegant dress. Rosario was not a woman to be messed about.

He smiled down at pretty little Frances wedged between them. The child took to Stosh right away as that was what children always did when they'd met him. He was a magnet for children because he was kind to them and never treated them like they were lesser beings.

He looked back at his horse trotting behind them and smiled as he addressed Rosario. "I am certainly happy to be off that creature." He rubbed his knees.

"If you do not grow up on a horse, it can

be difficult to adjust to them, señor."

"Stosh, please, ma'am, Stosh."

"Stosh."

She liked the man with the strange accent. She liked him even before she met him, as he helped Allingham crack the Webster case. She liked him now because he was gentle and gentlemanly and kind. He was also a Catholic and went to mass with her and she liked that very much, as, ever since the Irish brothers left, she had to go to mass on her own.

"When did you last see him, ma'am?"

Rosario thought hard about it. It had been too long and she did not like to say it for fear of it reflecting badly on her man Allingham.

She shrugged instead. "Oh, not for a pretty long time."

"How is he?"

She shrugged again then thought of how to best describe the situation. "He is broken."

She looked at Stosh Gorski and her eyes became wet. She blinked and rubbed them with the back of her left hand. "But I think he is living okay. Some people we have hired, they are Basques. Do you know of these Basques, Stosh?"

"From Spain, I think."

"Sí, they are shepherds. We hired them because we decided to add sheep to our ranch stock." She shrugged. "They are good friends with Allingham. They are the only ones that are allowed into his life now."

"Rebecca was very special."

Rosario let the tears come freely now. She did not mind the Pole bringing up Allingham's dead wife. Rosario was not like Allingham, and she'd not blot Rebecca from her memory, as she was certain must have been the case for the brokenhearted Capitan. She'd thought about Rebecca, just as she'd thought about poor Francis, from the Canyon Diablo times, and Hobbsie, every day of her life. She turned and looked at Stosh Gorski and sniffed and then smiled. "That is an understatement, my friend."

Gorski found himself talking, and that was natural, even expected, as Rosario had a way with people. Everyone who'd ever met her seemed to want to spill their guts after knowing her just a little while. "I lost my wife too." He felt a little foolish saying that, as if he were afraid he might appear to be keeping score, or seeking pity, which he was not. He really did not know why he said it at all.

His trepidations were quickly allayed, as Rosario covered his wrist with a chubby hand. "I am sorry for your loss, Stosh. I have lost many mates myself. Tell me, if it will not pain you too much, how did your wife pass?"

"Oh, female troubles. My wife was plagued by them all her life. Never could have children." He reached down and pulled the child onto his lap. He kissed her on top of the head. "That broke her heart worse than when the doctor gave her the news that she was dying." He shrugged. "Children are very important to Poles, Rosario. We love to have babies. Lots and lots of babies."

"I am sorry, Stosh." She turned and placed a hand on his cheek. "But she was very lucky to have such a good man as you for a husband. I hope she knew that."

"Oh, she knew it all right. We were best of friends. Soul mates, you would say. I loved her and never let her forget that. I guess we had a good time together, even if it was a bit short. It just, just wasn't long enough."

They arrived at the orchard by late afternoon. No one was there to greet them. The door was unlocked and the child sleepy. Rosario made herself at home, and put the little one to bed. Stosh wandered off to do some exploring.

It was a beautiful place, and different than

any other land he'd visited thus far in Arizona. Allingham's peach orchard was small but grand. Here and there, Gorski could see the ministrations of a loving hand. He did not know that Allingham had it in him to do such work. There were also buckets of water here and there, with a clean ladle for drinking. Stosh availed himself of some as it was quite hot this day.

Some movement caught his eye and he sat down alongside the road to watch a lanky fellow plodding along, a shovel over a shoulder, and a dark mule in tow. He looked to be somewhat of a derelict, and Stosh found it curious that, although the thought of it preposterous, he somehow knew this man.

At one hundred paces, the man picked up his pace, and at twenty, he called out. "Well, bless my soul, it is Stosh Gorski. Bless my soul!"

Gorski fairly reeled. "Allingham?"

He looked his old sergeant over carefully. The rustic clothes, the belt of hemp, the long beard and flowing hair, none of it made any sense to Gorski at all. But the sharpness of the eyes, the spring in the step, could not be doubted. It was most certainly his former sergeant and colleague Allingham.

Clarence dropped the mule's reins and

grabbed up Gorski in his boney arms. He hugged him with all his might and kissed him resolutely on the cheek.

Gorski stood back, flabbergasted. What had happened to the old Allingham? He held his tongue and waited for what was to come next.

"Come, come along, my friend. I want to see the girls." He placed an arm around Gorski's shoulder and literally pulled him along.

Gorski trotted to keep up with him. Allingham was gaunt, frail even, but nonetheless spry. Stosh finally caught a little break as his host dallied near one of the many water buckets. Allingham emptied it of a dead mouse then refilled it with one of his canteens, one big enough to hold more than a good piss, and Stosh remembered Hugh Auld's warning and smiled. Allingham had learned a lot since his days in New York.

"Have to make sure we have enough clean water for the boys." He grinned at Gorski who thought that it was a little queer. In all the time he'd known Allingham, he'd never seen the man so much as smile. Now he was grinning, a lot.

He was off again and Gorski did not have time to inquire about *the boys*. They were soon at Allingham's cottage.

"This used to belong to Webster, you know. I bought it from the bank." He ushered Gorski through the door. Stosh shuddered; a chill ran through him and the hairs stood up on the back of his neck. This was the former abode of a serial murderer, and Allingham now called it home.

Stosh looked about and was relieved. At least it no longer contained any of the vestiges of the diseased monster. It was plainly decorated and orderly and clean. It smelled good of wood smoke and baking, as Allingham had made them pies. He grinned again at Gorski.

"How about a nice trout dinner?" He did not address Rosario when she came out of the bedroom. He walked up on her and gave her a loving kiss and hug to rival the treatment he'd earlier offered Gorski.

"How's my baby girl?"

"She is sleeping, Capitan."

He waved her off. "Clarence, please, both of you, call me Clarence."

He smiled. "Rebecca always says, feed folks after a long journey. I know you're both probably famished" — he pulled out a bottle of Lucía's wine — "and thirsty."

Rosario watched him move about. He smiled and seemed pleased to have them, but there was something off, a little manic in his movements. She could not help but recall Francis the night before he died.

Allingham had everything in order, and would accept no offer of help from her. They sat down as he ran in and out of the parlor, performing various tasks.

Rosario looked at Stosh and shrugged. She leaned close in and whispered in his ear. "I never knew his Christian name."

"Me neither." Stosh scratched the back of his head.

The child was eventually up and they ate and spoke pleasantly as Allingham enjoyed his daughter. He was mesmerized. He looked up at Rosario and nodded. Nothing had to be said.

Rosario finally spoke to the child. "Frances, this is your . . ."

"Uncle! Uncle Clarence!" Allingham reached over and gave her a friendly pat on the head.

Rosario looked at him, incredulous and not a little angry. She held her tongue. This was her first attempt at bringing Allingham back. She did not want to overdo it. The man was even frailer than she'd anticipated.

They dined outside and enjoyed watching the sun go down. Allingham was animated and pleased that most of his pie had been eaten. Little Frances liked him, though it was obvious that his long beard and flowing hair were a tad off-putting to the toddler.

"Stosh, you should ride down to see the red rocks. They're just a little further south. Rebecca says that there is something magical, mystical, something otherworldly about them." He smiled.

Rosario spoke up. "Did you know that Stanislaus lost his wife, Clarence?"

"I did not." He reached out and grabbed Gorski by the hand. "I am very sorry, Stosh. How's she getting along?"

"She's not!" Gorski looked on, incredulous. "She's, she's *dead.*"

"Oh, oh, of course, but, she must come to visit you from time to time."

"No, Allingham, eh, Clarence. She does not. She's dead. She's with the angels. She visits no one. She's dead."

Allingham seemed to lose interest in the conversation. He sprang from his chair and ran through the doorway of the cottage. He retrieved a shawl and placed it over Rosario's shoulders. He pressed his hairy cheek to her face and gave her a loving kiss on top of the head. He skipped, like a child, to a nearby spring and captured a frog. This he placed in little Frances's lap. His little girl smiled and laughed when it hopped away.

"Tomorrow, I'll take you through the orchard. We might see some of the men there."

Stosh wandered outside and found Rosario tending a small campfire. She patted the chair next to her and he sat down. She pulled his cigarette pouch from his vest pocket and twisted him one. She lit it from an ember after placing it in his mouth.

"Can't sleep either, Rosario?"

She poured them a little wine and nodded her head.

"That place" — she pointed at the cottage — "it is not natural. It is, you know, where the evil Webster once lived." She shivered, though it was not especially cold this night.

"I heard that." He worked on his cigarette. He sat back and enjoyed the clear night sky. "It is a pretty setting, nonetheless."

"It is."

They sat for a while and said nothing, though each had a great deal on their minds. Rosario finally broke the silence.

"Stosh, did you ever know why the capitan left you in New York, why he came here to Arizona?"

"No, not really. I always knew something was wrong. Thought he might have consumption and came out to take a cure, but you know how he used to be. He'd tell nothing. Kept all his thoughts and feelings to himself. The rock of Gibraltar he was."

"He came here to die. He thought he had a cancer, and he came out here to die, and once he got here, it was then that he started to live." She looked back behind her to peer at Allingham's bedroom window. "Now, he is dying again." She threw another log on the fire. "I came here to bring him back home, to make him see what he was missing with little Frances, and to get him to help you to stop all the evil. But, now that I see him, well, I could not, do not have the heart to tell him of my husband, nor could I tell him of poor Joshua."

Stosh gazed into the fire. It made no sense to him at all. Allingham was the man with the cast-iron shell. He was unmovable, unemotional. All those years in Hell's Kitchen, Allingham never once showed the inkling of an emotion, good, bad, or otherwise. Now he was like a ghost of his former self, both inwardly and outwardly. It made Stosh a little angry.

"My God, Rosario, he dresses like a hobo! A rope for a belt, and the hair, all the long hair, all over his face and head, what, what on earth has become of him?"

"He used to dress so well." She laughed.

"Back at Canyon Diablo, my friend, you should have seen him." She stood up and marched to and fro, arms swinging like a tin soldier. "He would strut about in his fine suits, high collar, and that funny little derby on his head. Oh, how the bad men hated him!"

"Everyone hated him." Stosh laughed.

"Except us." She smiled but she was not happy. "I love him, always have, and I know you love him."

Stosh had to look away. He felt a chill, remembered the task at hand, remembered the photos in O'Higgins's office of the slain women and children, and he worried over Rosario and the child riding back to Flagstaff.

"Tomorrow, I'll, I want to ride back with you, Rosario."

"No, no. You stay a little while with him. Then go on to your business down south, as you planned." She patted her hip, where the pistol was secured in her pocket. "I will be all right."

CHAPTER 11
INTENDED TO ACHIEVE
ONE PURPOSE

Onan Graham abused himself as he sat next to a dung heap at the southern yard of his family ranch. With his free hand, he plucked the feathers of a live dove clamped resolutely between his filthy bare feet. It was a good late morning, as he was alone and no one was lurking about to clap his ears for him.

He'd discovered the joys of abusing himself since just after his thirteenth birthday and it was becoming his favorite pastime. In another couple of years his pa had promised to take him, for his fifteenth birthday, to the Birdcage down in Tombstone where he could become a proper man. He could not wait for that, as he'd heard all the stories about the whores in Tombstone, and even saw some bad photos kept by the hands in and around their bunks of women in various stages of undress. One of the fellows even had photos of men and whores fornicating. He could not keep those images off his dim mind.

One of the old men laughed as the boy quipped about having to wait so long, and offered him advice on the many virtues of sheep, and how certain parts of their anatomy was not unlike that of a woman. That piqued his interest, but there were no sheep around. The damned blacks, the Halls, were the only sheep handlers in the region, and his father had strictly forbidden the lowly beasts on any of his land, so sheep were regrettably out of the question in his quest to help slake the unnatural lust consuming his very soul.

A wave of rage coursed through his body at the thought of waiting so long for this great event and he savaged the dove, tearing its head off, reveling in the sensation of the quivering body's death throes against the soles of his feet.

Without warning, an explosion, louder than he'd ever heard, then another new, even stranger sensation assaulted his senses. He could not get his breath, and someone, or something, had punched him so hard on his back that it forced his head so violently forward that his forehead bore a little of the dead dove's blood.

He righted himself and looked down and now the dove and his lap and feet were red with bright scarlet blood. Something white, a chunk of breastbone, lay near the little pile of feathers.

The second shot was a little low, just at the base of his skull, and now, most of his lower face was gone, torn away by the big lead slug. Onan Graham, favorite son of cattleman Tom Graham, was dead. The patriarch would likely be the only one to mourn his passing. Everyone else would be relieved, or at best, ambivalent, at the wretched boy's passing.

A little further south John Gilliland rode the fence line and was pleased with the quick progress. In another few weeks, it would be ten times as long, but more importantly, it would separate the Hall ranch cattle from the water they'd needed and used for years.

He reached out and plucked the wire and was impressed at its tightness. This would certainly end the nonsense once and for all, and more importantly, break those damned blacks so that he could buy them out cheap.

Tom Graham was a genius and Gilliland was glad he'd met him. Glad he'd listened to him. And with O'Higgins's money, they'd soon have the whole valley to divide between them. Then he'd see what he could do to sell out himself. He could move back to Texas, where he was happiest, and start fresh. He'd like that, not having a man hovering over him, though he could not find fault with O'Higgins at all. The tycoon was a good boss, a good man, but there was just something about running one's own operation that appealed to John Gilliland.

He rode up a rise and was impressed with the Chinamen. They could run a straight fence all right, straight as an arrow and long, by God, it was long, and every cent paid without question by O'Higgins. He wondered at that. The man must have had an inexhaustible supply of cash. Gilliland would write check after check, and no one, not even the busybody secretary Tomlinson ever questioned him once. Never did anyone ever ask for an accounting of what he was doing, what he was spending the money on. He thought about what Graham once said, the old saying, better to get forgiveness than permission. Gilliland never, ever sought permission, and anyway, O'Higgins didn't really seem to care.

He stopped and looked on down the slope and then on to the next rise. He took a long drink from his canteen and wiped his mouth. They went on and on, neat as soldiers lined up in a row. He squinted and

further down, at the lowest point in the valley, there was something odd about a dozen
or so of the posts. He put his canteen back
and rode on. Heads crowned the posts here.
Eleven calves, decapitated and placed like
pike heads on each, their carcasses piled
nearby. A complete waste of prime animal
flesh, intended to achieve one purpose.
Those goddamned blacks!

He found his foreman at the end of the
gruesome line, or at least, his head. He'd
been missing for more than a day and
Gilliland was certain he'd been off to the
whores down in Holbrook. Gilliland was
half tempted to fire him when he'd not
shown up. Now he knew for certain how
he'd been waylaid. Eyes fixed skyward,
tongue hanging out like some swollen chunk
of meat that would not go down, by the
amount the red ants had carried away thus
far, it was fairly evident he'd been there
since around the time he'd gone missing.
John Gilliland vomited his guts out. It
would take another two days to find his
body.

Xavier Zubiri moved his flock along and
thought of his wife. He'd been away from
her too long and she'd made some mention
that she might already be pregnant, but that

did nothing to slake his desire for her now. Despite the time they'd been married, their desire for each other was as great, perhaps even greater than on the night of their wedding, the greatest night of the shepherd's life.

He pondered that. Growing up he remembered the old men quip about their wives, and his old father would joke as they walked back home after the day's work was done. He remembered his father's words so well. *They sit in the bar all evening instead of being home with their wives. No wonder their women won't do right by them, my son.* He'd pull Xavier in close, by his neck, lovingly, and speak into his ear. *You take care of your woman, Xavier, make being with you the best part of her day, and you will never know a marriage like that.*

He looked at the sky and quickened his pace. He'd be home soon, and the flock was behaving well enough.

Up ahead, standing between him and his home a Mexican sat ahorse and seemed benign enough. The stranger sat and watched the sheep envelope his mount and plod along, to his left and right. Xavier tipped his hat to the man and looked him over. He was a southerner, and Xavier had known a few. He sported a big sombrero and fancy vaquero leather and saddle. He had a machete tied just above the scabbard holding his Winchester. He was a vaquero of considerable means, and the Basque figured he must have been wandering up this way for the abundant work available to men in such a trade.

"Señor." The Mexican tipped his hat and nodded with great respect. "Would you sell me a lamb?"

"If you will take a ram." He'd sell him a Hall ranch animal and hold the money for Señora Rosario.

"I will, if you will eat some with me."

Xavier nodded. It was not ideal, as his wife was preying on his mind. Something told him to humor the Mexican and he resigned himself to an hour of inactivity as the Mexican worked on building a small fire.

Xavier killed the lamb and began breaking it down. The sooner he could get it cooking, the sooner he'd be on his way. He watched the Mexican prepare a frying pan.

They ate in silence for a while and the man began to dally too long. The Basque stood up and wiped his trousers clean.

"Thank you señor. I see, you are a long way from home, and I am certain you have things to do." He waited for the Mexican to respond, or at least look up. "I'd like to be paid now, and move on. I have much to do before the sun goes down."

The Mexican snapped back. "What's it to you where I am from, gringo?" He looked up tersely from a cigarette he was twisting. "What do you care if I am from the south or the north of the east or the west? I will pay you. Do you not trust Mexicanos, is that it, gringo?"

Xavier cast his eyes to the ground. He did not like to fight with men, especially ones well-armed. He pointed to the man's horse. "No offense intended, but I have been in the land long enough to know the things, the customs, the dress of the people of Mexico." Xavier shrugged and began to move away.

"Sorry, mister, I should not have called you gringo. You are a Spanish, are you not?" The Mexican got up and fiddled with a saddlebag. He pulled a cigar from his pocket and offered it to the Basque. "Here, mister, have a cigar, as an offer of apology. I'm sorry, mister, I'm, I'm just tired, and the gringos up here, they are always in my business, always suspicious of the Mexicano."

"I don't care for cigars."

"Then, here, here, I have good tobacco, for the cigarillos. Here, my friend." He dug some more at one of his saddlebags.

Xavier Zubiri did not see the flash of the machete as it came down.

Betty regarded the fine mahogany shaving stand atop her dresser and then a full half of her wardrobe taken up with Walter Druitt's suits. The tang of sweated and smoked-in garments washed over her and she turned to regard the sleeping man.

He awoke and it was far too early for Betty to do her duty. She regarded him with a look he'd not known in all the time he'd been with her.

He grinned uneasily and grabbed as much courage as he dared. She was his mistress, not his wife. He pointed at the objects that were new to her room.

"It makes sense. They're all off to England and, until the house is rebuilt, this is the most logical place for me to stay, Betty."

She recovered quickly. Betty was ruthless, but she wasn't stupid. She was not certain of how violently she could tug on Walter's nose ring, and she wasn't about to try just now. She smiled.

"Whatever made you say that, lover?" She dropped her dress to the floor and slithered between the sheets.

Afterward, they smoked cigars.

"You don't mind me staying here, then?"

He pretended that her answer would be genuine and that he would care one way or the other about the response.

She stretched like a queen cat and brushed up against him with a soft and baby-smooth thigh.

"Not a bit. But, darling . . ." She decided to change the subject, as there was no profit in sparring over the fact that he'd moved in. "I, I wanted to tell you, I've got an old school friend, from my boarding-school days" — she lied; she'd actually met the woman in a brothel — "coming to San Francisco, and, well . . ."

"You want to see her?"

"Yes." She did some things under the sheets to make him not capable of saying no.

He smiled. "How much?"

She held up two fingers, about an inch apart.

"That much?" His eyes widened. He got up and sauntered to the carpetbag. He opened it enough to let Betty have a gander at what it contained, and it had the desired effect.

"Where on earth did you get *all that*?"

"Oh, business, just business." He reached in and pulled a stack of bills, neatly wrapped with a paper band from the bank. He hefted it in his hand and regarded the thickness. "That looks about right." He tossed it playfully on her lap. He laughed a little to himself at the thought: *Just feeding the cat.*

"What's got you in such a good mood?"

"I don't know." He smiled and climbed back in bed. He wanted her again and that was a good sign. Money always put Walter Druitt in a good mood and it seemed his carnal desire was directly affected by such.

"So, the bank, and the fire, everything is working out, darling?"

"Uh-huh." He was distracted now. He wanted Betty to shut up.

He dozed for a while in her arms and when he'd awakened, he could not stop thinking of his wife and children. He took a deep breath and reached for the scotch by the bed. He took a long drink and breathed in the scent of Betty's hair. They all just as quickly evaporated from his mind.

"How long will you be in San Francisco?"

"Oh, I don't know." She played with the stack of bills and calculated how long they'd keep her there, in style, away from Walter. She quickly arrived at a rough estimate. She wanted to say a couple of months, and then thought that a tad too bold. Neither knew that the other would be relieved had the time stated been longer rather than shorter.

"I guess, a few days."

"That's vague. A few days, meaning, a few weeks, a few months, what?"

"Delores is off to Europe next, so she won't be around long. She's got to get to New York, then on the ship to Europe, to Paris, I'd say three weeks, then she'll be off, and I'll be back then."

"That's a long time." He lied. He'd be glad to be shed of her as he gazed around at his new bachelor apartment. He'd hoped it would be three months. There was a new young clerk working at the bank, younger and prettier and more bosomy than Betty, and someone mentioned she was partial to expensive perfume.

Betty finally pulled herself from the bed and he was missing her right away. She regarded the lust in his eyes and grinned a little cynically. It would be a good time to broach the subject.

"And, darling, may I have one more stack?" She leaned in and gazed at the carpetbag's contents, a twinkle in her eye. "I simply have *nothing* to wear."

CHAPTER 12
TO BE ALONE

The cart rode over a big rock and water splashed out, wetting Stosh Gorski on the thigh. Allingham walked a little ahead of him, leading the mule as they went. He turned and looked back at his old friend and smiled broadly.

"I still cannot believe you are here, Stosh." He turned his attention to the first bucket and emptied it of its contents. He wiped the ladle clean and then filled the vessel with fresh water. He moved on to the next.

"It's going to be hot, hot, hot today."

Stosh held his tongue and wondered at the great labor involved.

Allingham seemed to sense what was in his friend's mind.

"Every Tuesday, without fail." He nodded at the cart. "That used to belong to Webster, too. He used to transport his victims, or parts of them, at least. Had a devil of a time getting the bloodstains out. But I did,

I did." He patted his mule and sat down under the shade of a tree while Stosh twisted a cigarette. Allingham continued. "Webster got poor Mary Rogers in here, broad daylight, on a Flagstaff street." He shook his head slowly from side to side. "Damn terrible business was that." He brightened. "But she's all right now. With Hira, has little Frances." He thought for a moment. "Thanks in part to you, Stosh." He grinned and thought of a question. "How did it feel to see her, once you'd met her?" He didn't wait for an answer; instead he smiled and looked up the line at the buckets yet needing his attention. "Guess this is a bore for you, Stosh. Sorry. If you'd like to go back, I'll finish taking care of the boys."

"What boys, Alling— Clarence?" Stosh Gorski had a good idea, but asked nonetheless.

"The boys, from the war. They come see me. Not all the time, mind you, but now and again, now and again. We probably won't see them today." He looked quizzically at Gorski. "That's right, I've not told you. You were not yet in the States when the war came, were you Stosh? You would have been a grand soldier. Anyway, in the war, I was in a battle, in a peach orchard, just like this. Spent almost two days in the field till they could get to me. The men I was with, the ones who died . . ." He looked at Gorski a little confused. "Are you certain, Stosh, certain you don't ever see your wife?"

Gorski had had enough. He walked to the water barrel, took a ladle full and threw it with all his might into Allingham's eyes, causing his friend to sputter and cough, then smile uneasily at his companion.

"Why on earth did you do that, Stosh?" He wiped his face dry with an old handkerchief. "We might run out before we get to all the buckets now."

"Goddamn it, Allingham! Goddamn it, wake up, man! There are no men, there is no wife visiting you. My wife, my wife is dead, Allingham. She's dead and gone off to the angels, or to the great beyond, or is just dead, I don't know where she is but she doesn't visit me. Your Rebecca doesn't visit you, the men in battle don't visit you! God-damn it Allingham, get a hold of yourself, man!"

It seemed to have no effect. Allingham stared off at a line of trees heading east to west. He let the water drip from his flowing hair and beard. He finally spoke, a little quietly. "I know." He looked at Stosh and held out his hand for the Pole's tobacco pouch. Stosh twisted a cigarette for him. He did not want his tobacco to get wet. Allingham smoked and breathed in the smoke and blew a big plume with his comment.

"I might be mad."

Stosh sat next to him and put a hand on his old friend's shoulder. "I don't think you are mad, my friend. I think you loved your wife very much, I think you miss her very dearly."

The tears ran down his face, mixing with the water thrown by Stosh. "I, I just, I don't know, Stosh. I used to think, used to find order in things, used to think that there was order in the universe, that things turned a certain way, and now, now, I just, I just don't see any order, or well, fairness to life anymore." He smoked and stared at the ground in front of him. "I, you know, back in New York, it was quite easy. Everything was orderly, in order in my life. No worries, ever, really, just, my only concern, really, was not becoming bored, and then, then I came out here, and met Rebecca, and did some things." He cleared his throat and continued. "It just doesn't seem fair, Stosh. I, I, why did I ever even have to meet her? Why did that happen? I was going along fine with no one in my life, just me, alone in the world" — he stopped and smiled at Gorski — "except you, but, well, sorry, you don't count, Stosh." He thought for a moment. "And then, then Rebecca came along, and then she was stolen from me. It, it just doesn't seem fair."

"Fairness in life is a great cruel myth, my friend." He looked at the spot occupying so much of Allingham's attention on the ground at their feet. He went on, thinking of his own life. "My dear wife, I loved her Clarence, you know that, and she me. She loved me very much and we were, were better than husband and wife. We were soul mates, and the only thing missing was a child, and we could never have a child, Clarence, never, ever have a child, and it was always so close, the baby would come, would grow, and then, just when we thought we were on our way home, the little one would die. I have an entire cemetery plot full of my children, Allingham, and never knew a one of them." He laughed a little. "Remember the whores, Allingham. Remember how we fought them? Remember all the babies? The goddamned whores could roll in a wet spot and get pregnant, have a perfect little baby. Not one of them ever wanted a child, yet they'd sprout out of them like they were toadstools on a rotten stump. No, that's not fair. That's not fair. And then the dirty bitches coming in rooting them out with a wire. Remember, Allingham, remember the little pieces of corpses we used to find? Little ones, torn to pieces, lying in a little pile. No, that's not fair, but that's life, and that's what we've been given, my friend, and it's the way it is."

"But I miss her, so much."

"As do I. But my friend, she doesn't visit you, she doesn't, and you've got to move on." He waved his hand about. "This, this is all wrong, my friend. You are not a god-damned farmer; you do not tend to the needs of dead men. Jesus Christ, you live in an evil butcher's house; have his dogcart, in which he hauled his dead and dying victims around. *Jesus*, Allingham!" He thought hard about what to say. Wanted, needed to somehow jolt him into reality. "You've, you've, you know why Rosario, that wonderful lady came to see you, my friend?"

Allingham looked at him vacantly.

"She was trying to get you to come home. There's a goddamned war, my friend. And I, I'm in over my head. I'm, I need your help. Rosario's husband was lynched. Your friend, lynched, your friend treated so rudely, Rosario's husband, and it is not nearly as bad as it's going to get. This is just the tip of the iceberg, Allingham."

"Clarence." He smiled uneasily.

"Clarence, Clarence. Jesus, man, help us. We need you. You're, you're our only hope. We can't endure this without you." He sat down again and watched what effect his speech was having on him.

Allingham smiled a little cynically. He looked at Stosh through tears in his eyes. "The cemeteries are full up with men whom the world could not do without." He looked around a little, as if someone or something was about to come out of the shadows and accost them. "I, I, can't. I can't." He looked into Stosh's eyes and was likely the saddest man the Pole had ever known. "I'm sorry, Stosh. I want, I want you to go now. I just want to be alone." He turned and looked at the water dripping from his beard onto his lap. "Just, please, just leave me alone."

CHAPTER 13
THE BEST OF MEN

Dan Housman sat at the same place previously occupied by his now-dead brother, waiting for the tea to arrive. He was an older, taller, and more imposing version of young Joshua, with the same piercing blue eyes and sun-bleached hair. He was also not nearly so nice as his brother and this could not be hidden by Dan Housman. He was most certainly an imposing man.

He looked about the parlor and immediately spotted his brother's work as Rosario walked in and set the service down. She smiled and looked at the picture occupying his attention.

"It is good, no?"

"Very good, ma'am."

"Your brother was a great artist and a good man. I think he captured me well."

"Beautiful." The Floridian nodded as he tended to his tea. "It is easy with such a model."

She blushed a little. "You have a silver tongue, just like your brother, señor."

"No offense intended, ma'am."

"De nada."

They had tea in silence for a while and then Dan Housman was drawn to talk a little about his slain brother.

"Do you know why Joshua moved out here to Arizona, ma'am?"

"No, not really." She leaned forward and offered her undivided attention. She knew this to be part of the grieving process, and she'd be there for him to listen as long as he wanted to talk. Rosario reached over and pulled a cigar from Dan Housman's coat pocket, trimmed it, and lit it for him.

He smoked and stared at the tip.

"My brother and I used to be wreckers, ma'am, back in the early days. We've taken care of each other since my parents passed in a big storm, a long time ago." He smoked again. "That one storm took over four hundred lives. Don't know if you've ever been in a hurricane, ma'am, but my brother and I, we thought we were blessed for just surviving it." He hesitated a moment, remembering the terrible time. "Anyway, we used to go out to the shipwrecks, just small time, ma'am, all the big outfits had the good wrecks sewn up, but, well, ma'am

. . ." He thought of something. "Did you notice Josh never ate pork?"

Rosario shrugged. She did not know this about the young man.

"Well, he didn't, and anyway, well, we went to a wreck a few years ago, and ma'am, it was a dandy. A ship, an old one, one of the last sail ships, you know, they're all steamers nowadays." He shrugged. "It's what ruined the wrecking business, that and lighthouses. Steamships don't get blown onto the reefs like in the good old days. Anyway, this ship was resting on a reef, upright, just like it could sail away, except it had several tons of water in its hull, and a big hole punched just rear of the starboard bow, and well, that ship was carrying livestock, hogs, and those hogs, ma'am, they were kind of wallowing in that hull, just like they were in a great pile of pig slop and mud, except instead of muck it was seawater and there was just one big problem. A nice fat bull shark had swum right in there and he was just dining on swine to his heart's content. Pigs were bawling and squealing and that water was scarlet red. It was one hell of a sight." He blushed. "Begging your pardon, ma'am."

Rosario nodded for him to continue. "I have heard worse, my boy."

"Well, ma'am, I can say, we both, Josh and I, we were pretty shaken up by that, and I kind of lost my head, got into a bit of a temper" — he smiled a little coyly — "kind of known for my filthy temper ma'am, and I jumped in on that shark's back with the intent of stabbing him to death with my big knife, and well, ma'am, don't know if you know anything about bull sharks, but they are some quick devils, and that shark spun around and bit half the toes off my right foot."

Rosario looked down at the man's feet. "Ay chingao! That is terrible, my boy!"

"Yes, ma'am, but only due to my own foolishness and stupidity. Not the first time my temper got me into a bit of trouble, I can assure you. But that old shark swum right back through the hole in the boat and then all of a sudden, a great wave hit the hull of that ship and everything started breaking apart. Those hogs started swimming all around, some out to sea, some in circles, and we started herding them in to shore. Saved a few. Later on, our friends all went out looking for that shark."

He smiled at the tip of his cigar again. "Like a man hunts for a killer. Pretty silly, when you think of it. A shark's just being a shark, no need to track 'em down and bring them in for trial, like they're bad men. Shark's just being a shark. Anyway, my brother, he's got an eye for a face."

Rosario nodded energetically, remembering the story and how Josh related it to the stolen calves. "Sí, I know this very well, my boy."

He nodded. "Even the face of a shark, and do you know, ma'am, out of the hundreds those boys brought in, my brother recognized the right shark. We cut him open and out popped what was left of my toes." He held up a hand. "Swear to God!"

He looked like he'd cry and Rosario waited for him to continue.

"Well, ma'am, we got out of the wrecking business pretty soon after that, and started with the cigars. Guess Josh told you about the cigar business."

"Sí, my boy, he did. He told me he used to do the artwork for you, on the boxes."

"That he did, ma'am. And a lot more. Old Josh, you know, he was a workhorse." He regarded her drawing on the wall again, and thought of his brother's art. "But I couldn't hold him. Couldn't and he said he wanted to live where no shark could bite him and he used to read those silly old dime novels, you know, Wild Bill, and General Custer, and such, and well, that's how he came to be here in Arizona."

He sat and let a tear run down his cheek. He did not mind crying in front of Rosario. "I'm going to miss that boy."

Rosario led him to the bunkhouse and turned to walk away. She never invaded the men's privacy there. They were waiting for him when he came in and they all nodded respectfully. Long Jack even shook Dan Housman's hand.

"We—we're ma—mighty sorry for your loss, mister."

"You must be Harry." Dan gave him a warm smile and took his hand to shake.

The stuttering man blushed. No one ever acknowledged him, and Josh Housman had evidently told his older brother about him. He was humbled by that.

"Ye—yes sir. An—and this is Long Jack, and over there, the man coo—cookin' is Ang Lee."

He nodded and regarded the bunkhouse. It was just as Josh had described it, down to the last window sash.

"This here's Josh's bunk." Long Jack held out a hand as he regarded the bunk with the drawings pinned to the walls all around it. "Guess you can figure that out, sure enough."

"He was a drawing son of a gun."

"Ye—yes sir. He—he, you should see the paintings he di—did in Flagstaff. Barman there, Frenchman, got Jo—Josh to paint naked ladies. Qui—quite the sight."

Long Jack spoke up. "These are all his traps, mister. He was a frugal fellow, your brother. There's five hundred there and his six-shooter and Winchester. He's got another thousand in the bank, Miss Rosario can get it for you."

Dan Housman looked the things over. He picked up the six-shooter Josh had gotten in Florida. He remembered the day he'd bought it. He was proud of that gun. He picked up the Winchester and it had some of Josh's blood on it. He nodded to the men. "You boys divide all this up amongst you. Money too. Josh would have liked that."

"No—no sir. Don't ta—take charity, mister."

Dan held up a hand and nodded his head at the items on the bed. "No, you take it, take it as a way to remember Josh. If you don't want the money, give it to poor people; give it to some Indians or the like."

He looked at Ang Lee and nodded. "I'd like to keep the pictures, however." He turned to walk back to the ranch house and stopped. He looked each man in the eye by turns.

"Who did this to my brother?"

They shrugged. Long Jack spoke up. "We honestly don't know, mister. I swear to you, when we find out, they'll be hell to pay. Josh was a good man, and a good boss, and I, for one, won't let this go without someone answering for it."

Dan Housman nodded gravely. "Thank you for that, but, I'd say, just let it go. It will all work out. It always does with low-down dirty bastards like these. Just let it go, men, get on with your lives." He straightened a drawing just over Josh's bed. "If you know Josh at all, he'd want that."

He made it halfway to the ranch house and Rosario when Ang Lee called after him. The cook walked up on Dan Housman and looked him in the eye. "Mister, I want to say, your brother. He the best of men." The Chinese turned away. He could not linger any longer, or say another word.

Dan Housman read in his bed in the hotel room in Flagstaff. He removed Josh's drawings from the envelope and laid them flat on the table next to the bed. He read:

Dear Dan:
   Well, you know what happened to me by now. Dead. Sorry for all this. Sorry for ever

leaving you. I shouldn't have, but cannot deny that I had a good life here in Arizona. Just sorry that I was so far from you. You've been a good brother. Just needed to get away from those sharks. Funny thing, Long Jack dug out a big tooth in the desert, long time ago. Shark tooth in the desert. I thought you might find that amusing.

Those pictures in this envelope are some things about the seven men who did this to me. You know, you always said, I got a camera in my brain. I didn't tell the Hall people about these bad men. They've got enough to worry over. Maybe you could go on down to see that fellow Halsted in Flagstaff. Seems the only honest man in these parts these days. Don't know. Doesn't much matter now, going on to learn the grand secret. Hope to see you again someday.

Josh.

PS- Please don't get any fool notions of hauling my carcass back to Florida. It is too damned wet to make a good grave down there anyway. Rosario will take good care of me. She is a special lady. Give her a good kiss for me when you see her.

CHAPTER 14
SHE NEEDS YOU NOW

Clarence Allingham plodded along with a great deal on his mind. He had good peaches for the Basques, and felt a little more desperate than usual to see Lucía. The visit from Stosh Gorski had worn him out and now Rebecca had failed to visit him for two nights in a row. He was feeling especially sad and low-down.

For more than a year he'd been doing fine, alone, with his thoughts and his ghosts, and now, with his new friendship with the Basques, and especially because of the visit by Rosario and Stosh, and little Frances, things seemed to be literally unraveling in his tortured mind. Living souls seemed to do that to him. He was fine with the dead; it was the living that were so vexing to him.

He nearly bumped into Xavier on his way, or at least part of him, as the Mexican had very rudely propped the shepherd's head on the Basque's ancient makila, or walking stick, that never left Xavier's side.

Allingham dropped the reins and his mule wandered off a little ways to eat grass. The animal soon found Xavier's body nearby. The creature looked Allingham in the eye almost as if to say, *Here he is, I have found him. Your good friend is resting in the grass.*

Allingham removed the head and kissed Xavier on the forehead. He wiped some larvae away from the corners of each eye, then pressed the eyelids closed tight. He cradled the head in his arms, carrying it to the stream where he washed it off. He dried the hair and combed it with great reverence and care. He placed the head next to the body, then retrieved Xavier's grandfather's makila. He took it to the stream and washed it as well.

He put his friend in the dogcart and transported him back home. There he bathed him and spoke soothing words to him. He got his sewing kit out and re-attached the head. He put Xavier in his best suit, the handmade pinstripe one from the New York days. He pinned it in the back, as Xavier was much smaller than Allingham, but it all worked out, and soon he looked very well. He put a high celluloid collar around Xavier's neck to hide the sutures. He remembered it was one of the collars that Francis had forbidden him ever to wear, but the lad had missed this one, it had not been thrown away back in the Canyon Diablo days.

"Now you look very fine, my friend." He put the makila beside him and let Xavier rest in his bed until he could build a coffin of some nice chestnut he'd been saving for a clock case he'd intended to build one of these days.

He worked all day and through the night until morning. He should have stopped and gone back and told Lucía but didn't. Time had gotten away from him and he could only focus on the task at hand. By sunrise he'd finished the simple coffin, loaded it and placed his friend inside. He headed out to see the Basque's wife.

Lucía was waiting for him and knew her man was dead. She'd known if for a day and a half, as the sheep had wandered home and he had not. Xavier would not do such a thing on purpose, and this is why Lucía knew that he was dead.

She did not acknowledge either Allingham or the coffin. She simply turned to go inside. She undressed to her petticoat and climbed into bed. Allingham followed her as she held up the covers for him to join her. He held her and said nothing. They

145

slept all day and late into the night and Lucía said not a word. She did not cry or wail or ask what had happened. She slept and squeezed Allingham's hand and held it so as to keep him there. He'd not leave her side as she would not allow it.

He awoke to whispers in his ear and Rebecca was there, leaning forward, hands on knees like a fairy princess. She smiled warmly and was glowing all white. "Hello, my darling."

He turned to pull himself away and Rebecca stopped him. "Stay with Lucía, darling, hold her, comfort her, love her and be with her. She needs you now." She reached over and kissed him on his forehead. She gave him a loving pat and was gone. Allingham slept until morning.

CHAPTER 15
TIT FOR TAT

Hugh Auld was waiting in the road for Stosh Gorski as he traveled south. The Pinkerton stopped and took a long drink from his biggest canteen as a show to the prospector that he'd taken the man's advice. He extended a hand and Auld shook it. Gorski could tell right off that this was not a social visit at all.

"Stosh." Auld nodded his head.

"Hugh, you look like the weight of the world is on your shoulders, what has happened, my friend?"

"Tim Holt's what's happened, Stosh." He turned his mount to ride alongside Gorski. He continued. "Guess you've heard of the Graham boy's murder."

Stosh nodded. It was where he was headed now.

"Going to see him, and then on to Sheriff Owens."

Auld stopped him. "Stosh, it's all a big

frame-up. My friend, old Tim Holt, old buffalo hunter from a way back. He works for Gilliland. They say he shot the boy with a buffalo rifle. Shot him twice, just about destroyed his face. Couldn't even have a proper photo of him resting in his coffin."

"And why is this a frame-up?"

"Because I know Tim. Never killed a man in his life. Likes shooting guns, especially his big old buff guns, but he's a gentle soul, a good man, never hurt another human being, I swear it."

Stosh turned toward the Graham ranch, nodding for Hugh to follow. He looked over his shoulder. "Where's Holt now?"

"With some Indian friends." He didn't hesitate to tell Gorski, and this was not lost on the old copper. Auld trusted him implicitly, and Gorski knew he could do likewise.

He looked over at Hugh again and stopped. "Ride with me, Hugh."

"Do you suppose that's a good idea?"

"Does Graham know you?"

"Doubt it." Hugh shrugged. "But if he connects me to Tim, well, there'll be hell to pay."

Stosh held up a cautionary hand. "Let me do the talking, Hugh. Graham's likely pretty riled up, I know I'd be, and he's a loose cannon on his best day, certain enough." He nodded again. "I'll deal with him as regards the buffalo hunter."

They arrived by late afternoon and passed young Onan Graham's fresh grave. They were met by three hands, guards, armed with Winchesters. They were not especially friendly, but obliged the men by escorting them to their boss's ranch house.

Graham was there, on his porch, drunk and red-eyed from crying over his boy. He nodded just discernibly to the men. He did not know Hugh Auld, did not know the prospector was hiding the man he was after.

"I am sorry for your loss, Mr. Graham."

"Goddamn Gilliland's man." He began crying again and continued. "Son of a bitch thinks I'm responsible for his foreman losing his head, for the calves being slaughtered, and he sends one of his men to kill my boy. Destroy my boy." He held up a cartridge case the size of a grown man's index finger. "Destroyed my son!"

Stosh casually took the brass shell case from the man and, with significant sleight of hand, slid it into a vest pocket. It would be useful later on.

Graham, as if awakening from a dream, or at least a stupor, became lucid. He looked the men over, accusation and mistrust in his gaze. "What the hell are you two doing here? Goddamned Polock" — then he looked at Hugh Auld — "and a bum, what business is any of this to you?"

Stosh looked a little more serious than usual. "We're here to help, Mr. Graham. To get to the bottom of this. We're sorry for this tragedy, but fighting us is not going to help."

"Don't need your damned help. In this alone, first the nigger Halls, now Gilliland, probably your boss, the stinkin' Mick." He began crying. "I'll kill 'em, kill 'em all." He had a kind of little fit and dropped to the ground. Stosh and his companion turned and rode off. There was no point to any of this now.

"Tit for tat." Hugh Auld shrugged and looked at his new partner. He liked Stosh Gorski. The man was cool in a tight spot from what the prospector had seen so far. He grinned. "That was clever of you, lifting that shell casing."

Stosh pulled it from a pocket and held it up, regarding it as he turned it around in his hand. He'd never seen such a thing.

"One thing is certain."

"What's that?"

"Any man who'd shoot a boy like that, with a gun like this, was out to make a point. This was meant to do more than provoke or intimidate, this was meant to do exactly what it has done."

Auld nodded. He shivered a little at the thought of what the corpse must have looked like.

"Yeah, those big shaggies, they've got a lot of meat to go through. Need a big bullet for such, but" — he shook his head from side to side — "a boy, shot through the gourd, well, I swear."

Stosh had a thought and regarded Auld. "Hugh, where would you put your money on all this? I mean, if you had to pick a murdering faction?"

Auld scratched his head. "I'd have to consider that. What I know of it, Gilliland is dumb as a stump, and has been really doing all of Graham's bidding. Makes no sense that he'd be involved in this, but then again, his foreman getting his head chopped, well, that might motivate a man to do strange things." He pondered some more. "Then there's the whole issue with hanging it on my friend, the buffalo hunter. Too tidy. Too easy to make the connection, and, someone's done that. Someone's planted that seed in Graham's brain. But no, I don't think it's the Gilliland bunch."

"The Halls then?"

Auld scratched his chin. "Don't know. They've been victims sure enough, but far as I know, they're still licking their wounds."

Stosh thought about how much Hugh Auld knew about the goings on in the region. It amused him, like a small town that stretched many miles. Seemed everyone knew everything about this business in the territory. He was glad he had the prospector on this ride.

Auld continued. "But I know those people pretty well, the Halls. They've got no motive, other than revenge, to do something like this, but that would assume they'd known Graham had them set up, and I can't make a connection with that."

"How about Gilliland? Who do you suppose did that to his foreman, Hugh?"

Stosh was, all of a sudden, overwhelmed. Three different factions, and all victims of horrific murders. Now the latest news of the Basque losing his head. He stopped and took a drink from one of his canteens. He wished Allingham was around to help.

CHAPTER 16
THE LAND IS RUN AMOK

Allingham awoke to bright light under his bedroom door and walked into his parlor to find Francis sitting by a roaring fire, smoking a pipe and paging through a Montgomery Ward catalog. The former deputy smiled widely and nodded his head.

"Captain."

"Francis!"

"I'll be go to hell, Captain, you look like one of the Smith brothers." He touched his chin to imitate pulling on a long beard.

"Clarence, you call me Clarence."

"No, no!" Francis laughed. "Yer always *the captain* to me!" He looked around. "So this is where that murderous son of a bitch lived, is it, Captain?"

"It is."

"That's, well, pretty damned creepy, if you ask me, Captain. What the hell's with all that? And, while I'm at it, what the hell, Captain, what the hell?"

"What the hell, what, Francis?" Allingham sat down across from the apparition.

"Jesus Christ, Captain, people dying all around ya, and here you sit, on your ass with all the long hair and big beard, look like some kinda hermit or somethin', what the hell?"

Allingham leaned forward and smiled uneasily. He was pleased to see Francis, even if the young man was giving him hell.

"Well, I, I, you know, Francis, I married Rebecca, and, well, she died."

"Oh, yeah, know all about it, know all about it, Captain. Don't see what's that got to do with any of it. Jesus, Captain, that poor fellow, gettin' his head chopped off." Francis nodded his approval. "Damn nice job on the stitchin' though, damn nice thing you did for that poor man, gettin' him cleaned up an' all sewed back together for his wife. And that damned celluloid collar. Didn't know you had any of them left. Keep that boy away from flame, Captain. One spark, then poof! Remember old Sckogg." He knitted his brow. "Though, I guess he's beyond hurtin'."

Allingham sat back in his chair and regarded Francis. He was not certain how to respond to all that. He simply said, "Thank you."

"Oh, and Captain, thanks for namin' your babe for me. That was awful nice. Made me cry a little."

"My pleasure Francis. We all miss you, especially Rosario."

"And Hobbsie." He held up his hand. "I know he's gone on to the great beyond. Gone on to his Yaw—way, as they call him. The Jews, I mean. I know Old Hobbsie missed me somethin' terrible."

"Yes, he did go on." Allingham wanted to cry at the memory of old Hobbsie.

"But that still don't square it why yer sittin' on yer ass, raisin' peaches when the land is run amok with assholes."

Allingham smiled a little sheepishly. "I think that's a bit hypocritical, Francis."

"What's that mean?" Francis was still a bumpkin, and Allingham had forgotten how ignorant the boy could be sometimes.

"You, you getting yourself killed after poor Margaret died. At least I wasn't a suicide, Francis."

"Might as well had been." Francis tapped the dottle from his pipe into the fire then put it in a pocket. He shrugged. "Anyway, yer right about me. I shoulda lived. That was damned foolish and silly of me, gettin' myself snuffed by the whore. But that don't mean I can't give you hell about doin' the

155

same thing, though, Captain. Yer doin' the same all right. You say you're not killing yerself, but you are. You are, and taking a whole passel of good folks right down with you. At least I wasn't all that important and big as you are."

He sounded like Rebecca saying that, and Allingham couldn't help but grin a little at the compliment. "Don't feel very big."

"No, guess not." Francis stood up. "You look like hell, dress like hell, wearing an old rope for a belt. Jesus, Captain, clean yerself up. Stop all this nonsense; help that Polish fella out. What's his name Stosh?"

Allingham nodded. "Stosh Gorski."

"Yeah, he's a good man. You two could clean this mess up, sure as you cleaned up Canyon Diablo. Clean it up, Captain, clean yourself up, get a good shave and a haircut and then go and clean up this land." Francis started to leave, and then remembered something. "And another thing, Captain, burn this damned place down. It is a place of evil, a place of the devil himself. Just burn the whole goddamned mess down."

CHAPTER 17
NO ONE ELSE

Dan Housman studied his brother's draw-ings. They were good. Not his best work, as he made them while dying, but they were good, nonetheless. There were many sketches, some were men, some were the men's horses. Old Josh was a bright fellow with a keen eye, and he left clues for his brother wherever they existed. Some of the men were completely benign in their dress, and of these, Josh drew what was distinctive about their horses or their horse's tack.

He dressed and made it to the saloon that had been made famous by his brother's art. It was run by a rotund Frenchman who shook Dan Housman's hand energetically.

"I am so sad about your brother, my friend. He was a good man, the best of men."

"I've heard that stated before." Dan eyed the drink poured in his brother's honor. He stood back and looked the place over. It was a refined place and Josh's works hung on every wall. The Frenchman looked behind him at the reclining nude stretched out provocatively above the big beveled glass mirror across the back of the bar. It was imposing, at nearly twelve feet long.

"You should have seen your brother's first version." He pointed at the silk drape covering the subject's most intimate parts. *"Full cat!"* The Frenchman winked seductively and shrugged. "My wife would not have it, so Josh painted the drape over the best part." He shrugged again. "Just as well, the brothel business next door picked up considerably when we put Josh's work in here. Most of the men could not even hold a good conversation, as they were too distracted."

Dan Housman pulled out one of his best cigars, presenting it to the Frenchman.

"Oh, a Cubano?" He breathed in the aroma of the finest leaves available and nodded in appreciation.

"No, a Floridio." Housman lit his own from the fancy lighter on the bar top nearby. "Cuban leaf and Cuban workers, but made in Key West."

The Frenchman admired it as he smoked.

"I have a factory down there."

"Then we must do some trade, my friend.

The men here like good tobacco." He pointed with his head to another room. "Smoking room." He nodded. "It is good business, especially with your brother's art." He looked as if he might cry and swallowed hard. Josh was a dear friend.

Dan looked away and admired the saloon. It rivaled the finest places he'd known in Cuba and Key West. The walls, bar, and décor were all in the neoclassical style, heavy rich red mahogany polished and carved, with a marble bar top. Brass foot rails all around and spittoons polished so brightly one could use them for a mirror. On every open wall hung one of Josh's works.

His dead brother had always been fond of fanciful notions of women, always nude, always seductively posed, the place fairly reeked of sexual energy, and Dan could not help but be reminded of his brother's cigar-box art. He had to intervene constantly and tone them down. Josh was the artist, but Dan was the businessman. He knew the more puritanical buyers would simply not have such in their shops. But Josh absolutely adored the female form and could capture the most desirable, most carnal aspects of the fairer sex. One client even declared it pornography and Dan remembered Josh's

159

defense of his craft. His brother declared vehemently that pornography was only achievable through photography; it was not possible with pen or brush. Dan could never agree with that sentiment, as some of his brother's work was downright scandalous to even Dan, who prided himself on not being in the least prudish or put off by such images, fanciful or not.

His little brother had made his mark in Arizona, certain enough, and Dan was not in the least surprised. Josh had a way with people. He watched the Frenchman and felt certain he could trust him.

"Is there a place, Henri, where we can speak, in private?"

"Follow me."

The Frenchman looked the drawings over carefully. He did not know if he'd be much help. His clientele did not include many ranch hands or saddle bums. They could not afford it and that is why Henri had a nice establishment. He became a little animated at one of the illustrations, and tapped it with a chubby finger. "That man, or at least his horse, I know it, I know it."

He beckoned Dan Housman to another room and called for his wife.

"Adelaide."

"Oui?"

"This is Dan Housman, brother to Joshua."

"I am sorry for your loss, monsieur." She grabbed his arm and gave it a loving squeeze. "We all were very fond of Joshua. He was a fine young man."

"Thank you, ma'am."

"Adelaide, look at this picture. We know this man, or any of these other men?"

"Ah, oui. I know of him. He was the one to cause so much trouble, remember, last spring, at the, when the traveling show came to town. He was a terrible rogue."

"Do you know his name?"

"No, monsieur, but, I know where we can find out."

"Quietly, madame, quietly, please."

"Oui. I understand. There is much, many bad things happening now. I understand, monsieur."

Henri sighed. "If only Allingham were about."

Dan Housman gave a nod. "I've heard of this famous lawman."

"Ah, yes. He was the best, my friend." He looked at his wife through watery eyes. "But, alas, he no longer works. He would have the land right if he did."

"And there is no one else?" Dan Housman was beginning to appreciate the civility

161

of his own Florida home. It sometimes felt like the Wild West, especially along the docks on a Saturday night, but it was a pale comparison to the real thing. There was significantly more law and order there, at least. It seemed he was literally in the devil's own den.

"There is Sheriff Owens, but he is in the other county. He has no jurisdiction up here." Henri shrugged. "We cannot really trust the local law, and that was why Allingham was so good, so effective. He was a US marshal, and free to move about the entire land."

Adelaide interjected. "I am fearful, monsieur, that this injustice against your Joshua will go unchecked. The bad men will prevail and your brother's murderers will never be brought to justice."

She looked at Henri and gave a cynical smile. "It will be a long time before this land is civilized, monsieur. A long, long time."

CHAPTER 18
DREAM GOOD DREAMS

Clarence Allingham loaded the wagon that once transported the rotten blackheart Webster's victims. Now, instead of bodies or parts of bodies, or water for his dead comrades, it was filled with hay soaked in coal oil. He lit it and pushed it, with great purpose, through the front window of the cottage. He stood back and watched it burn for a while and was impressed that the flames could reach so high. The fire would be seen for half a mile. He turned slowly and led his mule, packed with all his worldly belongings, to the Basque cabin.

He felt very well as he plodded along through the crisp Arizona night. He touched his freshly shaven chin and smiled at Francis's admonishments. He missed the young lad. He knew that he'd never come to visit him again.

A lamp was lit and Lucía was sitting outside, almost as if she were waiting for him. She got up and wiped her hands clean with her apron. She responded with a little impish grin as Allingham looked very different with no beard.

He hugged her and she wept a little on his shoulder. It would be a long time before she stopped crying over Xavier. Allingham unpacked and settled his mule down for the night. Lucía had a big glass of wine and cigarette freshly twisted and waiting for him as he sat down.

He drank and said nothing for a while and Lucía finally began to talk.

"I thank you for your kindness and for what you did for Xavier, Clarence. I suppose it would be considered a shameful thing for a new widow to have a man in her bed, but, but . . ." She began sobbing and Allingham pulled her into his arms.

"Now, now. There is no harm in it, and no ugliness. It is just you and me and we loved your man, *our man,* very much and we are comforting each other. And that is all that needs to be said." He smiled and brushed a tear from her cheek. "And besides, my dear, Lucía, I must stay the night, so the scandalous behavior will simply have to continue, at least one more day." He shrugged. "I've burned my house down." He grinned a little devilishly.

"You've burned your house down? Why on earth would you do such a thing, Clarence?"

He shrugged. "A ghost told me to do it, and well, I did it, and here I am." He looked over all his things. "And anyway, tomorrow, we both leave to move into the Hall ranch, with Rosario." He nodded as if to assure her that arguing was not an option.

"I see." She looked around and everything reminded her of Xavier. She was half relieved to know she'd soon be away from the lonely and sad place. It no longer felt very much like her home, more like a jail cell.

He stood up and pulled her hands to his chest. He kissed her forehead. "Now, I need many things from you, my dear Lucía. I need a haircut, and I need" — he stood up and opened a great carpetbag, waving a hand across the contents — "all of these suits altered. I've lost so much weight, they're falling off me." He grinned and looked down at his bony form. "And I certainly can't use a hemp rope to hold up good suit trousers." He laughed.

She smiled and sat him down. She ran her fingers through his long hair. "I used to cut Xavier's hair for him all the time." She sniffed and cried at the memory. "You have beautiful hair, Clarence. Beautiful hair."

He grinned at the irony of any part of him being considered beautiful. He enjoyed her long, delicate fingers playing over his head.

"Were you a good barber?"

"Well, the people in my village, they said, it was good that I was not ever allowed near the sheep during shearing time."

Allingham smiled as he felt great locks of hair being cut away. Lucía was about as delicate as a lumberjack. He laughed out loud. "You can't do much to make me uglier."

Lucía smiled. She would not patronize him. Allingham was indeed an ugly man. "I think what is inside is much more, eh, great than what is on the surface, Clarence. And to me, you are a most handsome man."

He laughed. "When I was a child, they used to call me the ogre. Like in the fairy tales, you know, the big monsters that lived under a bridge."

"That is cruel."

"One time a prostitute called me a jug-eared carpetbagger bastard."

"What is this carpetbagger?"

He grinned a little. Lucía was snipping away with great gusto. At least she wasn't crying now, and Allingham was pleased at that. He pointed to one of his bags, made

166

of colorfully woven cloth. "It's named after that, and after the Yankees who invaded the south after the war. They came down with their Yankee ways, carrying their carpetbags, and took advantage of the broken south. Very bad business, Lucía."

"But you are not one of these men."

"Well, I *am* a Yankee, from the north, fought for the north, in the Grand Army of the Republic, and when I came out here to Arizona, well, there were a lot of displaced southerners in a town where I was the law, and they didn't like this big jug-eared carpetbagger telling them how to behave."

She finished and held up a mirror. It was a dreadful haircut. He smiled and nodded. "See, I was right, Lucía. Ugly as ever, now without the beard and long hair." He looked at his watch. "My goodness, it's after one." He smiled and Lucía, with some desperation, poured another glass of wine. She was not tired and did not want to go to sleep yet, as sleeping made her dream of Xavier, and she was just too mentally exhausted to think of that right now. This distraction was good for her and she did not want it to end just yet. She so enjoyed Allingham's company.

She pulled out one of Allingham's suits and held it under his chin, wrinkling her nose up, doubtfully. "Try this on, Clarence. I am better with a needle and thread than I am with scissors and comb." She ran to her bed and pulled the sewing kit out from a corner of the room. She began making marks with a chalk as she gathered up the waist on each side.

"You used to be a little fat?" She grinned as she liked teasing Allingham.

"No, just not so thin."

She got him to undress and he sat in his underwear and pulled out his gun cases. He laid his six-shooter on the table and began looking it over. It was clean, just as he'd stored it over a year ago. He removed the cartridges from the cylinder and inspected each one. They were intact and not corroded. He reloaded the gun. He checked his Winchester, then the big ten-gauge Rosario had bought him for his birthday a couple of years back. She said that a big man needed a ten-gauge, and it was the best weapon for dispatching bad men. It was just like the one she carried all the time.

He found Rebecca's pistol and it made him cry and he looked over at Lucía, leaning in toward the fire for better light as she worked on his suit trousers. She was even more beautiful now, and the fire reflecting on her raven hair gave it an almost auburn glow. She reminded him very much of Rebecca sitting there like that.

She caught him gazing at her as her petticoat had ridden up a little, revealing a well-proportioned leg up to mid-calf. She was barefoot. She did not mind at all, even if Allingham was old enough to be her father.

"Do you know how to handle one of these, Lucía?" He held up the six-shooter for her to see.

"Yes, I know. Xavier taught me, and we have one under the mattress." She looked in the direction of the bed, and Allingham got up to retrieve it. He looked it over, a relic from his days in the war. He walked back to sit down and handed Rebecca's revolver to Lucía.

"Take this one, Lucía. It used to be Rebecca's. It's better than yours. I want you to have it."

They worked until four. Finally, Lucía stood up and stretched her back the way Allingham always liked to see Rebecca do. Lucía was stunning, and Allingham found this curious, as he'd known her a long enough time but had not, until now, seen her for her beauty. It was the grieving, and now that he was beginning to live, he saw her as she was. He'd already known what was most important to know and appreciate about her: her kindness, her spirit, her inner goodness, but he did not notice that she was such an alluring young woman. He instantly felt a little ashamed for sleeping with her. It was just plain disrespectful to the memory of Xavier, and now he wondered if it would not be more fitting for him to go to the barn and find a place to bed down.

Lucía sensed it, as if they'd spoken of it outright. She walked over and took him by the hand. She once again led him to her bed and crawled in, holding the covers up for him to follow. They settled in together and he held her lovingly, her back pressed tightly to his chest, and he breathed in her scent, which was and simultaneously was not like Rebecca's.

She began to relax and wiggled, instinctively, pressing herself against him. She felt a stirring down below and Allingham was immediately mortified.

"I'm sorry, Lucía." He began to pull away, get out of the bed and leave her when she grabbed him by the arm, holding onto him so that he could not get away.

"No need to be sorry. You are a man and it is what a man does." She pulled his hand to her mouth and kissed it on his bony knuckles, wetting them with her tears.

"I am just sorry that I cannot do for you. I am sorry, Clarence, it is a cruel joke to play on a man. To lie down with him and not do more. It is a wicked joke to play on you, and I am sorry."

He kissed her on the neck. "It's all right, Lucía." He felt the flutter in his heart, not unlike the first time he lay with Rebecca. He never thought he'd know that feeling again. "It's all right. Just wish I could control myself better."

"It makes a woman feel very good to know a man wants her, Clarence. I'm, I'm just sorry."

"Go to sleep, Lucía." He kissed her on the temple. "Dream good dreams."

CHAPTER 19
CARVED FROM A PEACH STONE

Robert Halsted walked from his office to home. It was early, but he'd finished well enough for the day and thought, for certain, that little Frances would be home by now. He could not wait to see her as Rosario had taken her from him for more days than he could stand.

He did not mind so much that the child was with Rosario, as he trusted the Mexicana without question or hesitation. It was just that more and more, he was in need of the little one's company these days.

He heard about the visit to Allingham and how it did not go at all to plan. That disappointed him as well, as he'd grown very fond of his son-in-law over the past couple of years. He thought they'd be spending the rest of Robert Halsted's life together, and now that did not seem even remotely possible.

He also worried over the violence that

seemed to have engulfed the land. He'd do what he could with his Safety Committee, but things were different these days. Politics had come with a vengeance to their little part of the world, and now that the land was more civilized, there seemed to be a lot more at stake. Men were more motivated, to his mind, by personal gain, greed, lust for land and money, and it was difficult to get them to focus on the greater good. It weighed heavily on him, and he, like Rosario and Hira Singh, also held out some hope that Allingham would come around, come back to them and come back to society, to make it all right.

That was one of the most important things he'd come to realize and appreciate about his son-in-law. Allingham was terse, and rude, and initially, to Halsted's mind, a bit arrogant, and frankly not up to his dear departed daughter's standard, but now he knew better. He understood that Allingham was a great man.

He turned the corner to his street and saw the smoke and could not, at first, believe his eyes. He sprinted toward his home, toward the white picket fence he'd had built to keep little Frances from roaming out of the yard. He did not see, for all the haze, Singh and Daya, with the housekeeper and little

Frances off safe to the side, watching forlornly as the smoke rolled out of the windows and through the doorway. The entire house would soon be engulfed in flame. He rushed past them, as a man on a mission, and pulled the gate to when the explosion rocked their entire world.

Robert Halsted was down, his legs cleaved at mid-thigh, as if the lower half of his body had been run through one of his many sawmills.

Sheriff Commodore Perry Owens watched Stosh Gorski across his desk as he read the cryptic note the lawman had just received in the mail. Stosh looked up at him with a knitted brow. "When did you get it?"

"Yesterday. I checked the map. Looks like a crossroads. Funny, whoever wrote it put NM after the distance. Looks like miles, but never seen it written in such a way."

Stosh Gorski regarded the little figurine that had accompanied the note. "It's a pig." Stosh looked up. "Carved from a peach stone."

"Yes." Owens strapped on his fancy gun rig. He checked his six-shooters and holstered them. He picked up a Winchester and nodded to Gorski.

"Let's track down where this map takes

us, Stosh."

They did and in another hour were looking over the corpse of a trail rider, mutilated, as he and his mount had been recently set on fire. Nothing much remained but the upper chest and head, which had evidently been spared most of the fire's heat and flame. It was swollen and dark red gone to black, much like a beef that had been left on the spit too long and not turned with enough care.

Stosh Gorski went to work. He pulled the corpse from the pile and laid it out flat. He pulled what was left of the man's hat from his head. We washed the face and neck, freeing it of the clothing's ash.

"Well, he'd been shot through the eye. Doesn't appear to be the thing that killed him, though."

"How's that?" Owens looked over the Pinkerton's shoulder with great interest. He'd never investigated such a murder scene. It was as gruesome as the worst the Apaches could do, however, and he'd seen enough of that in his time.

"Because he's been hanged." Stosh pulled at the length of rope, imbedded in the man's neck. "Likely the cause of death. Asphyxiation, not separation of the spine. This man's been lynched, short drop. Strangulation."

"Tough way to die."

He looked around and found no means by which a man could have been hanged. "He was killed somewhere else, then brought here." He looked around. Gorski had learned a lot from his old boss Allingham about reading a crime scene. He pointed off toward the road going south. "From there, he was mounted on his own horse. He was killed and then brought here." Stosh looked the remains of the horse over. "Animal was shot through the head, fell over here and died." He felt the area around the kill site. He pulled a pile of moist earth to his nose and smelled it. "Ignition source was coal oil." He stood back and looked the scene over with a keen eye. He pointed at the ground. "Just one man did this. A man who walked funny."

Owens beckoned Stosh to a little pile of rocks. They'd been arranged near the corpse. On top was a flat sandstone rock. It had the image of a pig scraped on it like an old Indian petroglyph. "Pig again." He looked at Stosh with a little grin. "This is interesting, ain't it, Sergeant?"

"That it is."

Owens continued. "Those Hall men. One was lynched, the other shot through the eye, *and* the gut."

Stosh looked the corpse over and certain enough, found a gaping abdominal wound. "It all fits."

"Retribution?"

"Certainly."

"I wonder if they got the right man." Owens dug through the charred saddlebags. He pulled some papers out. Nothing identified the man. He shrugged.

"So, you don't know this man?"

"No. Likely a drifter. Likely just a saddle bum."

"Well, looking at the thorough treatment he was given, I'd say our man, the vigilante who did this, didn't do it to the wrong man. I bet this poor bastard's one of the gang who did for the Hall ranch men."

"I'm sure you're right. This fellow fits the bill. He's a drifter and ne'er-do-well, I'm certain of that. Has no connection to the place and was probably hired for the lynch gang." Owens took a long drink from his canteen and looked the remains over. "Bet he's not the last one we'll see like this, either, Sergeant."

"Nope, there were seven."

"Now six." He handed Stosh his canteen and twisted a smoke. "At least he's not stinking up the place. Burned like a roman candle on the fourth of July."

■ ■ ■ ■

The Hall ranch was looking more like a hotel these days than a hacienda, as Rosario made her boys move into the main house, where they'd be better protected, and where she could keep an eye on them. Now she had Allingham, Lucía, Hira and Daya, and, of course, little Frances, living under the same roof. It was good for them all, as the terrible tragedy of Robert Halsted's assassination, and the attempt on the rest of the family, weighed heavily on every one of them.

Rosario walked up on Allingham and gave him a loving kiss on the cheek. "I am glad you are here, Capitan." She took him by the hand and led him to one of her many guest rooms. She opened the door and held out her hand.

"Here are two nice boys I think you might remember, Capitan."

The Irishmen stood up and nodded respectfully to Allingham. "Captain, it's good to see you."

"And you, boys! Oh, ho, the bad men will pay dearly now!" He grabbed Mike up in his arms and gave him a sloppy kiss on the cheek. He did the same for Paddy. Both men looked on, incredulous. They'd only remembered the terse Allingham.

Allingham smiled at Rosario. "You are a sneaky one, my dear."

Rosario grinned at her Irish giants. "We need help, Capitan, and the O'Shaughnessy brothers are just what the doctor ordered."

"We are sorry for your loss, Captain. Miss Rebecca was as fine a lady as one could ever hope to know. She'll be sorely missed."

Allingham cried at the mention of his wife. He smiled and nodded. He could not speak just now.

Paddy tried his best to change the subject. "How may we help, Captain? Seems the whole territory has gone the way of Canyon Diablo."

Allingham led them to the courtyard, with the rest of Rosario's party. "You're right Mikey, you are absolutely right." He took a deep breath and continued the best he could. Memories of Rebecca were still very tough on him. He smiled cynically. "We don't know what or who is behind all this, but it seems the whole territory has lost their collective heads."

The Irishmen came out and mingled with the rest. They soon sat with Old Pop, now in his rocker, convalescing. He could manage a whisper by this time, and the two brothers were especially attentive to him.

Rosario considered Allingham as he surveyed her little refugee camp. He looked good to her. There was the old spark in his eye, even if he did have to cry now and again. She knew this was the best talisman for his pain and was encouraged by that. Allingham needed lots of puzzles to unravel, needed lots to think about to occupy that active mind.

Together they watched Lucía play with little Frances and the Mexicana poked Allingham a little hard in his bony ribs. "She would be a good wife for a certain someone I know."

Allingham nodded gravely. He moved his gaze to Pierce Hall sitting in a rocker on the porch, not far from his partner and adopted father, admiring the pretty Basque widow from a good distance away. The young rancher was obviously smitten. Allingham grinned slyly. He had learned to tease Rosario over the years. He nodded at the lovesick man. "He'd make her a good husband."

Rosario slapped him a little hard, at the back of his head. "You dunce!" She smirked a little at the look in his eye as he rubbed the spot on his skull. "You are no matchmaker, you are a lawman! You leave the love business to me."

"Oh, Rosario." He took a deep breath and exhaled a just-discernible sigh. "That poor child, she is even younger than my darling Rebecca. She'd not want an old fool like me."

Rosario turned to walk away. "I will not continue this conversation until you remove the mierda from between your ears, Capitan." She turned and squeezed him on the shoulder. "But I know when a woman loves a man, and I know" — she winked — "I know."

He thought on it. It was preposterous, yet he could not help but feel the flutter in his gut every time he looked in beautiful Lucía's direction. Rosario was right, there was something there, but Allingham just chalked it up to her aggrieved state. The poor woman had had a terrible shock, and Allingham was there to make it right, or at least as right as it could be made.

It was more a kind of hero worship, he thought, the kind of regard a child has for an adult who has come in and saved the day during a horrific, tragic time. He'd certainly known such a time or two in his day. He'd saved many a citizen back in New York, and the elation they felt would be directed at him, at least for a time. Those feelings, he knew well enough, were always self-limiting, and, as far as they related to Allingham, always gone away very quickly. It was absurd to think that the young beauty would want him in such a way. He shrugged and laughed a little to himself at the stupidity of such an idea.

But it all did make him feel very well. His time with Rebecca was the best in his life, and now that he was becoming more attuned to the reality that she was really gone, that he was a widower, it gave him the idea that being with another woman was a thought bearing consideration. It would do him well to try for a mate again someday, but Lucía, the more he thought on it, Lucía would not be the one. She was, to his mind, just too young and too beautiful to be held down by someone the likes of him. He looked over and saw Pierce Hall, caught the young rancher's attention and smiled, almost as if to say, telepathically, *Go on, boy, woo her, make her love you, have a family and begin living. Begin living with the lovely Basque beauty; just go on and begin to live your life.*

He watched the riders coming in. They stopped, or rather, were stopped and passed through the guard. Long Jack and Harry would let no one close to the place without passing muster. They were good pickets and ready to do what they needed to keep everyone safe inside.

Allingham nodded to Gorski then at Sheriff Owens. Owens he knew, but Hugh Auld was a stranger to him.

Gorski was pleased. He'd heard that Allingham had finally come around. "You look good, Clarence. You look damned good."

Allingham grinned and looked down at himself, at the suit, despite Lucía's best efforts, that still hung from him as if it had been a hand-me-down. No one would have believed it was hand-tailored just for him by one of the finest suit makers in New York. He appreciated the compliment, nonetheless.

"Thanks, Stosh."

They settled down to Old Pop's desk and smoked as they conferred about the war. Allingham had his notebook, his *brain,* as he called it, and wrote notes from time to time. He had a thought and called for Rosario. In short order, he had a chalkboard used to teach the children of the ranch. He made a grid on which he wrote, across the top: Hall, Gilliland, Graham.

Down the left side he wrote: Pierce Hall (shot at), UNK assassin; Old Pop (hanged), UNK assassin; Josh Housman (shot), UNK assassin; Xavier Zubiri (decapitated) by a Mexican; Gilliland foreman (decapitated), UNK assassin; Onan Graham (shot), Buffalo Hunter; Unknown cowman (shot, hanged, burned), UNK assassin.

He looked at Sheriff Owens and Stosh then at the Irish twins.

"Does that about do it?"

"No, your father-in-law, Robert Halsted, blown up, by an unknown."

"Right, right, of course." Allingham became embarrassed. He did not know why he overlooked the man. He had another thought. He needed Hira Singh. The Sikh was soon sitting in the office, by Allingham's side.

They all nodded respectfully to Singh, and Gorski reached out a hand. "I'm sorry about Mr. Halsted, and your home, sir."

"Thank you." Singh shook his hand gently. He reached for Sheriff Owens's hand. "Sheriff." He did the same for Hugh Auld.

"Hira," Allingham continued, nodding at the board. "Tell us what you think of all this."

"I do not know what to think."

Owens spoke up. "Looks like everyone's killin', or at least tryin' to kill everyone else."

Allingham held up a hand. He nodded. "You're right." He called for Rosario who

soon had Pierce Hall and Old Pop confer-
ring with the committee of lawmen.

Owens spoke up. "Marshal Allingham,
how do you know Mr. Zubiri was killed by
a Mexican?"

"Oh, just, just looking, Clarence, please,
and you are Commodore?"

"Just Perry."

Allingham continued. "He was
decapitated, one blow, by a very sharp
blade. Likely not a sword, few men carry a
sword these days. I'm assuming the blade of
the Mexican peon, the machete, and he left
clues at the little camp. He'd had a meal,
with poor Xavier, before he murdered him
and left cigarette butts all around, corn husk
instead of paper, and there were chilies in
the leftovers he'd thrown in the fire, all
point to a Mexican." He considered the
murdered foreman and looked at Stosh,
whom he could count on for careful analysis
of a crime scene. "What of your man, Stosh,
the one who lost *his* head?"

"Not one blow, Allin . . . Clarence. It was
sawn away, a sharp blade, mind you, but
not one clean blow. Same with the calves."

"So, likely not our Mexican. The Mexican
is, I'll wager, not part of this war, a drifter,
perhaps. Just attacked Xavier as a bit of bad
luck for my friend." Allingham cried at the

thought and it was curious to the Irishmen, as he made no attempt at hiding his emotions. This was, doubtless, a new Allingham.

He wiped his eyes and pulled himself together. "The murderer knocked some of Xavier's teeth out, he also took a ring Xavier used to wear. We might have luck if he tries to sell such." He nodded to Sherriff Owens. "Perry, can you get the word out, ask for help, ask for anyone in the region to let us know if a Mexican tries to sell such things."

"Will do, Captain."

Hugh Auld interjected, "Marshal Allingham?"

"Yes?" He smiled and extended his hand. "I did not have the honor of shaking your hand, Mr. Auld."

"Hugh." He nodded and took the marshal's hand. "I want to say, want to say right now that my friend the buffalo hunter did not kill that child."

Allingham nodded.

Stosh chimed in. "He's hiding out, Clarence, with some Navajos."

"Good, good to know." Allingham became a little distracted and turned his attention, looking directly at Pierce Hall and Old Pop. "You gentlemen, I want a square answer from both of you." He looked at the chalkboard. "Have you or any of your men done any of this?"

Pierce sprang from his chair. He was not so much offended as he was flabbergasted at the notion. "No, Marshal, I swear, no."

Old Pop chimed in with a whisper and a shake of the head. "Pierce is right, Captain. None of us, none of my men, and I know this to be a fact, have done any of these acts."

"And the man from Florida?"

"No, he's dead." Pierce looked on, confused.

"No, no." Allingham felt the old impatience well up. Pierce Hall could be as much a bumpkin as poor Francis from time to time. Just like the good old days, Allingham felt it, was compelled to do it, but he checked himself. He'd not be surly to the young man. "No, I meant his brother, the man who came out to settle his affairs, the cigar manufacturer."

"Oh," Rosario spoke up. She was neither offended nor surprised at Allingham's interrogation of her men. It was good to get it all out in the open. "I, one moment, Capitan." She rushed from the office, retrieving a letter from her room, she returned and handed it over to Allingham. "He could not have killed the burned man, Capitan. He was in Florida when this happened."

Allingham scrutinized the letter with great interest.

Rosario nodded. "Go ahead and read it, Capitan. It is just a thank-you for our hospitality, and for giving young Joshua a good burial."

The envelope was postmarked Key West, Florida, the day before the burned-up man was executed. It seemed evident enough that it was not Dan Housman, exacting revenge.

"Hmm." Allingham shrugged.

Rosario gave him a broad smile. She patted him on the cheek.

"What?" Allingham grinned, a little embarrassed.

"You are grunting. It used to vex Rebecca when you grunted, but I know, grunting is a good sign. It means the crimes will be solved soon." She took her letter back and replaced it in the envelope. She watched Sheriff Owens shrug.

"So, if it ain't you and it ain't Mr. Housman, who'd do such a thing?"

"Someone who wants to stir the pot." Paddy O'Shaughnessy finally spoke up. He nodded to Mikey. "Back when we were lads, back home in Ireland, there was a man who was trying to get all the others to sell their farms. He pitted one farmer against the other, by doing things, stealing sheep, breaking down stone walls, leaving gates open, spoiling the water, on and on, until all the farmers were caught up in their own squabbling. No farming or livestock rearing could be done, and many faced ruin, and then your man could come in, and pick up the pieces, buy cheap and take over the whole of the land."

"Sounds like that's what we've got here." Old Pop whispered gravely to the Irishmen.

Allingham had another thought. "Who do we know who has got a stake in all this, and who's not been a victim so far?"

"Druitt." They all spoke it together, Owens, Gorski, Pierce and Old Pop.

"Hmm." Allingham stroked his chin.

"He's had his house burned," Owens spoke up. "But anyone with half a brain knows he pulled that little caper off himself. Was insured to the hilt." Owens turned his head from side to side. "He's not, nor have any of his men been a victim like the rest."

They broke to prepare for dinner and to allow Allingham some time to review his notes and formulate a plan. He had six distinct crimes going and at least three different perpetrators, perhaps more. He had a potential siege on his hands, as there were certainly enough enemies of the Halls out there, determined to wipe the whole lot out.

He had, including himself, six good lawmen, three teams of two, and he'd work with Auld, the man with the least experience. He'd have Owens and Stosh work together, as Stosh was as good at investigating a crime scene as he, and Owens knew the people and the land. Auld would serve the same purpose for him. Allingham could use him certainly to move around the unfamiliar terrain.

That would leave the O'Shaughnessy brothers, and he knew they'd be handicapped by not knowing the land well, but there was nothing for it. It would be impossible to break them apart.

Hira and Rosario would defend the ranch; Old Pop would help in his infirmed capacity. Pierce Hall would just do his best. He was no fighter, but he was also loyal. Rosario would keep an eye on him. Maybe he'd have time to get to know Lucía better.

Allingham hated that thought. He swallowed hard and pushed the pain in his gut away. He was pining for her, and that was a just plain stupid idea. The boy was the right match for the Basque beauty, despite what Rosario might think. Allingham was full up with all this love business anyway. Maybe this next adventure would put him out of his misery, once and for all. Put an end to everything for him.

His scheming was interrupted by a knock on the door.

Rosario called out. "Capitan, there is a man here; I think you might need to see him now."

He stood in the sun with his hat in his hand. It had been a long time since Allingham had seen such a pitiful man. He was terrified and guilty and filthy dirty. He looked as if he might cry at any moment and Allingham's team of lawmen stood around him, like a pack of angry dogs, ready to tear a runt to pieces.

Rosario looked much the same. "Capitan, this hijo de puta is one of the men who hanged my husband." She walked up on the man and kicked him hard in the shin. "And who shot poor Joshua in the eye." She backhanded him across the mouth.

"I'm, sorry, lady, I'm sorry, sorry." He held up his hand to beg her to stop the attack. He looked on at Allingham and dropped to his knees. He crawled over to the marshal and clasped his hands together in prayer. "Marshal, Marshal, I'm sorry. Jesus folks, all a ya, you gotta believe, I'm sorry."

Old Pop limped up on him as he was still

fighting the paralysis in his legs. He pulled the miscreant to his feet, looking the man in the eye. He whispered, "Out with it."

"I, I was hired."

"By who?" Sheriff Owens spoke out without thinking much. He looked at Allingham and nodded for him to continue the interrogation.

"I, I don't know. I swear, I swear. I, we rode up, to the train tracks. Was told that a pair of rustlers was comin'. They said you two was bad men. They said they'd pay me twenty dollars and I went, I went, and the man who hired me, he was wearing his mask, his scarf on his face, I don't know him, me and my pards, three of us, we're from New Mexico, we was just driftin' looking for a ranch, a herd, and we was runnin' low on money, they offered us twenty dollars apiece, I swear."

"And now your pards are dead." Allingham stroked his chin. "And you're yellow and scared that whoever killed them is gunning for you."

"Oh, Jesus, mister help me." He flopped down on the ground again. He seemed to lose all control of his legs. Even Rosario felt a little pity for him now. The man choked on his tears and continued the best he could. "I, I swear, we didn't know." He looked at Old Pop. "Mister, I didn't know you had a ranch, that you was a good man. They showed us the irons you had on you, the stole calves, we just, we just thought it was the way up here, and then they shot that boy through the eye. Jesus, we all didn't want nothin' to do with it after that." He wiped his face with his scarf. "But they told us we was in up to our necks and we had to go through with it. Then, then, my God, we split up, and Andy got it first, Jesus, all burned up, then Al, the other day."

Allingham looked on at Stosh Gorski and Owens. "Looks like you'll be getting another letter." He looked at the groveling man. "What do you want with us?"

"I, just, just do what you want with me, mister, I turn myself in. I'll go to prison, I'll testify, tell you what I can, but please, please don't let that demon track me down. Jesus, I'm scared. I'm scared. I don't wanna get burned up, mister, I don't wanna go the way of my pards. Please, sir, please." He looked at Rosario and crawled to her feet. He pressed his face against her boot top. "Please, señora, I'm beggin' you, please don't let him get me."

Rosario pushed him away. "Don't touch me, gringo. Get away." She pointed and he crawled back, away from her, and crouched in the dusty yard.

Allingham shrugged. He looked at Old Pop, then at Pierce Hall and finally Rosario. "Up to you all. You're the aggrieved party here."

The groveling man spoke up. "But, but you're the marshal. You've got to follow the due course of the law. Jesus, Marshal, please, please, you, you *have* to help me."

"Is that what Old Pop here said when you and your pards were stringing him up? Is that the kind of compassion you showed him? Is it?" Allingham was furious now, scary and red in the face and Rosario knew now that he was back, the old Allingham was indeed back. He pointed a finger at the blackheart. "I'll tell you something, *boy.* I'll tell you something right now. This is a different kind of law, a law you and your kind made, and I'll not be bound to anything you think is right or wrong. You've made your bed hard, and now you'll lie in it." He looked at the Hall ranch folks again and pointed. "This is your lynch law, boy. These are the aggrieved party, right here, and they, not some ass judge in some courtroom, will decide." He nodded. "Old Pop, Rosario, Pierce, what say ye? What shall I do with this piece of garbage? You decide his fate."

Old Pop whispered. He pulled the man to

his feet yet again. Pierce retrieved the man's dusty hat and handed it to his partner. Old Pop put it on the man's head. "We'll let him stay at the old place until all this is sorted out." He looked at Rosario and pulled her to him, kissing her on the forehead. "We are civilized human beings, and this rat will not pull us down."

Allingham looked at the blubbering miscreant. He nodded. "So be it." He looked the man over with contempt in his eyes. "Better than I would have done for you. You're a lucky man."

That night, Allingham drifted off quickly and slept well, at least until he felt something, a hand perhaps, brush against his protruding right ear. He turned and smiled, expecting Rebecca. He grinned broader yet when Lucía motioned for him to make room for her in his bed.

He did and she shucked her nightgown, pulling it up over her head, revealing all that Allingham felt before, but now had the pleasure of seeing. His heart raced, and the blood pounded in his ears. His heartbeat was deafening. She did the same for Allingham, stripping him naked and then made love to him with a passion, a desperation that made him remember why he missed his departed wife so completely.

They rested, recovered in each other's arms for a long while, Allingham caressing the Basque beauty the way he'd learned over the years, under the tutelage of his one and only lover. He finally spoke.

"I guess we'll have to marry now."

Lucía looked him in the eye. "Why would you say that, Clarence?"

"Because I am an old-fashioned man, and you might become *great with child.*" He grinned coyly. "And I abhor the stigma placed on bastard children and their mothers."

She snuggled against his bony chest and ran a finger across his many scars. "Too late for that. I am already *great with child.* I am going to have Xavier's baby, Clarence."

He felt her body change as it pressed against him, and knew that she was crying. He kissed her on top of the head and held her more tightly. Reaching down, he wiped the tears from her cheeks.

"That's the best news I've heard in a long time." He lifted her chin and kissed her on the mouth. "You will make a wonderful mother. Why would that make you cry?"

She pulled away and looked at him again through her teary eyes. She shrugged. She did not know why she was crying. "Do you mean that, Clarence?"

"Of course I mean that." He shifted and again wiped her cheeks dry. "But I was just teasing about marrying, Lucía. I would not expect you'd want any of that from me now, or frankly, ever."

"Why not?" She was a little disappointed. She liked the idea of marrying Allingham.

"Because, *because* of me." He rubbed his temples and looked at the ceiling as he collected his thoughts. Lucía ran her pretty bare toe up his calf and rested it in the crook of his left knee. He was becoming distracted again. His heart fluttered at the realization, the lust and more importantly, the love and desire the young beauty was expressing for him, to *him,* of all people.

"I'm, I'm the ogre, Lucía, and you are, so, so beautiful, and young and desirable, and I believe just a little vulnerable right now. Xavier is not long gone, and well, I am afraid, I'm just afraid, that you are not thinking so clearly. You need, we need, more time."

She sat up and walked across the room, exposed and stunning in all her womanly perfection. And Allingham was now convinced that his assessment of the whole thing must be right. It was all preposterous. He was the beast, and now, just like before, the beauty was interested in him. But was it really so absurd? Wasn't Rebecca's love for him just as preposterous, outrageous, and insanely absurd?

But there it was. Rebecca was a lovely and intelligent woman, and she loved him as few ever know such love. And, he'd changed. He was different now, a better man. Perhaps, perhaps . . . and all of a sudden, Allingham felt very well.

She got a drink of water and looked at him through the silvery light of the moonlit room. It was a brisk night, yet Lucía lingered a bit beside the bed and the gooseflesh stood up on her pale skin, making him want her and want to hold her and make her warm and comfortable and happy. She saw the spell she was casting on Allingham, and thought a little seduction would not be such a bad idea.

She slaked her thirst and crawled back under the covers, to him, climbing onto and sitting astride him. She kissed him on the forehead and ordered him not to move or speak, until she was finished with him.

After a little while she spoke. "I have been talking with Rosario. You know well enough, Rosario has had many, many husbands in her time, and she told me, if I was to live in this Arizona land, that grieving is not a luxury that the women here have. I loved my husband very much, Clarence, you know this, but he is gone. He is gone and I will make a fine baby for him, so that a part of him may live on in this world but I will not waste my life grieving him. I am not wealthy, and my beauty will fade with time. I need another husband, and this is why I do not want to hear any more about waiting enough time. Rosario says the right things, Clarence, you know this, you know that she is wise and good and she has lived these things, and she is a good woman, a fine lady, and I will live like she has lived, so there is no reason to discuss such any further."

She moved about a little over him and soon had his full attention. She squeezed him when he tried to move and held up a hand. "Not yet, I am not finished my speech."

"But Lucía." Allingham was befuddled. He had difficulty finding the words. "I, I'm *so* old, and just a mess. There are so many younger men, good men who would die to have you for a wife."

"What men?"

"Pierce Hall, for one. He's smitten. I've seen the way he looks at you."

"He is a boy. He is a nice boy, but a boy, nonetheless." She shrugged and shuddered a little at Allingham's ministrations. She recovered enough to continue her little oration. "And besides" — she thought hard about how to break this news to him — "I, I, Clarence, do not think me wicked, but I loved you for a long time. Even before, before Xavier died."

"Oh?" He felt the flash of joy run through his gut.

He could stand it no longer and abandoned the discussion. They loved for a long time. The conversation could resume after the business at hand was consummated.

Afterward, Allingham collected his thoughts. He still could not understand any of it, not with Rebecca, and now, not with Lucía. He decided to just go ahead and ask.

"But why, Lucía, why?"

"Why, what?"

"Why me? It was the same with Rebecca. Why would a woman such as you want anything to do with a man such as me?"

"Oh." She shuddered again as she felt him inside her. "That is easy." Allingham was a good lover, better even than Xavier and Xavier was very good, even great, but Allingham was better yet.

"How is that easy?"

"You are a great man, Clarence."

"I am an ogre. I am a monster of a man."

"You are beautiful to women like me, and like your Rebecca. You have some *thing,* some, how do I say, a quality, an invisible power, a, what is the word, aura, yes, aura."

"That's silly." Allingham could feel himself blush. He felt as he did when Rebecca used to try and convince him of such things.

"No it is not silly at all, and it is this way with you and it is the way with women such as me and your late wife to love such men. You are a man of power and gentleness and love and greatness, and it is what women such as me find, find, well, just I, I cannot remember, don't know the word in your language, but it is not to be denied."

"Irresistible?" He felt ridiculous again, even suggesting such a word, such a quality to describe himself.

"Yes, yes, that is the word, irresistible."

He took a deep breath and let it out. He spoke under his breath, using Francis's words. *"I'll be go to hell."* He rubbed his temples again. He felt the elation rush over him, as a young woman finding him irresistible was an overwhelming thought.

"And when I learned more about you, from Rosario." She leaned down and hugged him around the neck. "Well, I knew that my first feelings for you were right. To know what you've done, done in the past, all the good and noble things, and how much Rosario loves you, well, then I knew, my love feelings for you were right."

He, reluctantly, pulled himself from her body and moved her onto her back. He reached down and felt her belly, still flat, still without a sign of a little being, growing inside. He immediately felt sad for Xavier, even though the man had never known that his wife was having such thoughts, such emotions for another man, and it weighed heavily on him. He felt he'd somehow betrayed the shepherd's trust. He spoke without thinking. "How on earth, my dear Lucía, could you possibly have loved me when Xavier was still alive?"

"Oh, it was not hard." She lay back and pressed his hand against her belly. It felt good and warm and comforting for him to hold her and the beginning of her child. She stretched and ran her foot up his calf again. "I fell in love with you when, the first time, when you came to our home and we had your trout. I saw your sadness and your kindness and your love for me in your eyes. Not a lustful love, I knew, you were not lusting for me, Clarence, but I could see that you saw how happy Xavier and I were and you were just, well, loving in how you appreciated what we, he and I had together, and it made me love you, Clarence." She shrugged. "I would never have done anything to harm my husband, and I would never have acted on such a love I had for you. I would have never let Xavier know about it. It was my little secret, Clarence. My little secret I kept inside, would have kept inside for the rest of my days, had Xavier not died. I loved him very much, and he made me very happy, but my love for you was very real. And now" — she reached over and touched his cheek — "now I plan to show it, live it, for the rest of our days."

Chapter 20
I Hate to Eat All Alone

Samantha Ford pondered her first train ride in first class as she sat on the great comfortable bed in the bridal suite of the Hollingsworth Hotel. It was the finest such establishment in all of Phoenix, really in all of the Arizona land. Druitt occupied the presidential suite next door. They were on the top floor. She was very pleased to experience such wealth and finery, as, in all of her time, she'd only known poverty and the things that such a station in life would bring. She straightened her back and thought that the world would turn differently for her from now on, and Druitt would be only the first in a long line of men to give her such wondrous things.

It was really quite easy, once she wrapped her head around the entire concept and thought it through. And now, it did not seem so terrible at all. She could pull it off. She already had, and she'd not had to subject herself to the things that she'd heard went on in the brothels. She was young and beautiful and she'd have a good ten years before those charms wore off. By then, with proper management, she'd amass a nice fortune.

She'd been in an orphanage since she could remember, and the one thing that the orphanage had taught her was that she could survive without love. By the time of her fifteenth birthday, the powers that be in the institution recognized her precocious development and further recognized that if Samantha were allowed to stay on much longer, they'd likely be birthing another bastard babe and have yet another mouth to feed. Therefore, young Samantha, or Sam, as she was called since she could remember, was spirited off to Chicago, Illinois, to learn the fine art of clerking, as she had a good mind for numbers, and could read and write well enough to collate and sort and file.

This is how she ended up working for Walter Druitt. She was not hired so much for her clerical acumen as it was for a figure that would have rivaled the most voluptuous denizens of the stage, and hair the color of spun gold, coupled with eyes the color of an iceberg that would have given her

Teutonic ancestors reason to pause.

At nineteen, she had reached the pinnacle of her feminine charm while not yet learning the pitfalls of working for the likes of her current employer. In fact, beautiful Sam Ford, by all outward appearances, seemed about as clueless as a newborn babe, at least to her new boss, and this is how Walter Druitt got her to ride with him, unaccompanied, unchaperoned to the newest hotel in Phoenix. The girl was quite literally overwhelmed by her good fortune.

She was not nearly as stupid as she let on, and this, along with a false zealotry, was her secret weapon. Men adored and revered her, and up until this time from afar, as, while Sam was a beauty, her religious fervor seemed to guarantee that anyone wanting in this petticoat would have to make the ultimate sacrifice.

She sat on the bed in her room all alone while Walter Druitt conducted some business somewhere. She bounced on it a time or two and wondered when he'd seduce her, as Druitt was quite famous throughout the land as a man who loved women. He was also famous for being a man who was married and had a family and said family was off to Europe or someplace far away. He was also famous for being a man who had certain lady friends and they'd come and go in and out of his life with regularity. Never ruined, or beaten, or injured in any way, and always, always well compensated.

She poured champagne from a bottle chilling in a silver bucket of cold water and she liked it very much. She walked around the room and admired the décor and she liked that very much as well. She felt a little drunk and that was good, as this would be the big day and a little liquid courage would help a lot. She looked at a bill of sale left by the man who delivered her dinner and the wine and she could see that the amount on the bill was more than she made in a week.

Sam was clever that way, as her whole life revolved around numbers and she had a habit, from a long time ago, to think in terms of how long it would take for her to make the money that things cost. The first-class tickets for the train, for example, represented two weeks' pay, and that was for just one of the tickets, one way. The hotel room was one week's pay per night, per room, and Walter Druitt had taken two rooms.

She laughed to herself at that. He was a clever fellow, and she knew that the ruse was all for her, so that she'd not balk at the idea. She also knew that the other room was likely not going to be used at all. She wished he'd just come out and say it, tell her he planned to deflower her and get it over with, and then he could have given her the money he'd spent on the room and everyone would have been better off. But he didn't and she'd have to figure out a way to extract the money now wasted on an unused suite.

She returned to the bed and sat down and bounced on it a time of two. She was a virgin, and she wondered at her inevitable seduction and its aftermath. She wanted it to happen. It was time, and she did not have a beau, and did not really have any interest in the men who found her interesting or attractive or of the marrying type.

She'd worked very hard to remain a virgin for so long, as many many men, from the time that she was around thirteen, wanted to render the service of defloration.

But Sam Ford did not want to be a clerk's wife or a blacksmith's wife or live on a working farm or ranch. She did not want to have to work for wages that would not buy even a cheap hotel room or a coach ticket on a rail line. She did not want to have a bastard baby and be ruined.

Sam Ford wanted what she had right this very moment, and she could see clearly enough, the way Walter Druitt ogled her, that she, at least physically, had what was needed to acquire such.

She'd have to be careful, however. She was rudely educated, spoke plainly, not poorly, but also not in the sophisticated way that Betty, the last one, could carry on. She lacked polish, and she thought that after she'd extracted what she could from Druitt, she'd leave Arizona and go on to someplace grand, San Francisco, perhaps, and learn to act and think and speak and dress like a proper lady, and then, the world would be her oyster. Perhaps she'd end up in the fancy places of Europe. She often had Paris on her mind.

That could all happen. With the growing new rich in society, there were scores of people teaching elocution, etiquette, poise, all the habits and behaviors that would make her not only look grand on the arm of a gentleman, but act well enough so that he'd not be embarrassed in the presence of the people Sam Ford wanted to live among. It was only a matter of having the funds, and time, to put it all together. She felt a little thrill at the thought, and wanted him to hurry. She had a lot on her mind.

She wondered how it would all play out. She was convinced that Druitt was certain that she had no idea what he had intended for her and that made her laugh. He would seduce her and she was curious how he'd manipulate things to make it look like it was in her best interest to let him bed her and deprive her of her virtue. Maybe he did not even know he'd be the first one. She'd have to work that into the conversation, as Sam was not worldly, but she was also enough in the know to know that men like Druitt held virgins in especially high regard, as if there was something sacred about copulating with a woman who'd never known another man. He'd be the first and best time for her and she'd hold him in great regard. She'd remember, for the rest of her days the great, god-like lover and all others afterward would pale by comparison. It was a fantasy worth a lot of money, and Sam would make him pay, oh how she'd make him pay.

At six there was a knock at the door and Sam waited to see if he'd try the door. He did, but finding it locked, and without his own key, he knocked again, a little more forcefully, and Sam could imagine the pounding in his heart at the anticipation. She stripped to her petticoat and put on a robe. She mussed her hair and looked herself over in the mirror. She adjusted the opening in the robe and pulled off her stockings. She rolled up the robe to reveal her shapely legs, up to mid-calf. She was ready, and opened the door slowly, peering through the crack between it and the jamb; she smiled coyly as she watched her future lover ogle the little she'd allow.

"Oh, oh, Mr. Druitt. One moment, please, I'm, I'm not properly dressed." She turned and left the door ajar. He followed her in as she rushed through the parlor, to the bedroom beyond.

He fixed a drink and waited.

She poked her head out. "Ah, Mr. Druitt, I, I don't know, sir, if this is really, my gosh." She poked her head out further yet and beckoned him to her room. "I, don't, don't know what is right to wear, to supper, I mean."

He followed. She smelled lovely. He looked over her shoulder and, tearing his gaze from the nape of her long neck, watched her point at the two plain dresses she'd brought along. She was irresistible.

"Neither one."

"But, I, have nothing else to wear."

"Then we'll get you something my dear." He eyed the bucket of champagne. "But not tonight."

"Oh." Sam Ford blushed. She looked at the floor and rubbed the carpet with her naked great toe. "Then, you, don't, don't want me to eat dinner with you?"

She looked as if she might cry and Druitt sprang into action. He handed her a full glass.

"My dear, no, no. I thought, well, we'll eat in our rooms tonight." He stood up and bowed respectfully as he watched the bared leg make lazy circles in the Persian rug. His heart was now in his throat and he coughed hard to clear it, a weak attempt to make his breathing and speaking easier and more coherent.

She looked at him plaintively, with an almost terror in her eyes. "Alone, all alone?" She welled up. "I, I don't *want* to eat all alone. I had to eat alone in the orphanage."

Druitt looked sideways. "You ate alone, *in an orphanage?*"

"Well, yes, when I was older, when I was the oldest, I had, they wouldn't let me eat with the other children, or the adults. I, I *hate* to eat all alone." She looked up and a little tear dripped from one of her beautiful blue eyes. "Mr. Druitt, I've, I've got to say. I, I know you're a nice man, and a good man, and I know you're being kind to me, but I kind of thought."

She stopped and rushed to the corner, behind a Chinese dressing screen. She wept a little loudly.

"What is it, my dear, what has you so upset, Miss Ford, tell me, please, tell me."

"No, no. You'll think I'm a fool, you'll think very badly of me, I think."

"No, I won't. I promise, please, please tell me."

She spoke over the screen, suppressing a laugh as she worked up the right tone. "I, thought, you were going to seduce me."

"Oh, no, no, my dear, my dear girl." He lied, but felt that he'd gone too far. Visions of the local sheriff, clapping him in irons, danced in his head. Druitt desperately thought for a way out. He began to back from the room and Sam called out.

"No, no!" She charged from behind the screen as her robe fell open. "I, was actually, hoping, Mr. Druitt, that you *were* trying to seduce me." She held up a hand for him to stop. "I, I think I might." She looked away again. "No, this is all silly. You're a fine man, a gentleman, and you have a wife and children, children not much younger than me."

Druitt pulled her into his arms. "You have made me very happy, Sam."

He was not very good at it and he looked like some kind of deranged animal bouncing and grunting and pawing all over her, and it was all over very quickly, and all Sam Ford felt during the whole sordid affair was an overwhelming desire to urinate. She thought a man who was so preoccupied with bedding women would be much better at it. She was wrong.

She looked down and saw the tiniest hint of blood and was elated as she could really play it up now and this is when she started the drama.

She broke down and sobbed and ran from the room, slamming the door to the bedroom behind her. She cried and told him not to follow her when she heard him turn the door handle. She suppressed a laugh when she heard the panic in his voice and she thought all of this would certainly be worth a new wardrobe.

Sam Ford looked at the clock on the mantel. It was time for bed. Tomorrow would be a most fun day in Phoenix, she was certain of that.

Chapter 21
A Stupid Jackass

John Gilliland loaded wire into his wagon, for what reason, he did not know. He could not find anyone, Chinese, Irishmen or Negros, at any price, to resume the fencing work.

He felt very low these days, as he was not as convinced as Graham that the Halls were the source of all evil in the world. The murder and decapitation of his foreman did not seem likely carried out by the Halls, and now the death of Graham's boy had driven a significant wedge between him and the grieving rancher.

He knew his man, the retired buffalo hunter Tim Holt, would never do such a thing. None of his men would do such a thing, but especially not Tim Holt. It was preposterous. Tim was a gentle man, an old-timer, a bachelor who cared for nothing but handling cattle and a little hunting and every now and again shooting off his old guns and bragging about the good old days when Arizona was really a wild land. He would not hurt a boy or even a man, for that matter. He'd never even killed an Indian.

Gilliland wondered how he was getting along with his old Navajo friends. He didn't have to worry. Tim Holt was having the time of his life and, unbeknownst to Gilliland, would likely never return to the hapless manager's ranch.

He hurried at his work as he wanted to get back on the ranch as soon as possible. These days he felt very strange, as if someone were looking over his shoulder all the time, and he'd heard that Graham spent most of his time these days in the saloon down the street. He did not want an altercation with his former friend.

But Tom Graham was waiting for him on the boardwalk outside of his favorite saloon. He'd pulled an all-nighter, and was still drunk, even after sleeping a few hours on one of the billiard tables in the back. He looked John Gilliland over with contempt. "Where's your murdering buffalo hunter, you bastard?"

Gilliland put up a hand. "Now, Tom, none of that. I tell you, Tim is not your man. None of my men killed your boy, so there's an end to it."

"Liar!" He went for his six-shooter and realized it wasn't there. He stumbled off the porch and fell on his face. He stood up and closed the distance between himself and Gilliland. "I'm gonna beat you till you tell me."

This was a bad idea, as John Gilliland, though not bright, was big, and younger by fifteen years, and sober. He also was good in a fight. "Come on, Tom, stop it. Just stop it."

Graham used his head for a battering ram, and charged at Gilliland, knocking the ranch boss on his backside. He began punching the younger man in the face and now Gilliland had had enough. He did not want to fight, but this had to stop.

He rolled left and jumped to his feet. He squared himself for battle and held up a hand. "Stop, Tom, please, just stop."

"You killed my boy. You and your bastards." He was crying and red in the face. He swung wildly and clipped Gilliland on the jaw. Gilliland returned a punch on his attacker's nose. The man went down, blood now streaming like a fountain from both nostrils. He sat for a moment and did nothing.

"Son of a bitch that hurts."

Gilliland wetted a scarf from the nearby trough. He held it to the man's face. "Pinch it, Tom, lean forward."

Graham complied.

They sat for a long moment and said nothing. Graham stood up and Gilliland steadied him. He put him in his wagon. He found his horse and hitched it to the back, they'd ride home together.

"Tom, there's something afoot." He thought hard about what to say as Graham was in a terrible state now. "I don't think the Halls are responsible for all this either."

"That's because you're an idiot."

"No I'm not."

"You are. You're the stupidest man I've ever met. You're so dumb, you're dumber than the dumbest nigger I've ever seen. You're stupider than the stupidest Indian squaw I've ever laid eyes on. You're a stupid jackass. No reason why you should ever be a range boss, you're so goddamn dumb. You wouldn't make a goddamn foreman in the worst goddamned Mexican rancho in the worst piece of shit state in the Sonoran desert, keeping an eye on a bunch of just as stupid pepper bellies. You're so goddamned stupid, you couldn't give out clean sheets in a whorehouse and keep it all straight."

He belched and swallowed hard to keep

his bloody stomach contents down. He started blubbering and his tears mixed with the blood still coming from his nose and now mouth. He got sick and vomited all over the floorboards of Gilliland's buckboard. He belched fetid breath and Gilliland now thought that he himself might start adding to the odiferous pile of detritus between them.

"God damn, I miss him."

"I'm sure you do, friend."

"Don't call me friend, you asshole."

"I'm not an asshole, Tom."

"You are. You are. You're an asshole and you're an idiot."

He cried harder and Gilliland pushed a canteen in the drunken man's face.

"Drink this, you'll feel better."

He did and cried and eventually began to nod off.

In a little while they were back at the Graham ranch and John Gilliland called for some men to put their boss to bed. Graham woke up and began pushing them away.

"I'm not drunk enough can't take care of myself." He stood up and fell over and onto the ground, opening up another torrent of blood, this time from the top of his skull.

"Goddamn it, goddamn it." He cried again. Gilliland waved the men away.

They sat again for a while and Gilliland got him to drink more water.

Tom Graham began to talk. "I know you didn't have my boy killed."

"Okay, Tom."

"But you're still an asshole."

"No I'm not."

CHAPTER 22
GOT YOU RIGHT

Harry led the miscreant along the road to the old place. He was not happy about it, as he hated the man for killing his boss and friend Josh Housman. He'd have been just as happy to be a member on the firing party to dispatch the wretch and just be done with it and send him on to hell, where he belonged.

He looked back at the miserable fellow and scowled. "Hur—hurry, up, y—you."

"I'm hurryin'."

The man rode up beside the old hand and tried to engage him a little. He'd lost some of his fear, and thought that being friendly would be the healthiest thing for him now.

"Pretty land you got up here."

Harry snapped. "Don—don't talk to me, mister. Y—you kilt the best man I ev—ever knew and I don't li—like this a b—bit. Sooner I get you settled the be—better."

The man became sullen and his voice

cracked. He wasn't nearly as tough as he thought he was. He could have been a decent sort, had he not gotten caught up with the wrong crowd. "I'm, I'm sorry, mister. I swear, I'm sorry."

Harry looked at the man and his pathetic demeanor made the old fellow a bit angrier yet. It would have been better, easier to deal with an unrepentant blackheart, it would have been better for Harry all around. Now the fellow's responses made Harry feel almost sorry for him and he didn't want to feel that way as he was too fond of Josh to have any kind of compassion for one of his assassins.

"Jo—Josh was from Florida." He looked down the trail as he didn't stutter so badly when he was not talking directly to another man. Sometimes, when he was out with just the herd and talking to them, or especially singing to them, he didn't stutter at all. The only man who kept his stutter down to a minimum was Josh Housman. He hardly ever stuttered around Josh.

He continued. "Jo—Josh was the best boss I ever known. And he was kind. He used to draw our pictures for us. Some of the boys used to send 'em home to their mothers or sweethearts. Jo—Josh was a g—great man."

He looked over and the fellow was crying

hard now. Harry kind of liked that. He went on. "He—he made great paintings at a Frenchman's saloon down in town. Grand pictures. Beautiful naked ladies. Ladies more beautiful than the likes of us c—could ever behold." He took a long drink from his canteen and wiped his mouth with the back of his hand. "The place was too rich for our blood. We never could af—ford to go in that place, just mostly rich men could g—go there, but one time the Frenchman and his wife let me in just to look over Josh's wor—works. They were grand."

He eyed the old place up ahead and knew they'd be there soon. The former assassin would be alone with his thoughts and Harry wanted him to have plenty to ponder while he was waiting for Allingham to do with him whatever the marshal had in mind. He looked the crying man in the eye as he pulled out a piece of paper from his work shirt pocket. He opened it with great care and reverence and pressed it flat on his thigh. He handed it to the bad man.

"He—here, mister, I, I wan—want you to take this for a while. It's a picture of Josh, h—he drew it lookin' in the ma—mirror, and then he gave it to me." He just as quickly pulled it away. "Do—don't you wrinkle it. A—and I want it b—back."

The man cried and took it. He wiped his eyes and said nothing. The only vision he could conjure of the foreman was of after he'd lost his eye. Josh Housman was a handsome man and now the fellow realized that.

Harry pulled the man's Winchester from its scabbard. "N—no rifle for you."

"But I'm all alone out here." He looked the little cabin over as if regarding his tomb. "What if, if the bad fellow comes to burn me up?"

Harry shrugged. "Order from M—Miss Rosario." He nodded. "Y—you can keep your six-shooter, w—we'll be by to check on you. Grub's inside, we—well's out back."

"But I need my Winchester." He whined like a little child.

"No—nope, Miss Rosario s—said you was a piss-soaked coward, and you might shoot one of us when w—we come out to check on y—you." He regarded the man as he turned to ride away. "Sh—she sure got you right."

Chapter 23
Follow Me, You Men

Mike O'Shaughnessy rode toward the mining operation and looked over to his brother and was pleased to see him awake. Paddy could sleep anywhere, even while riding a horse.

"Paddy, what do you make of Allingham?"

He shrugged. "Very sad, brother. Very sad indeed."

"I liked the old captain better. I like a mean boss. Keeps a man honest and straight."

Paddy could not disagree. He shrugged again. "I think there is the old terse Allingham, somewhere locked away, in that active mind." He shifted in the saddle and heard the explosions off in the distance. He looked at the sun. They'd be there by early evening. He looked at Mikey and decided it was good now to formulate a plan.

Allingham had a good idea the dynamite used to kill his father-in-law had come from the mining operation nearby. He put the Irishmen on it as he knew they'd get the straight story, and more importantly, any conspirators, had there been any to get.

"When we get there, Mikey, let's not tip our hand. Let's seek jobs, tell them we want to work at the mine. We can get more information if they don't expect lawmen sniffing about."

"And for how long, me brother? How long do we perpetrate this ruse?"

"Oh, not long. We'll go to the saloon. We should be there by suppertime. Men should be finished for the day. We can look them all over. Once we've done that, we'll show them our badges."

Mikey liked this idea. He rummaged through his traps and regarded his nightstick. It had traveled with him since Chicago. He trusted it more than he did his six-shooter. He pulled it out from the carpetbag tied to the back of his saddle, and tucked it under his arm. That would work. It would be secreted until he needed it and easily be gotten to if — and, more likely, when — the time would come.

He looked about as he rode along. He'd forgotten how much he liked the Arizona land. He liked it here, and was sorry he'd pulled his brother along to California, even though living near the sea was pleasant enough. Perhaps when this business was over and Allingham no longer needed them, they'd stay and seek out another adventure here.

The wives would need convincing. Mary in particular. She was not so docile as his own Kathleen and he smiled at his brother as he rode. Paddy was good for Mary. He was good for everyone. They were twins certainly enough, but in temperament there were never two men more opposite, except that both held good control of their anger, unlike their father who had the filthiest temper they'd ever known.

He laughed out loud at the memory of some of his father's shenanigans and his brother looked over his shoulder to see what was amusing him so.

"I was remembering Da."

"Why?" Paddy could not find any reason to conjure up memories of his dead father, good or bad, nor, for that matter, even one good recollection of a memory that would elicit a laugh. Fact was, Paddy was glad his bastard of a father was dead.

"Do you remember, brother, when Da could not get that wheelbarrow to roll right?"

Paddy shrugged. He could not.

"Da picked it up over his head and dashed it to pieces. Mother locked him out of the house until he calmed down."

"Oh, I *do* remember that. The old sot."

"That he was."

"What was he ever doing with such a device? A wheelbarrow is for a working man."

Mikey shrugged.

Their old man was the worst drunk in the village and that was saying a lot. He had many competitors for the distinction as the town's greatest inebriate.

And that was yet another blessing for the twins. The drink had no hold on them. They had their beer and stout and knew when to stop. They were good coppers and that is why they were here, helping Miss Rosario and Allingham.

The land reminded Paddy of Francis, and he had only just gotten over grieving for him almost every day. Francis was the most colorful, friendly, likable man the twins had ever known, and Paddy missed him.

He had to keep it to himself, however. Mikey could not bear to talk of their late friend, and this was especially difficult, for Mikey was Paddy's sounding board on all things that worried or vexed him. He'd had to manage his grief for Francis on his own and that was another good thing about coming back. He and Miss Rosario could talk about the young wild deputy, and they did well into the night since Paddy and Mike had arrived. It was good to talk of the old times, to talk about Francis. It was the kind of catharsis Paddy needed. He was an aficionado of wakes and grieving, as he liked to remember the dead.

As he rode, he thought about Francis. He'd think often about situations and wonder what Francis would do if confronted with them. On this occasion, he thought about the challenge awaiting them. Francis would go in, with that ubiquitous smirk on his face. He'd throw a few *I'll be go to hells* around and then proceed to vex and annoy the bad men. He'd accomplish the task at hand, but Paddy knew, when Francis was on the job, it was likely the nightsticks would be tapping a few gourds.

His reverie was interrupted when Mikey stopped. He watched his brother prepare. He nodded to Paddy to put his gun inside his pants and remove the badge from his sack coat lapel. They now looked like a pair of benign Irish immigrants, seeking wages in the mine.

The company store and saloon was a busy place. Here the miners could spend their

229

earnings freely and they did. The brothers walked through the door and a few men acknowledged them with a nod. The barman tipped his head.

"Gentlemen, what's your poison?"

"Just beer."

They drank and looked about as the men continued their conversations, seemingly ignoring the two giants. Paddy looked on and then addressed the barman.

"Who shall we see for a job query?"

A short man with darting eyes spoke up. He walked quickly from the other end of the bar. He looked up at the twins as if he were regarding a newly erupted pair of mountains, thrown up by some seismic disturbance. He liked big men, as he could get more labor from them. "That would be me."

Paddy took another drink of his beer. He did not extend his hand. He spoke at the barman and nodded for two more bottles.

"Me brother and me, we're seeking employment."

"At what?"

"Security."

Mikey looked at his brother, a little surprised. He thought they'd be continuing the ruse a little longer, but he knew now, Paddy must have seen something that would make him progress in such a way.

"What do you mean, security?" The little foreman stepped back as if he were regarding a pair of union men.

"Oh, you know, security, for thievery and such. You most certainly have a problem. That's without a doubt."

The little man blanched. He became furious and turned a reddish purple before their very eyes.

He glared at the Irish giants and pointed a shaking finger at the door."

"Out!"

Mikey nodded to Paddy as they continued to finish their beers.

"I don't believe we are welcome here, brother."

"Aye, me brother, and that is a shame. The beer is not bad" — he nodded his head at the cases of bottles stacked up high behind the bar — "and in good supply."

"Out!" The little man was bold, and dared to even put a hand on Paddy's shoulder. The big Irishmen grabbed it in his great meaty fist. He held the man's hand as if he were a small child, bucking his schoolmaster.

The foreman squirmed to get away. He cried out like an adolescent having a regular temper tantrum. "Let me go!"

"Not until you tell us, my good man, how the dynamite used to blow up Mr. Halsted got taken from your supply."

"That's a lie!" He struggled and Paddy turned to face the little man.

The foreman looked left then right. He ordered his men into action. One then another, and finally half a dozen, reluctantly rose to his defense.

Mikey turned to face them and, as if by magic, had his nightstick in hand. "Now, lads, no reason to become physical." He smiled and nodded to Paddy. "Me brother and me, we only want some answers." He ducked as a bottle sailed past his ear, hitting the barman soundly on the nose, it pouring blood as he fell back on a case of cheap whiskey.

Paddy knocked the little foreman senseless and pulled his own faithful club. He stood next to his brother as they each counted, dividing the gang between them.

"You take those three, Mikey, I'll do for the rest."

Soon fists were flying and men were falling and Mikey and Paddy were eventually back to back, the nightsticks twirling with deadly accuracy. They made it to the door and were out into the darkening night.

They looked about for their horses, now

nowhere in sight.

"We'll have to make a run for it on foot, me brother."

They were interrupted by a hiss and a call, as a Negro, bigger yet than the Irishmen, beckoned them to the shadows.

"Follow me, you men."

CHAPTER 24
HOW ABOUT A BATH

Walter Druitt was smitten. He was more in love, or at least more in lust with Samantha Ford than he'd ever been with any of the other women of his vast and carnally charged life. Physically, Sam was perfect. Mentally and emotionally, she was like soft putty in his hands. She worshiped him, or at least, so he perceived, and with Walter Druitt, when it came to the affairs of the heart, perception always took precedence over reality. She'd been deflowered by him. His heart spent most of his time in his throat when he was with her. When he was without her, all he could think about was bedding her.

They spent the day in Phoenix together and soon his carpetbag of money had dwindled to an insignificant pile. He didn't care. Sam was like a child, seemingly incapable of knowing the value of things. She'd point and he'd buy. He could deny her nothing, and soon she had a trousseau that would have made a Parisian courtesan green with envy. He loved buying her things, and the more he showed her, the more she seemed to need. He could not wait to take her someplace grand, perhaps San Francisco.

And Sam learned many things in this very short time as well. She learned that she cut a spectacular figure in fine clothing, and men liked it very much. She learned that drinking before fornicating made it much less difficult to endure. She learned, by some artful maneuvering, that certain parts of Walter Druitt, when properly positioned and controlled by her, could touch certain parts of her anatomy that made being with such a man much less intolerable.

He left her to nap after noon and went to the bank. This put a significant damper on his afternoon as he soon realized that the money he'd gotten was not nearly as much as he needed to keep his new Betty satisfied. He wished he'd not given the old Betty so much, and cursed her name under his breath. He emptied his bank account.

He finally made it back to Sam, his new Betty, and kissed her awake. She smiled coyly and stretched in bed, like a queen cat in heat. She kissed him hard on the mouth, sitting up enough to lose the bed coverings. "Miss me?"

"I did." She was taking his breath away. He presented her with a bowl of fruit and fed her grapes as if she was Bathsheba, and just as quickly carried the imagery to its most absurd conclusion. He stood up and beckoned her to the great parlor in his room.

"How about a bath?" He smiled proudly at the steaming copper tub, as if he'd hefted the water up to the top floor himself.

"Oh, goody." She lifted her slender foot up and over the edge of the tub, testing the water with her bare toe. "Just right." She slid into the water like an anaconda escaping the confines of the rain forest.

With trembling hands, Walter Druitt knelt behind her and began to thoroughly bathe his little prize.

"That feels good, lover."

He stiffened, and she could feel the strain radiate from his hands onto her lathered breasts. She waited.

"Don't call me that!"

"What?"

"Lover. I *hate* that."

"No, I'm sorry."

He went back to messaging her gently.

"It's all right. I'm the one who should be sorry."

"May I call you Walter?"

"Yes."

She turned and kissed him more seductively than he'd ever felt in a kiss. Of all the Bettys in all his time, Sam Ford was the best. She stood up and pulled him to her soaking body. She began removing his clothes.

He laughed. "What are you doing?"

"Come on in, it's a big tub, and the water's fine."

He did and now he held her in his lap, her back pressed to his chest. It was her turn to feed him grapes. She reached back over her head and waved each fruit around until she found his mouth. He sucked each finger clean. She dropped one and smiled. She turned to face him, pressing her breasts against his body. She reached down and caught the errant grape in her mouth, sucking it between her pursed lips.

"Like bobbing for apples." She smiled devilishly, then looked into the basket. "Oh, no apples, but here's an orange." She dropped it between them and it rolled down Walter Druitt's chest and immediately popped up, bobbing among the suds.

"Darn, oranges float." She tried a peach

and it floated. Finally, she happened on a plum. "Ah, that'll do it." They both watched it disappear. It rested somewhere in the depths of the tub.

Sam Ford smiled and took a deep breath. "Better go find it." She went under to search and was soon distracted by other things. She no longer bobbed for fruit. Walter Druitt lost his breath. He immediately wanted to marry her.

He was too tired to sleep and too exhausted to imbibe in any more of the girl's carnal offerings just now. He watched her sleep and his heart pounded as he gazed at her supine form. She was stunning and all he could think about now was bedding her.

It was a queer feeling, as Walter Druitt had had many, many Bettys and none had every evoked such a response. They always slaked his passion. He'd even get sick of them all after a little while, but Sam was different. He was, perhaps, for the first time in his life, genuinely in love. If not love, then at least at a heightened form of lust that made him almost happy.

He crept from the room and went to his own chambers next door. He dressed and shaved and looked at his watch. In another hour he could go to the bank. He looked the check over. He looked at the color of the ink and found a matching pen in his portfolio then fiddled around with the numbers. With significant craft, he slipped a zero in after the one, turning it into ten. He rubbed the word *one* lightly with an eraser and then carefully replaced it with the word *ten*.

He held it out at arm's length and grimaced. It wasn't right. He folded it in quarters then rubbed it between his forefinger and thumb. It looked better. He doused it with a little leftover champagne and the ink ran just enough. He blotted it carefully and was satisfied. They knew him well enough in town. They'd most certainly cash it.

Sam awoke and stretched and checked the bed. She was pleased as she was alone and stretched again and thought about the warm tub. She resolved to take many more baths and she resolved to keep Walter Druitt under her spell until his money ran out. She thought about him a little and could not remember his face. That was not so surprising, as she was not interested in Walter Druitt's face.

She got up and ate the rest of the fruit and found a new bottle of champagne. She aped the hotel waiter's actions and opened the bottle to a significant pop. She laughed as champagne ran down her front, soaking her breasts and pudenda and wondered what effect such a sight would have had on her hapless lover. She felt good and soon became distracted and began moving her hands over her wine-soaked body. The little convulsions led to a new feeling, as Sam Ford, for the first time in her miserable, albeit short life, experienced an entirely new sensation. She'd now known, for the first time in her life, the sensation of empowerment.

She washed up and dressed and combed her hair with the pretty tortoiseshell comb and brush set acquired just the day before. She doused herself with the French perfume and decked herself out in her new earrings and pearls. She called for breakfast and ate and then worked on another bottle of champagne and soon Walter Druitt was before her, like some deranged court jester hoping for an audience with his queen.

He thrust the bouquet of flowers in her face and she deftly moved them aside. She hiked up her skirts and pulled him onto her body. They made love again.

He recovered and let her rummage through the carpetbag at the piles of cash, neatly tied with paper bands, each one with the number one thousand stamped across them by the bank. She waved a pile, fanning her face and smiled.

"Samantha?"

"Yes, Walter?"

"Let's go to Argentina."

"All right."

CHAPTER 25
DUDE'S CARTRIDGE

Allingham stood in the gun shop with Hugh Auld, watching as the gunsmith turned the cartridge case over in his hands.

"Nope, never seen one." He harrumphed. "Dude's cartridge."

"How so?" Allingham looked at Auld and gave a just-discernible smile. The curmudgeonly shop owner amused him.

"Forty-five one twenty-five, dude cartridge."

"Not for buffalo?" Auld scratched his chin. He could not imagine such a massive bullet used on anything else.

"Yeah, well, it was made for the big shaggies and about ten years too late." He turned his head from side to side. "Sharps made it too late. All the big boys gone by the time it come around. Forty-five seventy's enough anyways, and you can get the ammo easy enough." He regarded the shell case and nodded again. "Definitely a dude. No real hunter'd leave cases like this lyin' around. They's worth their weight in gold."

"For what?"

"Reloadin'. All's you need's a primer, some powder and a good chunk a lead, and a mould. Make yer own. All the hunters did. Cheap bastards never did buy cartridges after the first box."

Allingham shrugged. "So, you've never seen or sold a gun or the cartridges for such?"

"No, Marshal. No, this is a dude's gun, and don't have no dudes for customers."

Auld nodded. They walked out.

Allingham thought as Auld talked. Auld liked to talk to the marshal as Allingham was still not so terse as he used to be.

"What do you make of it, Marshal?"

"Clarence."

"Clarence."

"It's a plant."

"You don't say?"

"Most certainly. Someone used it to kill Graham's boy. Next we'll see some bit of information leaked to Graham. We'll probably find the rifle hidden on the Hall ranch, planted there to make it look like they did it. They left the shell cases so Graham would find them."

"So my friend Tim Holt's in the clear."

"Yes, your friend was probably an irritation to the assassin. It delayed his linking the killing to the Halls and then Tom Graham went after Gilliland by accident. It slowed down the progress of this ridiculous war." He shrugged. "This assassin is a crafty devil."

"Indeed."

"But you still reckon that we have at least three different assassins?"

"Yes." Allingham looked at Auld and remembered Rebecca and how she used to work with him through the dialectic. He began to cry and didn't bother to try to hide his tears from the old prospector.

Auld became embarrassed and looked away.

"Don't be ashamed of my tears, Hugh."

The old-timer coughed a little and nodded. "All right."

Allingham cleared his throat and gained control of his emotions, at least for now. "As far as I can see, we've got the assassin who killed the boy, and that was the same man who killed Gilliland's foreman, and he also arranged the lynching of Old Pop." He rode along with Auld beside him. He handed the prospector his big canteen after taking a drink. "Then we've got the Mexican. He's just a loner, I think, then there's the one who's killing the lynch mob."

"And you say he's separate from the rest?"

"Yes." He took the canteen back and corked it. "But the big prize is the puppet master."

"How's that?"

"Someone's driving all this. Someone important."

Hugh Auld, as if he'd been hit by some invisible force, slumped forward. White bone protruded from just below the shoulder of his right arm. His limb dangled, useless, held to his body with nothing more than a strip of flesh. The big forty-five bullet had not found its intended mark, instead centering on the humerus of the prospector's arm. The shot cracked in the distance, causing Allingham's horse to skidder a little quickly forward. He looked off to the right at Auld and both simultaneously realized they were under attack. They kicked their mounts' sides, and took off for an arroyo up ahead, Allingham following close behind.

He got Auld from his horse and quickly tied the artery off. Blood stopped pumping with every heartbeat. Hugh Auld winced in pain. He looked down at his shattered limb and grimaced.

"God damn. Never seen the back a my

arm from this angle."

Allingham looked in the direction of the shot, peering over the edge of their little fortress wall. He saw nothing. He looked back at Auld and then at the sun. They were ten miles from the Hall ranch.

He pulled a bottle of whiskey from a saddlebag and held it up to the prospector.

"I know you don't imbibe, Hugh, and that might be a good thing. The liquor should affect you immediately."

Auld took a long drink.

He nodded at the bottle. "That's not bad."

"No, it's good quality. Got it from what survived the Halsted fire." He nodded and handed him his canteen. "Drink equal parts water and whiskey Hugh. Once the initial shock wears off, you are going to know some hellish pain."

Auld complied. He was losing color in his face but otherwise was in good trim. Allingham looked on at him and was impressed by the man's toughness.

"What do we do now?"

"First, I got to twist your arm back in place."

Hugh nodded for Allingham to proceed. He wound the arm back into place and the tourniquet slipped. Blood sprayed on Allingham's shirtfront and face. He once again stopped its flow. Auld grinned, doing his best not to cry out.

Allingham's mind raced. Out there was a man with a buffalo rifle and he was a pretty good shot. Auld's arm was no longer bleeding, but it needed attention. It needed to be cleaned and dressed at the least, and more likely, amputated as soon as possible. He knew Auld's only chance was Rosario. He looked at the sun again. He pulled one of his shirts from his saddlebag and made a sling. Once in place, he bound Hugh's arm to his chest. Auld nodded. He slurred his words.

"Feels better already."

Allingham looked the old fellow in the eye. He wanted to cry again, as Hugh had gotten to him. Hugh was one of the finest men he'd known, and he didn't want him to die.

"We've only got one choice, Hugh."

"What's that?"

"Wait until sundown and ride back to the ranch."

"Why not go now?"

Allingham knew the man was in bad shape, but Auld was the paradigm of logic. He was cool and calm.

"That ass of an assassin will pick us off if we ride again in daylight."

"Good point." He grimaced again as the anesthetic action of the body in its initial response to such a shock was beginning to wear off. The pain would soon be unbearable.

"You could go get him."

Allingham thought on that. He probably could, and the assassin wouldn't expect that. He shrugged. "I don't want to leave you alone, Hugh."

"Look, Clarence, I'm probably going to die from this, anyway. Jesus, man, look at my arm. Looks like it's been run through a rock pulverizer."

He did something Allingham would not expect from a man who'd just nearly lost his arm. With his good left arm, he grabbed the saddle horn and pulled himself back on his horse. He adjusted his feet in the stirrups. He pointed his mount in the direction of the Hall ranch and his only chance.

"Adiós, my friend. I'll give the son of a bitch something to shoot at. You do me a favor and gut him for me when you catch him." He was gone.

Allingham mounted up and watched the prospector ride like his horse's ass was on fire. A shot jolted him into action and dust kicked up thirty yards ahead of Hugh on the trail. The assassin was after him. Now

Allingham went into action.

He rode the edge of the arroyo so as not to be seen, off on a little oblique angle from the bullet's path. He heard shot after shot, but now Hugh was a good three hundred yards further away, and on a horse running full speed. The best shot in the world would not achieve such a feat of marksmanship.

Allingham could see the assassin clearly now, as the shooter was up high and the air was still and calm. Great puffs of smoke went up after every shot. He rode hard and wide. He'd come up behind him and the son of a bitch would not know what hit him. Allingham drew in a deep breath. With every fiber of his being he'd have to resist the urge to put a bullet through the black-heart's brain.

He slowed at one hundred yards and pulled his Winchester. He stopped at fifty and watched the man watch the horizon. Auld was gone. The assassin was now looking for Allingham.

"Behind you, asshole!"

The man twirled on his heels but the heavy buffalo rifle was too much to mount. He dropped it at his feet and grinned sheepishly, like a boy who'd been caught doing something he ought not be doing.

"What now?" The man was too calm.

"Drop your gun belt."

The man grinned and slowly backed toward the edge of the cliff he'd used as a shooting platform. He stared Allingham in the eye as he moved. He put his hand to his buckle and began pulling the tail of his belt through. He grinned more widely and went for his six-shooter. Allingham had him cold. This was the act of either a stupid or fearless man. Perhaps he was just plain out of his mind.

"Don't do it!" Allingham fairly shouted, as he took up the slack on the trigger of his Winchester.

The man grinned again and had the six-shooter in hand. He turned a little sideways and then stumbled. He tripped over a mesquite branch, regained his balance momentarily, then toppled over the edge. He screamed like a baby all the way down.

Allingham rode up to the limits of the precipice and looked over and down at the corpse crumpled in a heap a hundred feet below. He whistled between his teeth. *I'll be go to hell.*

Hugh Auld rode in sleeping across his horse's mane when the alarm was raised. Long Jack was on him and helped him to the ground. Soon half a dozen men had him and carried him to one of Rosario's comfortable beds. She worried over the man as they stripped him of his clothes.

He awoke and smiled and gave Rosario a little pat on the cheek with his good arm.

"Don't mean to bleed all over your house, ma'am." He hiccupped politely and covered his mouth.

"You don't worry over it, my boy."

Lucía was next to him at once. "Where, where is Clarence?" She was not ashamed of her actions. She could think only of Allingham.

"Oh, oh, he'll be along, ma'am. Went for the fellow who did this to me." He grinned a little uneasily at Rosario. "Sorry, but I'm drunk ma'am. Drank a whole bottle of good liquor. Clarence gave it to me. Beg your pardon, ma'am." He drifted off to sleep again.

Rosario worked quickly. She unwrapped the wound and surveyed the mess created by the great buffalo slug. She nodded her head doubtfully as Old Pop looked on, shrugging her shoulders in resignation.

"I can do nothing with this, my love. A good part of the bone is simply gone, and the rest is shattered."

Old Pop whispered and nodded gravely. "It'll have to come off."

They worked quickly and boiled the meat saw. Rosario had chloroform and began preparing it. Old Pop stood by as his wife's operating nurse. She awoke Hugh from his slumber.

"Mr. Auld?"

"Yes, ma'am."

"I am sorry to tell you, I must take your arm."

He grinned uneasily and looked at the horrific wound. "I know, ma'am." He smiled. "Knew it when it first happened."

"I have good medicine for you, Hugh. It will not hurt and you will be asleep. The wound is clean, thanks to Clarence. You will be asleep for a little while."

"I thank you ma'am."

Rosario soaked a sponge in the anesthetic and placed it at the narrow end of a funnel. This she held, cone down, several inches above the old prospector's nose and mouth. He breathed easily and soon fell back to sleep. Rosario watched the breathing slow; she placed the cone a little closer to her patient's face. She waited.

When he was insensible, she began.

She made a deep incision around the epidermis of the entire arm, careful to leave enough for a flap, just at the upper limit of the exit wound. She peeled back the skin, revealing the old muscles and sinews, veins and arteries and nerves. This she cut back a little further yet, leaving the shattered bone exposed for another inch. All of this she cauterized with a hot iron, fresh from the blacksmith's forge. Smoke and the acrid odor of burning flesh and blood and connective tissue filled the room. Pierce stood by with a big palm fan and waved it in Rosario's face. She could not risk falling under the influence of the anesthetic as she worked away.

She peeled back this material now and exposed the bone until it was undamaged. Old Pop handed her the saw and she cut quickly as Old Pop gently held the dead arm. When it was free, he removed it, placing it on a towel, with the reverence accorded a dead loved one. Pierce scooped it up and carried it from the room.

Old Pop nodded his encouragement and watched his wife work with the dexterity of a surgeon. She scraped the edges of the freshly cut end of the humerus smooth and pulled down the skin flap she'd made. She began sewing, until the whole affair looked very much like a turkey with its body cavity trussed, ready for the roasting pan.

She looked at Hugh Auld and he continued to sleep peacefully. She washed the wound clean and wrapped it round and round with a clean dressing. She nodded to Long Jack and Pierce who rolled the patient on his side. Rosario pulled the bloody bedclothes away, replacing them with fresh ones. They gently placed the old prospector on his back. He snored peacefully.

She nodded to the men. "Thank you, my boys. It will be a matter of time. If he does not get a fever, he will survive."

Old Pop reached over and kissed his wife on the forehead. He whispered in her ear as she washed the blood from her hands. "I love you."

Pierce Hall offered Lucía a cup of tea as she stared off into the dimming twilight. She refused it with a dismissive nod. She did not want him there now and did her best not to encourage him to linger. She'd keep vigil on her own. She thought ignoring him would be enough, but Pierce did not understand.

"I'll go after him in the morning, ma'am."

She pulled one of Rosario's rebozos tightly about her body and stared more intently at the horizon.

"He's a tough son of a bitch, old Allingham." He immediately regretted using such profanity and wondered at his own stupidity.

She turned on him with a savagery he'd not ever known in a woman, and scowled at him. "His name is Clarence. And do not call him an ugly name!"

"I'm sorry, ma'am. Just meant, just meant that he's a tough one. The marshal'll be along soon, I know it, know it for certain. You just wait and see, ma'am."

She cried and rubbed her eyes with the backs of her hands. She wanted him to go away.

"You love him don't you, ma'am?"

She didn't respond.

Pierce panicked a little. He'd been pining for Lucía ever since he'd learned of her husband's death, maybe, if he were honest with himself, long before that. He knew this was not the right time to broach the subject, and then, almost as if he could not control his tongue, sort of blurted the words out. "I, I guess it, well, ma'am, I guess you'd never, well, never . . ."

"I do not love you nor will I ever love you!" Her face changed as she glared into Pierce Hall's eyes. He was a disarming and kind fellow, and Lucía regretted treating him in such a rude manner.

She took a deep breath and tried to

control her quivering voice. She spoke in a tiny, quiet tone. "I am sorry, Mr. Hall. I am sorry, but no, I will not love you. I respect you and I like you very much, but no, I will not love you. I do love Clarence and he must." She looked again at the horizon, now black and featureless. "He must come back to me."

He backed away and looked about. He didn't want her outside on her own. He tried hard to think of something to say, but nothing sensible would come to him.

"Well, well, ma'am, you have, have a good night."

He retreated to the parlor and sat by the window. He'd keep vigil on the one keeping vigil.

Eventually, everyone was in for the night. Long Jack took up his post at the gate, and Lucía settled in one of the rockers. In a little while Rosario was out to check on her, startling her out of her light slumber as she covered the young woman with a blanket. She kissed Lucía on the forehead.

"How is Mr. Auld, señora?" She'd remonstrated herself all evening for not asking after the old prospector.

"He is sleeping, my child. I believe he will be fine."

"I am sorry for only thinking of Clarence.

That was wicked of me."

"No it was not." Rosario patted her, with a mother's love, on the back of her hand. She looked off into the night. "He will be with you soon, my girl."

"Do you believe that is true?" The tears were flowing now, and Lucía worked hard to gain control. "I love him so, and I am so worried he will die."

"I know, child. I know you are. Clarence is a resourceful fellow, and just plain too tough to die."

Lucía looked up at her, a little incredulous at Rosario's confidence. The old Mexicana smiled. "You only know the gentle and kind Allingham." She pulled up a rocker and sat down next to the young Basque beauty.

"Clarence Allingham is the most fascinating man I've ever known." She looked off in the distance and smiled. "He used to be the meanest man I'd ever known, and then he became the most loving husband I'd ever known, then the saddest man I'd ever known, and now, now, I believe he will surprise us all."

"I cannot help but feel that it is wicked of me to love a man so soon after my husband is dead." She cried as she stared into the night. "But I cannot help it."

"No, my darling. You must not think that.

257

As I have told you before, our lives are too short to grieve over the dead. We must move on, and you are a fitting match for Clarence. You are good enough for him, I think."

Lucía smiled a little at Rosario's candor.

"I do not say this to insult you, Lucía, but Clarence, he is a magnificent man. He is a man like not many other men, and despite his looks, he is a man that few woman can resist, once they know of his greatness."

"I know of his greatness." She cried, worrying and wondering when she'd see him again. "I know his goodness too, and that is why I love him so."

Rosario stood up and stretched. She was exhausted from the day's toils and the surgery and worrying over Allingham. She needed to get to bed now. She patted Lucía on the top of the head.

"You wait for him, my dear. He'll be along soon enough."

Singh was not sleepy as the surgery on the prospector had turned the whole place upside-down. He put his girls to bed and wandered about the place, checking to make certain all was safe and secure in the house. He walked up on Pierce, sitting and staring out the window at the Basque beauty. He put a hand on the young man's shoulder and Pierce nodded for him to sit down.

The young fellow started talking automatically. "Why's it, Mr. Singh, why's it, what do ya suppose?" He cleared his throat and stared at the young woman dozing in the rocker.

"She is smitten, Pierce, and that is all there is to be said. There is no logical explanation when regarding the human heart."

"I fell in love with her the first day I saw her." He shrugged and took a drink. "Course, I'd never a done a thing about it. She was married an' all then."

"Of course you would not."

Pierce became a little animated. He, as did everyone who knew the Sikh, felt compelled to spill his guts to Mr. Singh. It was as if the Indian was a kind of high priest, and everyone sought his counsel.

"I, I don't get it, sir. I mean, the marshal, he's a good man an' all, but, he's so, so well, old and, and danged plug ugly."

Singh smiled. He looked through the window and could see Lucía's profile in the moonlight as she slept. She was a remarkably beautiful young woman.

"I understand your consternation, Pierce. But Allingham, he, well, how do I say this. There is something about our friend Allingham." He thought hard about how to explain it to the young rancher. He continued. "The body, the human body, Pierce, it is made of many organs, you know this, and the skin, it is the largest such."

Pierce turned and dropped his gaze from Lucía as he gave Hira his full attention. "Yes sir, I understand that."

"And it is also the least enduring, when it comes to the affairs of the heart."

Pierce laughed a little cynically. "Beauty's only skin deep."

"That is correct." The Sikh was impressed with Pierce's quick mind. He always had been. "But the other great organs, the heart and the brain, and something that is not an organ, but just as important as the most vital organ, the soul, is what is beautiful about Clarence Allingham." He looked at Lucía again and marveled at how the moonlight played on her delicate features. "And you will not ever compete with that."

He stood up and stretched and did something that Pierce Hall did not expect. He removed his dastar and shook out his long dark hair, which cascaded over his shoulders and all the way down his back. He looked shocking, shockingly handsome, and wild, like a wild Apache warrior to the young man now and Pierce Hall thought that Mr. Hira Singh might very well be the most fascinating and wisest man he'd ever known.

At just after three in the morning, Lucía was jolted from her slumber by the loud and authoritative voice of her man.

"Hello in the house!"

Long Jack called back, into the night. "Marshal Allingham, come on in, sir! By God, it's good to hear your voice."

Lucía was on him, pulling him from his horse as she fairly devoured his mouth. She nodded to Long Jack who took Allingham's and the assassin's mounts. He looked on, a little confused as Lucía pulled the hero by the arm toward home, toward her cozy bed.

He called out after them. "I'll take care of the horses, Marshal."

She pulled his bloody shirt off, then the rest, and fairly yanked him into bed. She wasted no time and was on him, making love to him with a desperation he'd never known. She kissed him repeatedly and whispered in his ear. "I missed you, I missed you so much."

Afterward, she rested in his arms.

"The prospector is good, my love."

Allingham smiled. He nearly forgot to ask, as Lucía was quite distracting. He knew

Hugh must have survived, as Lucía would not have greeted him in such a way otherwise. He breathed in the scent of her hair. He'd not felt so good, so alive in a long time. He never imagined such a welcome home.

Hugh Auld regarded the little bag of meat, neatly tied and dangling at the end of his arm. He used to be proud of the strength in his right hand. He used to make money arm wrestling. He made a fair bundle doing that in his younger days. He thought about how hard it would be to learn to become left-handed. He could do nothing worthwhile with his left hand. He grinned a little at the thought of what a challenge it would now be to wipe his backside.

He coughed a little and Allingham woke up in the chair next to the invalid's bed. Allingham smiled uneasily, as here was another man maimed and affected because of him. He nodded and worried over the bandaged stump. "Hugh, I'm sorry, friend."

"Aw, just some bad luck." He shrugged. "When you think about it, could say good luck. If that boy had not pulled the shot, you'd be fitting me for a box and not a prosthetic arm."

He looked Allingham over and saw the

weariness in his eyes. The marshal had a new shirt, and had washed, but some of Hugh's blood remained, dry and caked to the marshal's fleshy right earlobe. He pointed to it and Allingham wetted his fingers and rubbed it off.

"Did you get the blackheart?"

"He got himself, Hugh. Stupid bastard tripped and fell off a cliff, and I couldn't get to him. It's just too damned ugly terrain where he lay."

Hugh pretended to spit in disgust. "Good! Good resting place for the bastard. He'll be carrion, wolf shit by the end of the week." His brow furrowed in doubt. "But you won't be able to identify him now, or pick up any clues he might have had on him."

"No, but I doubt we'd get much. He had nothing, and I mean nothing on his mount. Saddlebags clean, nothing to identify him in any way. I'm asking the Halls to investigate his horse's brand, but I doubt it's from around here. I got a good look at him, so we have that much." Allingham shrugged. "One thing, Hugh. He didn't have one of those fancy Sharps rifles like the gunsmith talked about. He had an old Remington, a Rolling Block, forty-five seventy. That's what he shot you with, Hugh."

"I'll be." The prospector looked at his arm. His missing hand all of a sudden throbbed, then itched. He wanted to scratch it. Instead, he took a swig of laudanum.

CHAPTER 26
A DOGGONE TOUGH LAND

Four parcels awaited Sheriff Commodore Perry Owens when he arrived at his office with Stosh Gorski in tow. He opened one and handed another to his Pinkerton partner.

"More peach pit carvings." Owens emptied the others. Stosh looked on.

"A moon, a cat, a little snake?"

"I think probably a worm."

"And a turtle."

Owens laid out the maps. "I know these places well enough."

"And I'm sure I know what we'll find when we get there."

"That makes five, and the bastard who turned himself in is six. Means there's one left."

Gorski smiled cynically. "Bet that boy's sphincter is puckering, whoever, and wherever he is."

"Indeed."

And, as if on cue, a knock was heard at the office door. The jail keeper escorted a sallow man holding his hat at his side. He was quite shaken.

The jailer announced the young man to his boss. "This fellow's been waiting for you, Sheriff. Wanted to turn himself in, I told him he'd have to wait for you. I've been lettin' him sleep in the cell in the back. One we been usin' for storage."

"That's right! Want to turn myself in, Sheriff."

Owens looked at Stosh and then at the miscreant. "For what?"

"Tryin' to lynch that rancher, up north, and shootin' that boy in the eye. I was part of it."

Owens nodded for him to sit down. He instructed the jailer to unsaddle the man's horse and bring all his traps into the office. Once this was accomplished, Owens began rummaging through it while Stosh Gorski emptied the young man's pockets.

They took his six-shooter and Winchester and just sat and looked the man over for a long time.

He was a young man and nervous and pretty well without means. He had six cartridges in the loops of his gun belt and only two in his Winchester. His six-shooter was loaded with five. He had sixty-three cents to his name.

"What's your name?"

"S—Smith."

Owens stood up and backhanded him across the mouth. The lad fell onto his backside and rubbed his jaw, then checked his hand for blood. Owens wasn't finished with him. The sheriff reached down, pulling the man by his shirt collar to his feet. He punched him hard just above his gun-belt buckle, and the man grunted in pain and fell back down. Owens pointed at him with a finger, shaking with fury. "Lie to me again, shithead, and I'll make you wish you'd got caught by the man who did for all your lynch gang friends."

"I, I, my name's Smith, mister, I swear, I swear."

Stosh Gorski handed Owens the man's wallet. There was a receipt for range pay in the name of Robert Smith. Owens ignored it and continued.

"Your first name."

"B—Bob, Robert, Robert, I swear, I swear."

"Go on out of here."

Stosh Gorski looked on at the sheriff, then at the boy. He was enjoying Commodore Perry Owens a little now. He was a good performer.

"What, what do you mean, sir?"

"Just what I said. You deaf? Get the hell outta here, now!"

"But, but the bad man, the man who's killed all the others. He's going to get me, he's going to get me, I don't want to be burned up, Jesus, please, you gotta arrest me."

"Bullshit. I don't have to do anything. You did the crime up north, out of my jurisdiction. Got nothing to hold you on. You're free, like a bird, now, fly." He waved the boy out the door, as if he were shooing flies. "Ride on up to the sheriff in Yavapai County. Sure he'll welcome you with room and board and a nice soft pillow on which to rest your weary head."

The boy looked at his traps, strewn everywhere. He began gathering them up in his arms.

"Leave them."

"But I need my saddle, and guns. Jesus, mister, you're sending me on to my death. Can't even defend myself."

"Yeah, well, it's a hard goddamned life, ain't it son? Hard for those two fellows you lynched, now hard for you."

The boy dropped to the floor and sobbed. He cried and when that had no effect, he groveled at the sheriff's feet. Owens kicked him hard, once again, this time across the mouth.

"Get away from me you little bastard."

Stosh Gorski spoke up. "Tell us of the man who hired you to do this."

The boy looked up, hope in his eyes. "I'll tell you, I'll tell you everything, just please, please lock me up."

Gorski escorted him to one of the cells, opened the door, and the boy jogged in. He gripped the bars, as if to assure that they were made of good steel. He was safe now.

"He was some dude, not from around here, spoke funny, like he was from up north somewheres, don't know where."

"What did he look like?"

"I don't know."

Owens threw an old cup of coffee in his face and the lad sputtered.

"He, he, wait, he, he had kind of yellowish hair, and, and mustaches. He wore a kind a like derby and, he, he wore a brown suit, with stripes in it."

"What's his name?"

"I, I don't know." He held up his hands in surrender, preparing to fend off any other attack from the sheriff. "I swear, I swear, never heard his name."

Owens looked at Stosh Gorski and then at

the jailer. "Sounds about right, Stosh, what do you say?"

Gorski looked at the pathetic man. "Sounds about right." Gorski nodded to the jailer, who opened the cell door. He pulled the fellow back out.

"Start walking."

The boy looked at them all and stood, dumbfounded.

"Go, get on your horse, you can keep that." Owens reached over and threw him his wallet and the few coins the man had on him. "You can take that, as well. And your horse's bridle, just consider yourself lucky I don't make you try to ride him without that."

The boy stopped in the doorway. He turned with tears in his eyes. "You men are sending me to my grave; you know that, don't you?"

"Good riddance." Owens slammed the door in his face.

Stosh twisted a cigarette and smoked and then twisted one for Owens. He nodded toward the door. "Shall I go fetch him?"

Owens did not smile. He looked at Gorski and then at the young fellow's traps. "Not on your life, Stosh, not on your life."

Stosh blew smoke at the ceiling. He shook his head slowly from side to side. "This is a doggone tough land, Sheriff Owens, for certain, a doggone tough land."

CHAPTER 27
A BUTTERFLY

The old place was a proper jail certain enough. Granted, the henchman had enough to eat and good water to drink, and even good coffee, but he was exhausted as every time he closed his eyes he either saw Josh's shot-out eye, or the sketch the stuttering cowhand gave him, or heard noises outside that were most certainly those of his assassin, coming to do him in.

When he did finally nod off, all he had were nightmares, nightmares of a great conflagration, and he in the middle of it. Every time he had this night terror, he'd awaken soaking wet, as if he'd stuck his head in the open door of a blazing coal stove.

He took to pacing, as that was the only thing that he found any comfort in. He was terrified to venture outside, and did so only to use the jakes or fetch fresh water. At night he'd let the place get cold, as he was fearful of starting a fire or even going out for wood. He let his horse wander, and threw bag after bag of feed near the stable. The animal gorged itself.

At one point, when he'd reached the furthest limits of his frayed nerves, he lashed out, frenzy-like and yanked the picture of the young range boss from its spot on the wall near his bunk in order to tear it to pieces; he even went so far as to crumple it a little in his fist. Then, as if the paper were on fire, he released it, remembering the warning from the stuttering man. *Do—don't you wrinkle it,* And, as if the stuttering man was somewhere, hiding in a corner, waiting for the slightest misstep, the prisoner pinned it back on the wall, pressing it flat with the palm of a grubby hand.

He did not bathe and did not shave and soon his clothes reeked and he looked like the true saddle bum that he was. He wondered how his life had gotten to this lowly state. It was all so promising when he started out from his home in Nebraska. He had over three hundred dollars saved. He learned horses and was told being a cowhand would be fun and profitable. It was neither. He hated it right away, and then he learned of the game faro and that was his downfall. That and the whores. The whores, where he'd obtained his carnal knowledge. It was the most fun he'd ever had, and they were so willing, all he needed was cash and cash he had, at least for a little while.

He found some cards and played himself in faro. He even lost when he did that. He rummaged around the old place and found some playing cards without the markings. Instead, they sported images of women in various stages of undress. This got his heart thumping pretty well and he thought that at least he could pass the time by pleasuring himself. This seemed to be a pretty good idea. He went to bed and settled down and then the greatest insult of all befell him, nothing would work the way it should.

That's when he broke down and cried like a little child. He wept and soaked his pillow with his tears and gave himself a terrible headache. He looked at the cards and then tried to remember every whore he bedded, every detail, down to the last nipple, down to the rank odor of sex and dirty female bodies and unwashed pudenda and cheap perfume and the smell of liquor on a whore's breath and still nothing happened.

He stood up and threw the cards in the air then proceeded to wreck the old place. He broke every chair and every table and broke out every window in the cabin. He threw his foodstuffs everywhere and then he finally burned his rage out and sat in the flour and coffee grounds covering the floor and cried again. He began hyperventilating and then vomited and aspirated some of the detritus and hacked and wheezed and considered that this was how he very well might die. He eventually got his throat clear and he could breathe again and fell into an uneasy sleep.

He awoke with a start and it was dark now but something made everything glow orange around him. He looked out in the front yard of the old place and his horse was a giant pyre. It lit up the night and the corral and the cabin front and the jakes off to the side and he could smell the horse fat burning. The animal's stomach swelled and popped and hissed and blew hot steaming oats all over the ground next to the carcass. The ruffian wailed a long and unnatural wail.

He ran to his six-shooter and pulled it and shot over and over at nothing until he was out. He tore the loading gate open and pushed the empties out, fast as he could. He reloaded and began firing again at nothing. The gun jammed up at the third shot and he saw that the loading gate had flopped open as it was wont to do as his gun was old and worn-out and he did not have the money to have the gate spring replaced. He reached over to close it, simultaneously yanking the trigger and the flash of the fire between the ill-fitting cylinder and frame belched a lightning-hot flame that tore a trench across the palm of his left hand, down to the bone. Blood poured freely and the pain was unbearable. He absentmindedly ran out into the night and dunked his hand in the water trough. He dropped his six-shooter into the coffin-shaped vessel and then could not find it. He was unable to defend himself now.

Off in a distance he heard a whistling. A human being whistled a tune and the saddle bum soiled himself. He ran back into the cabin and fell to the floor and smashed the stool that had filled his trousers till it rivaled the biggest cow flop he'd ever encountered. He crawled into a corner, pressing himself between his bed and the wall. He drew his knees to his chest and threw a blanket over his head and waited. He could not get the odor of greasy burning horse out of his nostrils. Even the stench of his waste, wafting up between his dirty collar and neck could not overpower it. The whistling got closer and he held his breath and cried.

Harry rode up to the old place to check on his prisoner. He saw smoke a good ways off and this did not hurry his progress. He knew what he'd find and was not surprised in the least, as he knew it was only a matter of time.

The henchmen's corpse was atop what was left of his horse. He'd been shot through the eye, hanged, shot through the gut, and thoroughly burned up.

Harry tied his horse off and wandered into the wrecked cabin. It stunk of human waste and spoilt food and body odor. He looked for Josh's picture and found it, hanging on the wall, ensconced in the terrible vapors. He pulled it from the wall, folded it carefully and tucked it into his shirt pocket. He found a peach pit toy on the bad man's unmade bed. It was beautifully painted, and carved into the shape of a butterfly. Harry put this into his pocket with Josh's likeness.

He rummaged around the cabin and found a fancy Sharps rifle. He picked it up and it weighed nearly twenty pounds. He opened the action and pulled out an empty shell casing. It read forty-five one twenty-five on the head stamp. He put this, as well, in his pocket.

He wandered out to the yard and took a drink from the trough and as he did, a glint in the bottom caught his eye. He rolled up his shirtsleeve and fished it out. He looked the six-shooter over and then into the corpse's vacant eye sockets. "Miss Rosario was right. Nothin' b—but a piss-soaked lying coward. G—good riddance, you mi—miserable bastard. H—hope you're b—burnin' in hell."

Allingham moved about the place and then looked up at Harry and his bosses, and then back at the wrecked interior of the cabin. He nodded and pointed.

"The assassin threw a rope around his neck here." He pointed at the spot where the man lay in his stool with the blanket over his head. "He dragged him outside." The marshal walked along, observing the scraped-up floorboards and disturbed ground. "They stood, face-to-face for a while."

"A conversation, Marshal?"

"A sentence, or at the least, a mock trial. More likely a mock trial."

Harry looked over at Pierce Hall and then at Old Pop. They watched Allingham's eyes as the lawman looked up and saw the makeshift gallows. "He used that block and tackle, hanging from the ridgepole extension on the barn. He hoisted him, and let him dangle for a while."

Old Pop's throat tightened. He pulled at the band collar around his neck. He swallowed hard. Allingham continued.

"When he was almost dead, the assassin shot him through the eye, but look." Allingham reached over and moved the denuded skull at an angle, so as to show his audience in the most excruciating detail. "He shot him so that the bullet would just take his eye out, then pass through the very front of the skull." He shook his head from side to side. "This fellow was going for revenge on a grand scale."

"Je—Jesus." Harry, much to his chagrin, felt a little sorry for the poor devil.

"Yes, and the worst of it, the poor beggar was alive when he was thrown on the burning horse. Thrown there, then shot in the gut, but like Josh Housman, not a fatal shot. The fire, that's what did him in. He was burned alive."

Despite not being a Catholic, Pierce Hall absentmindedly blessed himself, as he'd seen Rosario do about a thousand times since he'd known her, whenever such grim occasions called for it. He watched Allingham wipe his hands clean with his handkerchief and proceed back to the inside of the cabin.

"You say the peach stone butterfly was on his bed, Harry?"

"Ye—yes sir."

Clarence Allingham smiled broadly at the stuttering man. He patted him on the back and nodded. "Good man."

Harry stood a little straighter. He nodded gravely. He was proud to be of use to the lawman. He pointed off to one side. "An—and this is we—where I found the Sharps rifle, Captain."

Allingham picked it up and hefted it in his hands. "Heavy contraption, isn't it?"

"Why'd he leave it, Marshal?" Pierce looked at Old Pop and then at Harry. It was all too confusing.

"I don't know." Allingham thought on it. He had a good idea but did not want to articulate it to anyone just now. The rifle was of the same caliber as the one used to kill the Graham boy. It had to be the same gun, based on what the gunsmith had said. Dude rifle. It wasn't like there were scads of them lying about.

It was confusing, as it was counter to the conclusions of his investigation so far. He was certain the man rubbing out the lynch mob and the man who'd killed the boy were not the same.

He turned and walked away from the three men. He left them standing by the burned-out corpse and horse carcass. He mounted up and rode back to the ranch. He knew what he had to do. He needed to write in his book, his brain, and he needed to parse this out with Lucía, his new Rebecca. He needed to engage in some good old-fashioned dialectics.

CHAPTER 28
I'LL KILL 'EM ALL

John Gilliland stared vacantly at the purchase order held in front of his face, too closely to read, by Tom Graham. He took the paper from him and held it out at arm's length. He looked up at Graham and shrugged.

"It's for cartridges, you fool."

Gilliland shrugged again.

"Forty-five one twenty-five." He cried and spoke with a certain desperation in his voice. "The same cartridge that killed my boy, you stupid idiot!"

"Oh, oh!" Gilliland sat up a little straighter in his chair. He read more carefully. The bill was made out to the Hall ranch.

Graham tore it from the dull boss's hand. He crumpled it and held it in his clenched fist. "I'll kill 'em all, by sweet Jesus, I'll kill every black one of 'em. I swear to Christ, I'll kill 'em all."

He broke down and cried like a child.

Gilliland sat, stupidly, not knowing what to do. He reached out to pat the rancher on the back, then thought better of it. He stood up.

"I'll get you a drink of water, Tom."

"Damn your water!"

Gilliland's slow mind raced. He thought of a pretty good question. "How'd you get that, Tom?"

"What the hell's it matter how I got it. I got it. I got it, and it shows who killed my boy. My boy, my good good boy."

He kind of deflated and sat, slumped over in one of John Gilliland's office chairs. He pulled a flask from his coat pocket and began feeding on it, like a baby pulling on the teat.

Gilliland was confused by all this, and by Graham's constant inclusion of him in his ongoing war with the Halls. He didn't want to fight with the Halls. The more he thought on it, the more he realized that he didn't want to fight with anyone. Hell, none of it was his anyway to fight over. He was an employee, a hired hand and doing the work for O'Higgins. None of it was worth breaking the law over, nor was it worth all this contention and misery.

He even regretted stringing the wire, and when he thought on it, that was never his idea, or the idea of his boss in the first place. It was all Graham. Graham was the key to all the unhappiness it seemed. Certainly his boy being murdered was a terrible thing, but maybe, in a way, Gilliland thought, Graham's actions were somehow a cause, at least in part, for the boy being executed in such a cold and terrible way.

His musings were interrupted by Graham's sudden outburst.

The now drunk rancher sat up in his chair and pointed off, north, toward the Hall ranch. "It was all good, all good until that goddamned war was lost."

Gilliland was confused. "What war?"

"The goddamned war between the states, damn your simple stupid mind."

"I'm not stupid, Tom. Don't say stupid about me."

Graham harrumphed. "You're right." He looked into John Gilliland's eyes. "I'm sorry. I'm genuinely sorry."

"That's all right, Tom. I know you're upset."

Graham continued after taking a healthy swig from the flask. "Calling you stupid is an insult to stupid people." He glared at him and continued. "The war between the states, idiot. The war. The war. Now we got niggers treated like they're human beings, goddamned foreigners, papist, miscegenation."

Gilliland cocked his head, kind of like a curious birddog. "What's that?"

"Miscegenation, mixing of races, damned whites and blacks, niggers, Indians, Mexicans, breeding together, making everything come apart." He shoved his finger toward north again. "Just like you got with those damned blacks! Those goddamned Halls." He sighed and belched and let out a little sound like an animal who'd been gut shot. He glared at Gilliland through inebriated eyes.

"This is why the Knights were formed up, down in the broken south. This is the kind of thing that needs to be done here, done here to dispense justice, and stop all this nonsense."

"What knights?" Gilliland could only think of old England, and he knew that was not what Tom Graham was referencing.

"The knights of the circle, the Ku Klux Klan!" He took another drink. "If we had an order here, we'd get to the bottom of all this for certain. *And* put an end to it."

"But, my boss, O'Higgins, he's working on that. Brought the Pinkerton, that fellow Gorski in."

"Another goddamned papist foreigner.

You think a drunken Mick and a Polock are going to care about us? They bow down to the Catholic dagos in Italy," he sneered and then shook his head in disgust. "Why the hell am I talking to you about this? You're an idiot. You're an idiot, and you don't know shit from shoe polish."

Gilliland sat up a little straighter. "I'm trying to understand, trying to learn what's got you so torn up, Tom. Tell me. Tell me, so's I understand."

Graham stood up and steadied himself on the edge of Gilliland's desk. He weaved and blew whiskey breath at the range boss. "We need to wipe 'em out."

"Who?"

Graham became red in the face. "The Halls, you imbecile, the Halls!"

"But what did they do, Tom? What did they do?"

He threw his hands up in disgust. "Everything! Everything! They cut your man's head off. They're going around burning all those boys up! They're bringing in sheep to destroy the rangeland. They're mixing the races up, and soon the whole place'll be chock-full of Catholics and greasers and Jews and, and God knows what other kinds of foreigners. That bitch Mexican who runs the ranch, she, she was married to a Jew, for Christ's sake, a filthy goddamned Jew. And now she's the wife of a white man!"

Gilliland sat and scratched his head. He looked at Graham, incredulity in his eyes. "A Jew? Serious?" John Gilliland wondered at Tom Graham. He was a smart man, that was certain. And everything he said made sense. "What should we do, Tom? Tell me what we should do."

CHAPTER 29
A GOOD MAN

The brothers followed the Negro along a winding path, between great piles of crushed rock, until they were deposited into a little camp, a shanty town of sorts. This is where the Negros lived, and the Irish twins' towering savior was the unofficial mayor and benefactor of the place.

The big man beckoned them to a small shack with no windows. Once they were inside, a lamp was lit, illuminating a room full of black men. The leader nodded for the brothers to sit down. They served up beer and soup and the Irishmen ate, despite a lack of appetite.

"Name's Henry Simms."

Paddy nodded respectfully. "Mr. Simms, we thank you."

Mike looked the man over. He was taller by at least six inches than the brothers. He could not have weighed less than three hundred pounds. He was powerful and dark, and spoke with the acumen of a preacher.

"You gentlemen are investigating the stolen dynamite, what was used on Robert Halsted in Flagstaff."

"We are."

"I can help you."

Paddy looked on at Mike and nodded. The plan worked, more or less. He rubbed his jaw and wondered if they could not have been a little less physical about carrying it out. He turned his attention to Henry Simms.

"I run the blasting here." He looked at the rest of his companions and they all nodded, as if to verify the big man's credentials.

"About two months ago, I saw a man talking to the foreman," he smiled. "I like the way you thumped him, by the way."

Mikey smiled sheepishly. He'd actually gone easy on the man.

"The foreman sold three cases of dynamite to a man. I didn't hear much of the conversation, but did hear him referred to as Walter."

"What did he look like?"

"A gentleman. Middle-aged, perhaps in his mid-forties, well dressed. He did not do physical work for a living. In fact, he would not even pick up the boxes. Men loaded it on a wagon for him."

"Ay, and can you describe his horse, his wagon, anything that might help us track him down, sir?"

Henry liked the Irish. Once they knew he was an educated man, they generally treated him well. He particularly liked Mike and Paddy. They were tough enough and gentlemanly in their own right.

"Ah, yes. Horse was a dapple gray gelding, not easily overlooked. And the wagon, let me try to remember. Corning body . . ."

An old man spoke up. He had no teeth and spoke accordingly. "Thilver thtar on thides, boss."

Henry smiled at the old-timer. "That's right, Sam." He looked back at the Irishmen. "The buggy, it had big silver colored stars on either side of the body, just below the seat. It had initials engraved on them. W.D."

"And why, Mr. Simms, would you say that this was a shady deal? Why do you say your foreman was doing something wrong?"

"Oh, the owners, Mister . . . ?"

Paddy stood up. "We are very rude, gentlemen. O'Shaughnessy. Mike and Paddy. We're brothers." He grinned at his little irony.

"I see that." Henry smiled back. "No, the

mine company, they guard our dynamite with great care. They do not resell it, and we keep careful records. They don't like to waste money, Mr. O'Shaughnessy. The foreman forgets that I can read and cipher. He doesn't know that I know when he's been altering the books. But he has, gentlemen, he most certainly has."

Paddy stood up. He nodded to Henry Simms. "We thank you for your hospitality, gentlemen, but we should leave here, now. We don't want to make trouble for you. You've done enough for us."

Henry nodded and two men dashed out. In short order the brothers' horses were waiting outside. Simms escorted them out.

"I'm sorry to hear about Mr. Halsted. I met him once. He was a good man. He treated people well."

"Your information will help bring his killers to justice." Paddy reached down from his horse to shake the man's hand. "My brother and me, we are much obliged, sir. We'll hope to repay the favor someday." They rode out, disappearing into the night.

CHAPTER 30
THE PUPPET MASTER

Lucía watched Allingham from her bed for a long time. He sat at a card table and had chess pieces and the peach pit toys that Stosh Gorski and Sheriff Owens had delivered to him, along with the butterfly Harry had found on the most recently slain man's bed, spread out before him.

He put Hira Singh's carved ivory king at the top. Under this he placed ebony pawns. A slip of paper was placed at the bottom of each. He had a pawn for Josh and Old Pop, then another for Xavier, another for Gilliland's foreman, one for the Graham boy, one for Hugh Auld, and a final one for Robert Halsted.

Off to one side, he had the peach pit figurines laid out in a row, next to ivory pawn pieces. He had one ivory pawn piece placed without a toy. This represented the hapless young man who tried, but failed to get himself arrested by Commodore

Perry Owens.

He stared at these pieces for more than an hour, and Lucía got up and had a pee in the chamber pot and stood over his shoulder, looking on at what had so much of her new lover's attention. She rubbed his neck and he reached back to cover her hands, patting them lovingly.

He grunted and leaned a little forward. He wrote, in a bold but fine hand, above all the representations of the victims: *At least three assassins.*

"What are you doing, my love?"

He was ready to share with her now. He needed to talk about it. Speak it out loud to test the veracity of his theories.

He pointed at the king. "This is the puppet master." He pointed to the space occupied by his writing. "These are, at least, some of his minions."

"At least three."

"Yes, the Mexican, who killed poor Xavier, the one who burned up the latest man at the old place, and the man who shot Hugh, and then died himself." He pointed to the other pawns, the ones with the peach pit figurines. "And then there's the one or ones knocking those boys off."

"I see. She reached over and picked up one of the pawns, the one that represented

293

her husband. Tears ran down her cheeks. She nodded and looked over at the last one in line. "And that one, is your father-in-law."

Allingham nodded, then picked it up and remembered Robert Halsted. "We had a contentious relationship, Lucía. He, well, he was a good man, but well, I'll just say that he loved his daughter very much, and I, I was not his ideal."

She put the chess piece back and kissed him on top of the head. "You are my ideal."

Allingham blushed. He could not see that in himself.

"Promise me something, Clarence."

"Anything." He turned to face her and pulled her onto his lap. She was tiny and did not weigh much; she easily fit on one knee. He ran his hand down over her belly, checking to see if he could detect any swelling yet. It was still too soon.

"Promise me you will be careful. Promise me you will not take undo risks to avenge my Xavier or your Robert Halsted." She cried hard and held him around the neck. She cried into his ear. "Promise that."

"Oh, not to worry." He sat up and brushed the tear-soaked hair from her eyes. He kissed her on the nose. "I am too mean and tough to die."

"You are not mean."

He laughed and thought about all the years, all the confounded and angry people he'd encountered. He thought about his terseness, even his arrogance on more than a few occasions. Then he thought about his little breakdown. He had become more human, nicer, more compassionate, but the meanness was still there; Allingham was a son of a bitch and he knew it and knew that, like some dark demon, lurking deep down in his psyche, it was there, and he could rely on it to be conjured up, like some great monster from another world, when he needed it.

He patted Lucía gently. He leaned back, like an old soldier regaling young boys with his tales of battle. "I've been shot, stabbed, slashed, bitten, kicked, punched, hit with a metal ash can, and thrown off a bridge, Lucía. I've been called every dirty name in the book, in several languages. I've been spit on, had the contents of chamber pots thrown on my head, and once someone even tried to set me on fire." He grinned at the memory, back in the earliest days of his time in the Five Points.

She looked up at him and just now seemed to notice how many scars his ugly face bore. He kissed her again, this time on the mouth.

"But then I got nice, but that doesn't

mean that I'm vulnerable." He ran his fingers over the chess piece in his hand. "You don't worry about me, darling. You worry about the dirty blackhearts, because, my darling, there will be hell to pay when I find them."

Stosh Gorski felt very low. The final boy, number seven, had been found, burned, shot, hanged, like all the rest. The Pole looked at Commodore Perry Owens up ahead. The sheriff seemed unaffected by the fact that he'd not arrested and protected the lad. The little peach pit toy of the sun felt heavy in the Pinkerton's vest pocket, and in reality, it weighed almost nothing.

He rode and finally got a little angry and kicked his horse until it moved up alongside the sheriff's mount. Owens looked over at Stosh. He knew what his new friend was thinking, and Owens, though not a particularly articulate man, decided he needed to come up with something for Stosh to think about.

"This land is a lot different, from a law enforcement perspective, than what you've known, Stosh."

"Oh." Gorski thought for a moment that he was going to be treated to some sort of self-righteous diatribe, and he did not feel much like being patronized at this moment. He held his tongue, nonetheless.

"How many people did you have to keep an eye over, Stosh, I mean, back in New York, back in Hell's Kitchen?"

"Oh, I don't know." Stosh knew down to the exact amount, but he did not feel compelled to share it with Owens.

Owens continued. "I'd guess it was a lot, in the thousands, and in a little space."

"Yes."

"Well, we got a few people and a lotta space here, Stosh. My jurisdiction is measured in miles, not city blocks. In that jurisdiction are good people, good hard-working people just trying to scratch out a living, make a go of it here in Arizona."

"I understand that."

"I've also got the most savage wild Indians, outlaw Mexicans, whores and their pimps, gamblers, leftover idiots from the war, cattle and horse rustlers, petty criminals, and some not-so-petty criminals, all over the span of miles of the most unforgiving land that God felt compelled to create. On top of this, I border Mexico, California and New Mexico. No fences, no way to keep the worst miscreants out from these places." He stopped and took his hat off and wiped his brow. He took a long drink from his canteen and handed it to Stosh. "So, I get all the assholes from those places wandering in and out, too."

"I understand, Perry. I understand."

"It is just barely manageable, Stosh, what with the fact that the Federal government doesn't much care about us here in Arizona anyway. We're no state, we are mostly a liability, and we don't make the government any money." He grinned. "Starting to wonder, with all this talk, why I even live here myself."

"But that boy, we, I don't see how letting that boy get killed helps you in your enforcement of the law, Perry. I don't see that at all."

"Well, I'll tell you. I don't need lynch mobs helping me, Stosh." He looked at Gorski as one veteran lawman to another. "I know you know what lynch mobs can do. I know you've had 'em in New York. Know what they've done to the Negro up there. And, Stosh, I won't have it. I simply won't have it."

They rode along and Owens looked his new law dog partner over. He liked Stosh Gorski. Stosh was a good and decent man, and had not been affected negatively by his time fighting crime in New York. Owens regarded him respectfully, as Stosh still retained a high regard for humanity, and that was a rare trait in a man who'd dealt with all that Stosh had endured in Hell's Kitchen those many years.

"But we'll make it right, Stosh. I promise, we'll make all this right, but that boy, he needed to be set up as an example. I don't need vigilantes running amok, hanging good men, following some ass around, some gang leader, calling the shots. When we find him, we'll put an end to this range war, I'm certain of it."

They made it to the office and a letter was waiting for them. It was written out in a feminine hand. It reeked of French perfume. Owens opened it with great interest as Gorski looked on.

"Well, this is interesting." He handed it to Stosh. Gorski read:

Dear Sheriff Owens:

I have information regarding the case of the Pleasant Valley Range War. I will speak only to you and Marshal Allingham in person. Please come to the Hollingsworth Hotel. Ask for Miss Smith in room 310. Hurry, Sheriff Owens, if you want to save lives.

A Friend

Stosh Gorski opened the envelope with

one hand and, putting it to his nose, breathed in the alluring scent coming off the page. He looked at the handwriting again, then at Owens with one eyebrow raised. He tossed the letter on the desk and reached in his vest pocket, turning the carving over between his thumb and his forefinger as he regarded the postmark on the envelope.

"I guess we're heading to Phoenix, Perry."

"I guess you're right, Stosh."

CHAPTER 31
A PARALLEL UNIVERSE

Stosh Gorski decided to stay behind. He felt something in his bones. Something was not right and he did not see much use in going all the way to Phoenix just to interview some high-priced whore. Allingham and Owens could handle that without him.

He thought that he could be of some use to the Halls, though, and likely, more than any other reason, just wanted to be by Hugh Auld's side. The prospector made a great impression on him, and now that the man was in such a state, Stosh just felt compelled to be there for him.

He watched Allingham prepare for the ride to the train station. The marshal and Owens would then ride the rails on down to Phoenix. Stosh grinned as he observed his old friend working away. Allingham had learned a lot since leaving his home in New York. He finished tacking up his mount and he was competent about it. But then again, that was Allingham. Stosh Gorski thought that Allingham might very well be the most intelligent man he'd ever known.

He twisted a cigarette and watched the evening unfold on the Hall ranch. Despite the siege-like state, this was a happy clan. He looked down toward the gate at Long Jack and the stuttering Harry. They kept a good watch.

He saw Rosario making her rounds. She was the true boss of this outfit and everyone knew it. Pierce Hall sat, brooding over Lucía and that was not so pleasant. But the young man would eventually find his love; it would just be a matter of time.

Stosh watched Hira Singh with his wife and little Frances. They were a good family and Allingham still, out of respect for both the Sikh and his wife, would keep his distance from the child. The little one did not yet know that this kind couple were anyone but her mother and father, and Allingham had every intention for it to stay that way. The toddler was just too much of a reminder of Rebecca, and Allingham was still quite frail in that respect. No one thought any less of him. Frances had good parents and she was loved. And as a tribute to Daya, Allingham had vowed to spare her heart as well. The young woman was barren, and she needed to have the love of a child, even if it had not come from her womb. He'd not tear little Frances from Daya. It would simply be too cruel.

Stosh watched Lucía fuss over Clarence as he prepared to ride out. She was a beauty and this amused Stosh. In all the time he'd known Allingham in New York, he'd never known the man to exhibit the slightest interest in women, nor had he known any woman to ever show interest in his terse friend. He laughed to himself at the memory of his departed wife, who, one time, said that Allingham's great problem was that he'd not had regular relations with a woman. She was convinced that it was what made him so mean, and Stosh Gorski could not disagree with her on that point one bit.

Now Allingham had buried one beauty who, by all accounts, had adored him, and had another, hanging on his every action and word. Stosh cast his eyes back to Pierce Hall and watched his heart break and Gorski turned his head from side to side as he twisted a cigarette. "Poor bastard," he muttered to no one in particular, under his breath.

Allingham finally sat down beside him.

They'd had so little time to talk lately. Stosh handed him a cigarette and they blew smoke together at the porch roof.

"How do you like Arizona, Stosh?"

"It's a hell of a place, Allingham."

"Clarence."

"Clarence."

"When all this is settled, I want you to run for sheriff of Yavapai County, Stosh."

Gorski threw his head back and laughed. "I don't know that this place is ready for a Pole and a Catholic in such a high position, Clarence."

Allingham smiled. "Most people around here don't even know what a Pole is. They'll probably think you're from Wisconsin, think you're a Swede with that accent and those blue eyes."

Gorski laughed. The compliment was not lost on him. "Thank you, Clarence. That's very kind."

"I mean it." He looked Gorski in the eye. "You're a good man, Stosh." He nodded. "Owens told me about the last boy, the one in the lynch mob, and, Stosh, I can say, I don't agree with what he did, but he told me about you, about your reaction to it, and, he's, well, I think you got to him. He's mighty proud to work with you, Stosh."

"I know this is a tough land, Clarence. I

understand why Perry did what he did, but you're right, I don't agree with it. I don't think lawmen should go about dispensing justice in such a way. We become no better than the criminals when we do that." Gorski worked on his cigarette and looked at Allingham. "I should have intervened. I should have not let that happen, Clarence. I regret that."

Allingham stood up. He slapped his friend on the knee. "No matter. This place is not like the real world, my friend. Sort of a parallel universe and some things happen that shouldn't but, frankly, that boy would have ended up dead, one way or the other. It was just a matter of time."

Lucía walked up on them. She put her arm around Allingham's waist and kissed him gently on the cheek. "My darling, it is time."

"Gotta ride, Stosh." He grinned. "Sounds like a dime novel, doesn't it old friend?" He became serious. "Keep a weathered eye, Stoshy. I need you to keep 'em all safe here." He nodded, and Gorski could swear he saw a tear in the tough lawman's eye. "Please do that for me, friend."

Harry stood with Long Jack at the gate and let the riders pass. Clarence Allingham nodded as he followed Sheriff Owens close behind. "You boys keep sharp, keep 'em safe. We'll be back."

Harry watched Long Jack and was compelled to say it. He was proud of the dour man. "Y—you know, L—Long Jack, you ain't bitched one t—time since all this started."

Long Jack didn't look up. He was working on a reata. He was pleased nonetheless. It was a great compliment and true. He'd not bitched, as was typically his wont, one time since the self-imposed siege had gotten under way. This all was just too serious to bitch about, and he didn't want to cast doubt on anything or anyone. He'd do his best to make it all right.

He finally regarded Harry and was glad they were posted as sentries together. Harry was a good man. Because of his stutter, he was often dismissed, overlooked, but Long Jack knew, Harry was a smart and competent man.

He tried to recover from the compliment, and make light of it. "Ain't much point in complaining, no one ever listens to me anyway."

"I da—do, Long Jack. I da—do."

"I know it, Harry." He looked back toward the house. "When's that Chinaman going to get here with our grub, my stomach's pasted to my spine, I'm so damned hungry."

"He—he'll be along, Long Jack. He'll be along."

CHAPTER 32
CLAP HER IN IRONS

Betty held court in the presidential suite, unbeknownst to her, in the very room her former lover had deflowered his most recent flame. She looked grand in her San Francisco fashions and even Allingham was impressed with the high-priced prostitute. Commodore Perry Owens was not so taken. She'd work on him, however, despite his ambivalence.

"You men have a pleasant journey down?" She opened a box of Cuban cigars and presented them to her guests. Owens waved her off; Clarence picked two out and trimmed them, handing one to his partner. He lit the other and drew on it hard.

If he did not know better, Clarence could swear Betty was a little starstruck by the long-haired lawman sitting next to him. Owens had developed a significant reputation as a tough customer, and quite a specimen for the ladies to ogle, even if he had eyes only for his wife.

"What is your business, miss?"

"Smith. Elizabeth Smith, but please, call me Betty."

"What do you want, Betty?" Clarence regarded her through the cigar smoke hanging between them. He got up and poured a big whiskey for himself and Owens. He sat back down.

"I want to do business, Marshal. I want to give you something valuable, as it regards this range war and all these assassinations."

Clarence smiled. He'd been studying Betty a bit more than she could have ever anticipated. "I guess the old saying goes."

She leaned a little forward with a knitted brow. "What saying's that, Mr. Allingham?"

"Hell hath no fury like a woman scorned." Allingham looked at the end of his cigar.

Betty's face flushed. She was not being a good poker player now. "I'm sure I don't know what that means."

"Oh, sure you do. Walter Druitt traded up for a younger little chickie, and now you're left out in the cold, sucking hind tit."

She stood up, a little angrier than she'd like to be. "Now see here, Marshal, I don't need to listen to this."

"Shut up and sit down."

Owens looked over at Allingham and suppressed a grin. He'd heard stories of Allingham, but had not seen him in action until now.

Betty complied. She was not used to dealing with such powerful men. She kind of liked it this way.

"Now, I'm too old and have too little patience these days to play a lot of silly games. You're Walter Druitt's whore. You were jilted because he found another whore several years younger, prettier, and more bosomy than you. That's what we know. I also know you've got no money left, you're three weeks behind in paying for this overpriced hotel room, and you've got creditors beating on your door. I know you know something and want to sell it, so, let's cut all the bullshit and get to the facts."

She smiled. Allingham was getting to her, getting to a certain, primordial spot that made her all warm and tingly inside. She liked this one in a perverse way. She took a deep breath.

"Walter's been getting money from a certain person." She looked at both men with conviction, as if it was imperative that they believe every word she said. "I don't know the man, or the organization or whatever it is, but I do know that Walter's been doing some things to get the hornets' nest stirred up."

"Such as?"

"I don't know that."

Allingham stood up. "This is a waste of time." He nodded to Owens. "Sheriff, clap her in irons."

"What?" Betty lost the flushed pink in her cheeks.

"That's right. You're going to jail, prison more likely." He nodded to Owens. "Ten years in Yuma will take a toll on that pretty face and figure, wouldn't you say, Perry?"

"No doubt." Owens pulled out his handcuffs and held them at the ready. He was enjoying the play.

"Hold on just a minute, hold on, Marshal, Sheriff, I, I'll tell you everything I know." She pulled out a canceled check and handed it over. "This is just one document. I have more."

Allingham looked it over with interest. He'd not seen this name before. He folded it and put it in a pocket. "And, what of the rest?"

She jumped up as if shot from her chair. "I've got many things, Marshal, many things." She stopped abruptly and gave him a little smile. "I, I was hoping for a little reward, I mean, many people have died because of Walter Druitt. I thought it might be worth a substantial reward to help bring him to justice."

"How much?"

"Oh, a thousand dollars or so." She gave a little look, and Allingham could have sworn, that just for a split second, her tongue darted out like a serpent's from between her pursed lips. She was a thoroughly corrupt young woman.

"I'll give you fifty."

"Okay."

CHAPTER 33
THE WORST IS YET TO COME

John Gilliland rode uneasily next to Tom Graham along the road to the Hall ranch. He looked back over his shoulder now and again and was impressed by the little army the rancher had pulled together. They were a terrible-looking lot. They were from all over, some were men who were friends or relatives of the slain men who'd been on the botched lynching of Old Pop, and these were bent on exacting revenge.

A half a dozen men were from down near Tombstone. They ran with a gang known as the Cowboys, and these were the men responsible for all the trouble in those parts. And then there were the Mexicans and Indians. All told, there were thirty hired bad men.

Graham looked over at the hapless Gilliland in disgust. He looked back down the road long enough to take a long draw on a silver flask. He warmed his insides, then sneered at the vacant and frightened look in his companion's eyes.

"Yeah, they're a sizable lot, and mean as they come." He harrumphed. "I see you brought no one."

"My boys are cowhands, not vigilantes, Tom."

"Your boys are a bunch of gutless bastards."

"No they're not." Gilliland, all of a sudden, wondered why he was there at all. He looked ahead. By four in the afternoon, they'd be at the Hall ranch. He did not know what Graham was planning, once he got there, but whatever it was, John Gilliland was certain he would not like it.

Graham seemed to read his mind. "We ain't going to hurt women or children, or livestock, Tom." He drank again. "I just want that damned old man, and the nigger Indian Pierce Hall, and anyone else we figure had a hand in any of this. The rest'll be left alone."

"Why do you need thirty-two men to do that, Tom?"

Graham ignored him and kicked his mount's sides. He rode up ahead of his band of derelicts, and picked up the pace. This could not happen soon enough as far as he was concerned.

"What do you want?" Rosario stood with her jaw out, cradling her ten-gauge in her arm.

There was a line of them, many men, and they stood fifty yards from Long Jack's sentry post. He trained his Winchester on the nearest man.

Tom Graham called out. "We want to speak to a man."

"You will speak to me and tell me why you are on my property."

"We want Old Pop and Pierce Hall and all the able-bodied men on your ranch, chica. Hand them over, and we'll leave you and your ranch be."

"For what purpose? You are no law."

"We are the Pleasant Valley Ranchers' Association."

John Gilliland cocked his head. He'd never heard of such an organization, and wondered when he'd become a member. He thought he'd ask, then thought better of it.

"I have never heard of such a thing. You go home, Mr. Graham, go home and get sober and you may talk to Marshal Allingham when he returns from Phoenix. He will help you then."

"Goddamn it you stupid Mexicana whore. I'm telling you now, send out the men or face the consequences."

"Come and take them."

Tom Graham pulled his Winchester. He raised it and then thought better of it. "I've never killed a woman, but I'm tellin' you now bitch, if we come in there, we're comin' in shootin' and we won't be particular about targets."

"Then you will be riding to hell, muchacho, we will send you all straight to hell, and I guarantee you, we *will* be particular about targets."

Harry sat up from his perch on the roof of the hacienda. "G—go on outta here, y—you. W—we don't want an—any trouble."

A Mexican bandit pulled his Winchester and began drawing a bead on the stuttering hand. Harry dropped down, using the hacienda's ridge pole as a rest. He let loose with a round from the great Sharps rifle. The Mexican's head came apart, blasting his companions with a spray of blood and brain matter. Several horses skittered at the odor of the gore. Graham cursed them and turned. He rode off with his band of derelicts following close behind.

Rosario stepped off the porch and looked up at Harry, shading her eyes with her free hand, as the fellow was backlit by the sun.

He expected to be chastised, and held up a hand in apology. "S—sorry ma'am, couldn't let him c—call you a b—bad name and get away with it."

"Good shooting my Harry, good shooting, my boy."

They called Long Jack back to the house and began barricading the windows and doors. They settled in for a proper siege and everyone pulled together for the long night's wait. It was unlikely the bad men would try anything after sunset.

Rosario and Old Pop met them all in the courtyard as they ate the evening meal. She called for everyone's attention.

"We are sorry this thing has happened and we will tell you, as it will be dark soon, we do not expect an attack tonight. But tomorrow, there will be the devil to pay." No one stirred. They ate and sat in silence and listened to the matron of the ranch.

"If anyone would like to go, they are welcome with our blessing. We do not want anyone hurt or in a position to hurt another without it being their choice. We thank you."

She turned and walked into the house, Old Pop limping close behind. They had guns and ammunition and bandages to prepare.

But no one attempted to leave. It was futile anyway, even if they wanted to. The bandits would probably catch them up as they tried to escape and dying would not be the worst thing that could happen to them.

Rosario nearly bumped into Old Pop, preparing rifles and shotguns and six-shooters. She gave him a kiss on the cheek as he rushed by.

She made it into Hugh Auld's room. He was awake and dressing himself. He smiled sheepishly.

"Guess I'll be about as worthless as a one-armed paperhanger" — he looked at his bandaged stump — "but we'll give 'em hell, won't we, ma'am?"

She checked the sutures holding his wound together, and they were intact. She didn't try to get him to stay in bed, as she knew such an effort to dissuade him would be futile. She redressed his bandages, then nodded at him gravely and tried her best to put on a serious air. "If you get that stump to bleeding, those silly bad men will be the least of your worries." She patted him on the shoulder and saw Lucía standing in the doorway. She nodded to the young woman. "You take care of Hugh, my dear. Take care of each other."

Hugh nodded and smiled. "With pleasure

Miss Rosario, with pleasure."

Daya Kaur sat and watched her husband pray. He came out of his reverie and noticed she was in their bedroom standing behind him. She nearly panicked when she saw his face, wet with tears.

"My husband, what's the matter?" She reached for him and he held her with a desperation she'd not known since Rebecca's passing.

"I'm afraid."

She kissed his forehead and removed his dastar. She beckoned him to rest his head on her lap and she began combing his hair with the kanga.

"Tell me."

He pressed his face into her fleshy thigh and held her leg tightly.

"I do not want to fight. I do not want to lose you or little Frances. I'm, I'm afraid my wife, I'm afraid, and now I am ashamed. I've stopped thinking of God, and I'm only thinking of myself and of you and our little girl and I'm afraid."

She rubbed his back and thought of something to say. She still had a lot to learn about her new faith, but she was a good student and Hira had repeated many times that his wife knew Gurbani, the teachings of Sikhism, better than many he'd known who'd lived it for decades. Daya Kaur had been studying for fewer than three years.

"I think this is a very trying time, my darling, but we have to remember, remember that we're together and we are with God and this corporeal life is not what is important. It is not the flesh and bone, it is the oneness we have with God, now, isn't that right?"

He sat up and dried his eyes. He looked into Daya's pretty round face and kissed her on the forehead. "How is it that I have been so blessed with such a wise wife?"

"You're just lucky, I suppose." She walked to the wardrobe and began rummaging about. She found some black material. "Tomorrow, we'll crown you in black. It is a better color for battle."

He grinned a little. "That's what Francis said, back in Canyon Diablo. He said my saffron turban was a target."

She pulled her nightgown over her head and then pulled him into bed after her. "But for now, we have other things to do, my love."

He awoke at three. The house was quiet and only a few men were stirring, still keeping a weathered eye. He dressed quietly but could not keep from awakening his wife. Daya smiled at him and got up without dressing. They made love again and she combed his hair. She pulled out the black material and began to crown him. In a little while he was ready.

She regarded him in his black turban and kissed him on the mouth. "I've forgotten how handsome you look in black." She pulled herself away as there was no more time and she did not want to wear him out. He had bad men to slay.

She checked his kirpan, then loaded his pistols for him. She pulled out his big sword, from the corner of the wardrobe, stored in oilcloth. It had been passed down through his family for four generations. It was as pristine and sharp and shiny as ever. Then finally the chakra, the razor-sharp disc that had been used to dispatch the villain Webster when the devil had held Daya captive, it seemed a lifetime ago.

She finished the ensemble by pinning a khanda, the symbol of the Sikhs, to the front of his turban. She stepped back and looked her lion over. He was beautiful and deadly. She nodded and, with every fiber of her being, resisted the urge to cry.

"I'll leave now." He looked outside and it was a dark night as the moon was in its first quarter. He kissed her again and smiled. "I'm not afraid anymore Kaur."

He was gone.

Rosario lay with Old Pop for a good hour after making love. She kissed him and he whispered to her how much he loved her. She stretched and felt him pressed against her body.

"This is better than the last time I was under attack, my love. That time, I was with Francis, and he had a broken heart. I like this way to prepare for a fight much better."

"Me too."

"Rosario, tomorrow," Old Pop whispered the best he could, "if I die, well, I just want to say now, I want to say, you're the best thing that's ever happened in my life. My time with you has been the best in my entire time on this earth. I love you."

"And I you, my darling, but tomorrow will not be the end for either of us."

"You're certain of that?"

"I am." She stretched and pulled his hand to her breast and wanted him again. They'd love and pass the night loving as neither could sleep.

The Irish twins had beer and smoked cigarettes as they'd run out of pipe tobacco.

They said their acts of contrition and did a little patrolling, wandering up to Pierce as he stood guard over Lucía's door. They nodded and wished him a good evening.

Paddy saw the look in the young man's eyes and thought sitting with him a while would be good for them all. He nodded to Mike and they settled in as they watched the dark.

"I'm sure sorry to get you boys pulled into this mess." Pierce spoke at the gate separating them from the bad men.

"Oh, it's our pleasure," Mikey lied. He was thinking of his wife in California. He looked at Paddy twisting a cigarette.

Paddy looked up and gave Pierce a fatherly smile. "It's all in a day's work, Mr. Hall, all in a day's work."

"You call me Pierce, please. Both of ya, call me Pierce."

"Pierce." Paddy looked the place over. "You have a fine family here, sir. You have a fine ranch and a good life. Most certainly worth fighting for."

Pierce straightened his back. He'd not thought of it that way. He'd spent so much time dwelling on the injustice and unfairness of it all that he did not look at it as something bigger than all that. He should be outraged by the treatment he and his family had received, but instead, he'd just been feeling sorry for himself. He looked into Paddy's eyes.

"Goddamn it, you're right, Paddy." Anger washed over him. He sprang to his feet and Mikey watched him with some amusement as the young rancher shook his fist at the night.

"Of course we're right, lad." Mike pointed off in a distance. "They can all go to hell, and we'll send them for their trouble."

Pierce slumped down, as if he'd been deflated. "Ain't never killed a man."

"Well, it's like having your first beer."

"How's that?" Pierce was not quick, but was convinced the Irishman must be having a little joke on him.

Mikey continued, deadly serious. "Oh, you know, when you're ten or eleven and you've been drinking buttermilk and sugar tea and have gotten the taste of sweet things all your life, and you have your first beer. It is salty and bitter and just seems awful, but then, by the time you're twelve or thirteen, you wonder how you ever drank anything else. Killing is like that. You shoot your first bad man, it becomes easier after that."

Paddy guffawed. "Now, Mikey, don't be makin' jokes. Taking a life is a serious affair."

"I've never seen it have a deleterious effect on you, me brother."

Paddy shrugged. That was true; killing bad men never fixed a bad image in the mind of either one of them. "Well, I guess, but . . ." He thought of something and nodded gravely at Pierce Hall. "Me brother did not start drinking beer when he was ten, Mr. Hall."

"No?"

"He was five."

Mikey sat up, and spoke defiantly, "That was only milk stout, and does not count."

Stosh Gorski joined them and sat quietly and enjoyed the Irishmen. They were like his Irishmen back in Hell's Kitchen. No wonder Allingham hired them. When there was a pause in the conversation, he spoke up. "I've never killed a man, either."

Pierce Hall jumped, a little surprised. "Mr. Stosh, didn't see you there." He cocked his head to the side. He was flabbergasted that the lawman, working all those years in the Five Points, had never taken a life. "Are you serious?"

"Yes, serious." He worked on a cigarette and passed around a flask. The brothers took a few sips, but did not imbibe enthusiastically. They wanted to be sharp for battle. "Oh, I've thumped a few," he grinned, "been thumped a few times myself." The brothers gave a knowing smile. Anyone who'd been a copper knew what Gorski meant. "But I've never had to take a life."

Pierce grinned, then was distracted by a shadow off in the distance. He watched Mr. Singh silently make his way, like a Bengal tiger, past the gate. The Sikh turned and gave an old-fashioned military salute, reminiscent of his days serving the British crown. Pierce returned the gesture. He looked at the Irishmen and then toward Gorski.

"Jesus, boys, I would not want to be a bad man this night."

John Gilliland awoke to cursing, forty-five minutes before daylight. He was up and watched Graham rant and rave about the mess the Sikh had left them. The Indians and Mexicans were dead in their beds, throats cut deeply and each corpse staring skyward, looking much like a hog, freshly slaughtered and ready for the scalding tank.

One of the bad men handed the boss several calling cards. On the front they read, *Hira Singh, Esq.* On the back there was written, in a crisp hand: *The worst is yet to come.*

John Gilliland vomited all over Graham's

boots. He wiped his mouth and tried to pretend the loss of his stomach contents had not happened. He belched vomit breath at his partner in crime. "How many's left?"

"I don't know, goddamn it!"

Another henchman spoke up. "Nineteen. Six been killed in the night, the Mex yesterday, and six run off this morning."

"Well, that's it." Gilliland mounted up. "You can call it eighteen. I bow out."

Graham pulled his six-shooter and pointed it at the middle of the range boss's back. He fired and Gilliland tumbled to the ground. "Goddamned right about that."

He looked around him. "Anyone with an idea that they want to run off, look at that piece of shit and think hard about it." He looked at his watch and climbed up on the rise separating him from the Hall ranch. "Come on you men, we have rustlers to bring to justice."

They rode hard and fast and Long Jack was on the dinner bell, beating it for all he was worth. When everyone was up he climbed to the roof and took up a place next to Harry. "Morning, friend."

"M—morning, L—Long Jack." Harry had the big Sharps, but it was too much gun and slow and ponderous to use and only a single shot. He grabbed Joshua Housman's Winchester and levered a round into the chamber. He drew a bead on the lead bad man and fired. His horse toppled to the ground. Harry spit in disgust.

Long Jack smiled. "Nice shooting, Harry."

"Weren't aiming for the horse." He squeezed off another round and missed. "H—hate shootin' horses."

The rest of the folks started firing, and all hell broke loose. Men were falling from horses and the din of rifle and pistol fire was deafening. Smoke soon filled the front yard and it became difficult to choose targets.

Rosario calmly walked about, ten-gauge at the ready. She looked on at the Irishmen and Pierce Hall, firing until their rifles heated up. They changed to six-shooters to give them a rest.

Out his bedroom window, Hugh Auld ponderously worked the six-shooter with his left hand. He fired again and again, and Lucía was behind him loading gun after gun. He looked back at her and gave a confident smile. She crouched down, resolution in her eyes. She was angry and no longer afraid.

Daya Kaur followed her man about, covering his back. He was planning to mount up, fight ahorse with his khanda, but this was no longer necessary. Most of the bad men lay dead or dying. There was not much fight in them left.

Tom Graham was the only one to breach the fence. His horse vaulted over the gate and he rode back and forth, looking for targets to shoot. He was resolved to die trying now. He no longer wanted to live, and finally, mercifully, his mount received a rifle slug to the skull. It dropped as if poleaxed, spilling the rancher to the ground.

Rosario was on him at once. She pointed her ten-gauge and waited for him to surrender. She could now confront him. "Why'd you do this terrible thing, Mr. Graham?"

"Because you killed my boy. You and your damned bunch of bastards. You killed my boy."

"We did no such thing."

He went for his six-shooter, and Rosario called for him to stop. "Don't do such a stupid thing, Mr. Graham. You will not survive."

"I know." He jerked the gun and pushed the muzzle under his jaw. He fired and the slug ripped off a good part of the top of his head.

Rosario's eyes widened and she whistled

through clenched teeth. "I'll be go to hell."

They'd celebrate that night. Allingham and Owens had returned to a raucous crowd. The defenders of the ranch had slain the dragon and were happy and exhausted and emotionally spent. Rosario had two hogs slaughtered and the food and drink would be enjoyed by all. Allingham watched them in their post-battle reverie.

He enjoyed watching Lucía taking care of Hugh Auld. They were warriors, tested in battle, they'd fought bravely together and survived. He enjoyed seeing such a bond, and he enjoyed the new attitude in his future bride. She looked more confident, more mature. He no longer saw a young woman. She'd aged, at least in maturity, by a decade.

Even Pierce Hall seemed a different man. Neither he nor Stosh Gorski could say they drew blood. With all the bullets flying and the smoke and the dust, it had been impossible to determine exactly whose bullets found their marks, but they'd fought bravely and faced the bad men down.

Allingham walked up on his Pinkerton friend and extended his hand. "Not bored yet in this Arizona land, Stosh?"

The Pole smiled as he removed his sweaty

hat, wiping his forehead with a silk scarf. "No, Clarence, not bored." He looked around and was himself just now settling down from the battle high. His voice cracked a little as he watched Rosario glide by. "Not by a long shot."

The Mexicana stopped and regarded Allingham. "Capitan" — she nodded, then looked over at Lucía — "you need to get your woman to bed for a few hours, and then get cleaned up for the fiesta."

Allingham's face reddened. He was still not accustomed to speaking so freely about such relations. He dropped his head and felt his cheeks flush, yet simultaneously thought it a splendid idea. "Yes, ma'am." He gave a little salute with his right hand.

He, automatically, as if Rosario's command could not be denied or even delayed by one moment longer, took his woman by the hand and escorted her into the hacienda where he bumped into Singh, carrying little Frances outside.

"How's my sweet girl?" He reached over and kissed the child on the cheek, then pushed his great rubbery lips under her chin, pretending to gobble up her neck. She laughed and scrunched up her shoulders and patted Allingham on the head. She turned and whispered into her Indian father's ear then hid her face in his long beard.

Hira smiled. "She wants to know if you have brought her any frogs."

"No sweetheart, not this time." He grinned at Hira and the tears ran down his cheeks. He recovered the best he could and nodded at the khanda pinned by Daya on the Sikh's headwear the night before. "Fine medallion." He stepped back and regarded his friend. "You look good in black."

"Thank you. Francis would be proud. He always said my saffron turban was a target. Daya suggested I wear black." He moved along out into the sunlight and over to the men slaughtering the hogs. Little Frances was keen to watch the activity.

In bed Allingham held Lucía and kissed her all over. He cast his eyes about and realized what danger she'd been in as the bullet holes could be seen everywhere, scarring up every wall and door and window frame. He cried again and she held him, lovingly.

"Why are you crying, Clarence?"

"Oh, I just thought about what happened. How I could have lost you."

"But you did not."

"No, I did not." He pulled her onto his body again for another go-round. He smiled. "I think you might be magic."

"Hmm." Her eyes rolled back in her head as she bit her lip. Allingham triggered sensations she'd never known. "How, how is that?" She shuddered a little then collapsed onto his chest.

"Because all I want is you." He kissed her neck and then forehead. "All I want is to be like this, just like this, and to do nothing else."

"That is not sorcery, my darling. That is called love."

CHAPTER 34
YOU CAN ONLY HANG ONCE

The three lawmen sat waiting in the fancy Chicago office and smoked good cigars. Harold Tomlinson, the tycoon's terse secretary, waited for his boss to arrive. He never had a lot to say to strangers and said nothing to these men now.

Clarence Allingham stood up and wandered about the opulent chambers, admiring O'Higgins's taste in art. He was about to say something to Stosh Gorski when the tycoon burst in on them.

"Gentlemen!" He smiled and reached out to take Allingham's hand. "The famous US marshal, we finally meet!" He shook Allingham's hand energetically. "I'm proud to know you, sir."

He went to Stosh Gorski in turn. "How are you my friend?" He did not wait for a response, instead addressing Owens. "And Commodore Perry Owens!"

The sheriff blushed and O'Higgins

understood the frontiersman's confusion.

"The fame of your auburn locks precedes you, sir!"

"Oh."

They all sat down as Tomlinson milled about. O'Higgins clapped his hands together, then rubbed them as if warming himself by a fire built up on the blotter covering the mahogany desktop before him.

"What do you have for us?" He smiled broadly at his secretary, hopeful for some good news. He thought certainly there must be something important to report, to have all three prominent lawmen here at once.

"Oh, I think we should let your man tell." Clarence nodded at the secretary.

O'Higgins turned and gave a confused smile. "Harold? What would Harold know about any of this?"

Stosh Gorski stood up and moved to cover the office door. He reached into a pocket and put a hand on the grip of his six-shooter. He kept it concealed in his pocket as he nodded for the secretary to go on.

The man burst forth with a maniacal laugh, twisting up his face in a hateful grin. "Yes, all right, all right." He wandered over to a leather upholstered chair, poured himself a large scotch and proceeded to tell.

"I'm the reason why the range war happened."

"You and Walter Druitt, at least initially," Gorski corrected him.

Tomlinson scoffed. "That buffoon! He thinks only with his dick. Worthless bastard."

O'Higgins stood up. He looked Stosh Gorski in the eye. "What's going on here, Stosh? What's going on?" He looked on at his secretary, as if the man had broken his heart.

Allingham spoke up. "Yes, well, Mr. O'Higgins, it seems your man is not satisfied with the generous salary you pay him. He's the one to start this range war. He hired assassins . . ."

"Just one." The secretary spat his answer at the marshal.

"No matter." Stosh looked at the secretary, then at Allingham and Owens. "Can't hang but once." He beckoned O'Higgins to sit back down. The tycoon's color was not good and Stosh worried that the man might collapse. Stosh continued. "He hired a man to stir up trouble down there. Pit one ranch against the other. By the way, I regret to inform you, your manager, John Gilliland is dead."

"I heard from him, just yesterday, by

wire." O'Higgins swallowed hard.

"That was my wire," Allingham spoke up. "I didn't want your devoted secretary to vamoose before we could get here to lock him up."

Gorski chimed in. "Yes, and well, sir. He's made a horrible mess down there." Gorski had a thought and looked with disdain at Tomlinson. "What of the Mexican? The one who decapitated the shepherd, Xavier Zubiri?"

"Just a bit of good luck." Tomlinson sucked down another scotch. "He and then the one who killed all the men on the lynch mob. He wasn't mine, either. I only hired one man and he had an assistant, but that was it. And now they're both dead." He nodded at Allingham. "The one fell off a cliff while this jug head was taking him in, under arrest, the other I killed just yesterday when he came up here with his tail between his legs. The stupid son of a bitch tried to blackmail me. Me! But I fixed him well enough." He shrugged. "Could never get Druitt to do anything but fornicate with whores, and cheat me out of thousands and forge my checks, the gutless bastard."

O'Higgins was parchment white. "But why, my darling, Harold, why?"

The secretary began to cry. He lashed out

337

at his benefactor like a spoiled child. "Because, because you treat me like a toy, like a, like I'm nothing to you. A monkey on a stick and you wind me up and tell me what to do, what to wear, what entertainments to seek, I, I wanted something more, something of my own." He coughed and looked at the lawmen with hatred in his eyes. "And these bastards, all of them, they found it out. I was going to be rich. I was going to go in and pick up the pieces, buy everyone out," he sneered and pointed a shaking finger at O'Higgins, "*and* with *your* money!"

"The railroad is planning big things down there, Mr. O'Higgins, big things." Allingham looked the tycoon over and felt sorry for him. He'd been betrayed on a monumental level.

"And that land'll be worth a hundred times what I would have paid for it, but for those damned Halls and you three bastards."

"And, so he killed dozens of innocent people, wasted thousands of *your* dollars, just to do this, Mr. O'Higgins, just to do this." Allingham had a thought. "You even tried to kill Stosh here, didn't you?"

"Yes, and my buffoon shot the wrong man, some inconsequential prospector and

338

not you!" He looked over at Gorski with hatred in his eyes.

"And that *inconsequential prospector* now has one arm, you devil."

Tomlinson nodded his head dismissively. He didn't care.

"But, but I would have done anything for you, darling." O'Higgins was beside himself now. He stood up and walked toward the terrible man.

Tomlinson held up a hand. "Don't come near me. Don't touch me. I'm sick, sick of you, sick to death of all of you." He glared at Gorski. "You say I can only hang once, well, that's a lie."

He pulled a little pistol from a vest pocket and pointed at his temple. "I won't hang at all." He fired and flopped over, a pink smoky haze filled the room.

"Oh, Jesus, Je—sus!" O'Higgins was on him, holding him in his arms. He pressed his palm to the hole in the man's head, trying his best to staunch the effluent. Tomlinson was dead.

Allingham pulled the Irishman away. "Come on now, Patrick, come on now, he's gone. Your man's gone."

He held O'Higgins in his arms for a long time. He patted him on the back and the Irishman wailed. "I loved him so much. I loved him so."

"I know you did, my friend." Allingham nodded to Owens who covered the corpse with a blanket.

Allingham looked up into his lawman companions' eyes. He breathed deeply and whispered. "I'll be go to hell."

CHAPTER 35
LA CHARADA CHINA

Sheriff Commodore Perry Owens had received word that a Mexican had tried to sell gold teeth and a ring from the Basque country in a saloon on the New Mexico and Arizona border. Now he stood with Stosh Gorski watching a little adobe hut.

He turned to a sallow man with a pockmarked face. "He alone?"

"Yes, except for two whores."

"How long's he been in there?"

"Three days. He orders food and whiskey. He hasn't come out once, not even to shit."

Owens nodded to Stosh Gorski who made his way around to cover the back. He then called out to the occupant of the little hut.

"Come out now, and we won't kill you."

"Go to hell, gringo."

"No."

"I have two women. I'll kill them if you don't let me alone."

"Go ahead, they're only whores."

"Okay." The Mexican fired a shot. Owens put two rounds through the decrepit wooden door.

"Stop gringo, stop. I was just kidding. I didn't kill no whores."

"Send them out, then you come out, hands high."

"Okay."

The door slowly opened and a bloody woman emerged. She wore no clothes, except for sandals. She jogged toward the sheriff. When she was within ten feet, the Mexican fired, striking her between the shoulder blades, tearing apart her left breast as the bullet passed through; she was dead when she hit the ground.

"God damn it!"

Owens fired again.

"Hold on, gringo. I got another whore. I won't kill her if you let me go."

Stosh Gorski kicked open the back door. He pulled both triggers on Allingham's ten-gauge, and the Mexican nearly came apart at the waist. The whore ran out the front. She'd survive.

Clarence Allingham and his new bride arrived at the cigar factory office on a crisp clear morning at the end of Amelia Street in Key West, Florida. They'd lie over for a day before heading to Cuba, then on to Spain. They were escorted to an open room cooled by many ceiling fans. Dan Housman soon greeted them wearing a tropical suit, waving a Panama hat like a fan. He beckoned them to sit down.

Allingham handed him a gift, wrapped in colorful paper. Dan Housman blushed. He'd not expected such.

It was a cigar box containing seven colorful peach pit toys and Allingham was impressed that Dan Housman lost no color in his face as he regarded them. He stood up and poured Lucía a mint julep and lit a fresh cigar. He trimmed another and handed it to Allingham, lighting it for him.

"When did you figure it all out?"

"Oh, right away." Allingham worked on the cigar and then regarded the glowing end. He enjoyed the odor of the fine Cuban leaf. "Your red herring letter to Rosario was pretty good, but not good enough."

"Please, indulge me, Marshal." He had a thought and became a little grave. "My secretary, she knew nothing. I just sent her the letter and asked her to post it. She's not guilty of any of this, Marshal; please don't pull her into it."

Allingham waved him off. "I knew that." He continued on with his explanation. "NM

343

in your letters to Perry was the first thing. Nautical miles." Allingham turned his head from side to side. "Seaman in Arizona, not very probable. And you favor one foot, evidently due to your run-in with the shark. You left a pretty good clue wherever you walked." He pointed at the box. "And the toys, well, they were a dead giveaway."

"How so?"

"La Charada China." Allingham smiled and nodded at the box. "Sun, butterfly, moon, cat, worm, turtle, pig; the numbers one through seven in the Cuban lottery system, derived from the Chinese. And, Mr. Housman, Cuba is just ninety miles away." He looked about them. "Really not even so far." He waved his hand around. "The Cuban influence, well, it's everywhere here. You've probably got more Cubans than Americans working for you."

"I'd have never, in a million years, expected anyone to know that in Arizona."

Lucía smiled as she took a sip of her cool drink. "My husband is a genius, señor."

"That he is." He sat down and admired Lucía. "I don't suppose you'd model for one of my cigar boxes, Mrs. Allingham."

Lucía blushed but before she could answer, Dan Housman spoke up. "What do we do now, Marshal? I won't give you any trouble, you want to clap me in irons, go ahead, I've no regrets. I won't give you a fight."

Allingham stood up and looked at his watch. They had a ship to catch. He nodded to his wife and helped her up, as her belly was now quite round with Xavier's baby. She, of late, had a bit of a time extracting herself from chairs.

He smiled at Housman. "In the bottom of that box is something from one of the ranch hands, Mr. Housman. He wanted you to have it."

Clarence Allingham looked about the office. "This is a fine place you have here, an impressive factory with many workers relying on it for their livelihoods." He nodded again. "Take care of it and take care of your people, Mr. Housman." He reached out to shake the man's hand. He and Lucía turned to walk out. "And Mr. Housman?"

"Yes?"

"Stay out of Arizona." He and Lucía were gone.

Dan Housman pulled the paper from the bottom of the cigar box. He flattened it out on his big cherry wood desk with the palm of his hand and thought about his brother and cried.

EPILOGUE

Walter Druitt never did own a bank. He lived with Sam for a brief time in Argentina, until the money ran out, and then Sam ran out and he was all alone. He got pretty good at forging checks and then started a bogus insurance company with some shady characters where he bilked shipping companies out of thousands of dollars with false claims and false shipwrecks, but then his partners cheated him and he, yet again, lost his shirt. Eventually, like his father, the cigars and alcohol and pork and sedentary life caught up to him. He died quite unexpectedly of hardening of the arteries. He was forty-nine. No one cared.

Betty made it to Europe and then to the Ottoman Empire. Her fair features were a hit, and she soon landed a count who immediately added her to his significant collection of concubines. She didn't mind. She lived out her days in meager opulence and relative obscurity, but at least did not have to resort to providing sexual favors in the twilight of her life.

Sam Ford stayed in Argentina for a few years longer and perfected her ability to dance the Tango. She eventually moved to Paraguay where she became a general's wife. She outlived the general and then purchased a hotel catering to European adventurers. She was a celebrity and rubbed elbows with the country's few elite. She founded an orphanage and staffed it with loving caretakers. She learned to fly aeroplanes and died at the age of ninety-one.

Rosario and Old Pop, and of course Pierce, finally sold out to the railroad. The couple moved to Mexico. Rosario outlived yet another husband and decided she'd had enough. She took a few lovers here and there, and doted on her grandchildren and then great-grandchildren. Nearing her eightieth birthday, she fought alongside Emiliano Zapata and achieved the rank of captain in his revolutionary army. She died in her sleep on her ninety-third birthday. The entire town turned out to bid the feisty Mexicana farewell.

Pierce Hall found love and married a young Indian girl. She gave him eleven children, five boys and the rest girls. With his fortune from selling his ranch to the railroad, he moved to California and started an orchard. He never again handled a gun for the rest of his days.

Patrick O'Higgins continued to grow his fortune and gave the majority of it away. He lived out his retirement in San Francisco. He never returned to the Emerald Isle.

The Irishmen never were to return to their homeland, either. They brought their mother over to America and she helped raise sixteen grandchildren. Mike and Paddy started a fine restaurant and eventually parlayed the proceeds of that to purchase a fine brewery of Irish-style ale. They lived in a duplex and were never more than a dozen yards apart. They outlived their wives and worked to make conditions better for Irish policemen.

Stosh Gorski rebuilt the little cottage Allingham had burned to the ground. He tended the peach orchard and lived out his days in sunny Arizona. He and Commodore Perry Owens remained friends for the rest of their lives. Stosh gave up the Pinkertons and refused, despite repeated requests, to run for sheriff of Yavapai or any other county. He, like Pierce Hall, never again touched a gun.

Hugh Auld became an employee of the mining company visited by the Irish twins. He took over the job of making certain the equipment, and especially the dynamite, never again got into the wrong hands. He no longer wandered alone into the desert, looking for treasure and because of this, he found a special treasure in the form of a lovely Hopi named Soyala, who turned out to be every bit as feisty and capable as Rosario, and, though she was too old to give Hugh babies, she made him a happy home.

Hira Singh and Daya Kaur raised Frances and continued to live in Flagstaff. They periodically took trips to England and one to Hira's home in India. Daya passed away from Bright's disease at the age of forty-one. Hira became a doting grandfather and taught Frances and her children how to be close to God. He passed away in his sleep at the age of seventy-one. All of Flagstaff mourned.

Clarence Allingham became a shepherd in a settlement just outside of his bride's hometown, in the Basque region of Spain. He lived out his days loving his wife and growing family.

Sometimes on clear nights, up in the hills, at the foot of the Gorbea, when he was all alone, Rebecca would come to visit him, but only in his dreams. He learned to play the dultzaina and became thoroughly absorbed in the community of shepherds, where he was affectionately known as erraldoi, or giant. All of his children would outlive him, as would his Lucía. He was happy and content, for the rest of his days.

ABOUT THE AUTHOR

John Horst was born in Baltimore, Maryland, and studied philosophy at Loyola College. His interests include the history and anthropology of the Old West.